THE LODESTAR

THE LODESTAR

DANIEL HAGEDORN

atmosphere press

PART ONE

Everything looked magnificent, ultraluminous, lit up splendidly like the liveliest place in the world, either imagined or as some amalgamation. And though I felt an immediate sensory overload, I was awakened too, by the magnificence that surrounded me.

Buildings were perfectly designed and varied, here a sculpted façade with double glazing creating a honeycomb effect, there a curved lattice like structure with greenery on the sides next to a simple building with Doric columns and an interior courtyard full of flowers. Little details stood out, lower floors visually connected to the streets, from the wrought iron balconies on one to the intricate patterns of another, the lines of each building arrested the eyes to see its shapes and feel its life flowing through the walls to the world outside.

Tree-lined streets lit by lamps, fuchsia hung from posts, outdoor cafés with matching tables and chairs, the little glints of light patterned on the water; all these things, these splashes of color and effect came greeting me like strangers suddenly familiar, triggering some great thought that I opened my mouth to muse aloud when it happened. I paused, a feeling suddenly trickled inside that approached nausea, rose up then subsided, leaving a trace of terrible.

The images flickered as if blown by some centrifugal force, blurred then brightened, faltered then faded, dulling into an eerie darkness that revealed like stratum, the world underneath as a shabby construct, cracked and crumbled, barely held together, before shimmering black to life again with new found glory, rendering that semi-dark drabness as merely a momentary lapse, some fault in the construct. Dilapidated buildings reformed into what they were, what they had been, spectacular beyond belief with their stained glass and vertical aesthetics. A sudden relief filled me, replacing my discomfort, but I still felt uneasy as I walked.

I squinted, wondered what I had just seen, what it really was and why it was suddenly gone, though the sickness remained in my mouth. When I blinked that netherworld wasteland flashed into existence then once again dissipated as it had before, and everything was illuminated magnificently as it had been, as it was, that stretch of tree-lined streets, the outdoor cafés, the buildings, the flowers, the colors of life everywhere enriching my every breath. I glanced to the waterway, saw the boats moored to cleats all down the line, then back again to the explosions of color like sweet breaths.

Where I was, strange yet familiar, a place I must have known, but if the names came to me, then they recalled such things only unconsciously. While that other world, that sickness numbed me at the thought. I shuddered for a moment in the streets until the world brought me back to life with its vibrancy, color and light and buildings connected to the landscape like everything was a part, an essential piece in a puzzle, even me. That other stuff was all in my imagination, for who could argue what I now saw and not what I thought I saw that was the more real? What was now, or what was merely this partial separation?

I walked towards the light at the center, felt the life of the city, the hum of its energy, of hearts beating and pulsing as the magnificent buildings shrank in size while still retaining an irresistible charm. Off to my left, the water shimmered and voices from boats on the canal lingered in the air, hanging as these sounds, these luscious sounds that I strained to hear but could not, though it mattered not. It just felt good to hear them. And though I didn't really know why, I felt alive, more alive than I had in a long time as I breathed in the air.

A soft breeze kept me calm as I walked, my dark shoes slapped against the sculpted stone pathway and created a pleasant tone. I looked in the windows of shops closed for the night, boutiques with brightly dressed mannequins, little intimate restaurants where cozy conversations were being held. Surely, they were just as surely as at one time that might have been me.

I came upon an open windowed restaurant and bar, although full of people, the conversations did not ring loudly out into the night. Something about the place drew me in, perhaps its pendant lights and crystal fixtures or something else, something I knew but didn't know. The flooring resembled a maze of interlocking tiles, and as I walked in, I had the sense I was getting into something and I needed to be sharp so I could think my way out.

The tall bartender with a slight beard nodded to me, and when he approached, we exchanged pleasantries. I didn't quite understand it, but it seemed like we knew each other, yet I couldn't be certain. Looking around at the people, I was struck by how beautiful everyone looked in evening dresses and entertaining attire, how happy everyone seemed to be with their drinks and dramas, laughing or smiling or just listening to some story, to some bit of conversation that added up to a good time. I felt a bit self-conscious, like this was a private party, but I knew none of the people. I was not only alone but uninvited, and I didn't think I was otherwise special enough to be there. In time, I would be found out, singled out as the one who didn't belong.

Everyone was with someone or in a group, no one alone, except for one other woman, dark haired, a drink in front of her that she must have sipped slowly because the ice had almost completely melted. She fastened her gaze on me. I looked away to my right, at what looked like a secret code embedded in a copper plated sculpture on the far end of the wall. The name of the bar suddenly made sense. Kryptos. When I turned back, she still stared.

She was on the opposite end of the bar but directly in my view in a normal glance. I surveyed the room again to see if there was anyone else alone, for anyone I recognized, but there was not, only she and I. She even smiled at me, which was something that never happened. I figured she was looking at someone else or thinking about something, and it just happened to be me in her vantage. I sometimes found myself smiling for what appeared to be no reason, but there was always a reason, it just wasn't visible. Like code, hidden.

The bartender had brought me a drink, indicating to me with a knowing nod that it was something that I would like, which suited me just fine because I didn't know exactly what I would have ordered or wanted or what I even liked. I had felt drawn to come inside as if there was some invitation I was answering. And perhaps there was. It was not necessarily for want of a drink, but now that I was here, it sounded good.

I took a sip of my drink, a whiskey drink of some kind. I was never good at placing tastes, so I couldn't say what else was in there, though it was quite delicious. When I looked up again, across the bar to that dark-haired woman, she was gone. She was, in fact, just sitting down next to me, eyeing me cautiously as she did so. Once again, I wondered if I knew her. I hadn't even realized the seat next to me was vacant. The seat where she formerly sat was now occupied.

"Are you looking for someone?" she asked, looking to me briefly before looking around the room, then once again fixing her eyes upon me. "Well, are you?"

"Not that I know of, but I could be," I said. "It's sometimes hard to know."

She fixated on me, studying my expression and my response, which I hadn't meant to say at all. Normally, I kept as much as I could to myself. It seemed easier that way, easier to not reveal hardly anything to anybody. And here I was mumbling something that almost defined interest, which was clearly not the case. My mind and body were in two different places with a chasm between that could not be bridged, though I apparently stretched without stretching, reached because a part of me wanted to regardless of what the other half felt.

"I feel like I might know you, but maybe not. It's like I am in a dream," I added, as if to clarify and communicate something more intelligible.

She looked away from me now, as I did her, to the direction of the bartender, but not for any particular reason, rather it was just a place to look so that we were not looking at each other, since I had accidentally made the moment awkward.

"Marta," she said, turning her head towards me, smiling as she did. And it was at that moment that I really noticed how lovely she looked. Before, when I glanced at her across the bar, it didn't really register. I noticed her smile, but now I felt there was something about her that was intriguing. She certainly was direct.

"David," I responded, after a pause, perhaps the slightest hesitation. Usually, when someone says their name it is an obvious cue that you follow with yours, and yet, for a moment I wondered if that was really my name. I definitely didn't want to tell her that. For surely then, she would realize she made a mistake in talking to me, that I was just another weirdo because everyone knew their own name. But I actually wasn't sure that was my real name, and I hoped the bartender, who seemed to know me, wouldn't blow my cover.

"You look kind of dazed," she said, somewhat concerned. "Is everything okay?"

"I'm a little disoriented. And I don't know why. Either I've been here before, in this exact spot, or I have not. All of this is so familiar yet strangely foreign at the same time. I suppose that does not make any sense. I feel like I am at two wits."

"Two wits?" she repeated.

"You know, like two minds and they are both battling for control, one against the other," I said looking to her. "I'm sorry, you must think I am out of my mind."

"It's okay," she said. "I think I might understand."

"Really?"

She nodded, went back to taking a slow, measured sip of her almost empty drink. As if on cue, I did the same. It really was quite a wonderful drink. I sensed the taste of bitters now, a whiskey with bitters. When I asked the bartender the next time he came around if that was it, he corrected me, puzzled. I was way off. That was something I was supposed to know.

"It's a whiskey sour with fernet. One of your favorites."

One of my favorites, I thought. And then he moved on. Marta asked me if she could have a taste as her drink was nearing the end but had not really interested her all that much. I nodded and she reached over, briefly touching my hand then the glass, startling me but shooting a jolt of electricity through me too. Had she meant to do that, or was it just some innocent thing?

"Good choice," she said after taking a sip and returning the glass to me. "Would you like to try my drink? It's gin and something, I forget. But evidently, it is not my thing."

I didn't necessarily want to, because I knew that I hated gin, but at the same time, I wondered about the taste of gin. I knew there were lots of variations, generally though, juniper berries were part of the final concoction. I didn't know why I knew this either or why I hated gin. The sense was prominent. Like tequila.

"Sure," I said, then added, "Yeah, not so much my thing either," after I tasted what I was sure was some kind of pine tree in liquid form. "Is that a Christmas tree I am drinking?"

"A Christmas tree?" She asked, somewhat amused. "What's that?"

And what *was* a Christmas tree anyway? I thought about it. I thought everyone knew what a Christmas tree was. Maybe they didn't. Okay, this was starting to make a little more sense. I had seen some signs that things were awry, the world not quite right. And something like this confirmed it. Everyone knew what a Christmas tree was. Maybe she was joking. But when I looked at her for a sign that we could laugh about it, there was nothing. Okay. She didn't know what a Christmas tree was. Did I? It was just a simple noble fir with pesky pine needles that fell off the longer it sat out of water, but I had the feeling I could have told her anything.

Definitely just a dream. It had to be. All of that stuff earlier too. Just a dream. And if I was aware that it was a dream, that meant this was a lucid dream and I could do anything I wanted, no matter how rash or drastic such an action was deemed to be, not that I would, but the thought occurred to me that I could simply lean over and kiss Marta and that would be perfectly fine because it was a dream and she would like me. I already knew she liked me because she smiled at me then came over to talk. Something that would only happen in a dream. That should have been my first clue.

"What's so funny," she mused, obviously noting my smirk. "That I don't know what a Christmas tree is? Well, I don't. Enlighten me."

Maybe she was just messing with me. To be sure, I had to find a light switch. Now that might have been some old wive's tale, but in a lucid dream, you were supposedly unable to turn light switches on and off. You flipped the switch back and forth and nothing ever changed. I needed a light switch to confirm this. Only when I glanced around the room, I didn't see any. And I didn't want to appear weirded out more than I already was, so I let it slide until further notice.

"A fancy name for a pine tree," I finally said. Though it had taken me a long time to respond, she didn't seem bothered by it. That was one more thing in my mind that meant this was actually a dream. Time didn't seem to matter. And another thing, what a world too. It pleased me that I could imagine such a place to begin with, full of beauty and attention to detail, inhabited with attractive people who all seemed to be having such a great time. It didn't bother me too much that I didn't recognize anyone, though in a dream, I would have thought there would be lots of people I knew.

"Oh," she said. "A pine tree. I guess gin does have that kind of taste to it. What's with this *kristmas*?"

"Christmas?" I repeated, not directly responding to her. I really didn't know what the holiday signified other than gifts. That seemed like a terrible explanation. I wondered why I couldn't say anything else about it.

I looked around some more, focused in on things, the pendant lights that hung from the ceiling to illuminate the bar, the mirror above the bar surrounded with intricate metal work, the paintings on either side, the copper plated sculpture, the texture of the wall that added dimensionality and so many other things that were marvels of design much like the world outside that I could glimpse with a slight turn. And all the while, Marta watched me, content to say very little but seeming like any moment she might say something of importance, like she was on the cusp of some great utterance.

"I'm only saying this because I can," I said as I looked at her, her lovely eyes looking back to me as I continued on, "but I know this is a dream."

"What makes you think that?" she shot back at me, rapid fire like.

"Mostly because it has to be. It's the best explanation for a lot of things that happened before this and after, including why you are talking to me."

"So, I wouldn't normally talk to you?" she asked.

"I don't think so. I am just not the kind of person that someone comes up to in a bar and starts a conversation with."

"Why do you say that?"

"I don't know. Because I am not remarkable or striking in appearance. I am distant. I don't even know why I am telling you this except that it is a dream, so maybe this is some kind of therapy, some form of self-analysis."

"Well, if this is a dream, as you say it is, then you must know me or you must have seen me somewhere before. I must not be a complete stranger."

"That's true. My projections would need some kind of base. Although, you very well might be a combination of a couple of people, a composite."

"Like Star?"

"Star?" I echoed. But that was interesting. I knew Star. I knew all about Star. Suddenly, I thought of Star, pictured her, but Marta was nothing like Star. I loved and hated Star. I looked more closely at Marta. She knew something I didn't. She knew something about me, but I knew nothing about her, except that she was nothing like Star. This suddenly didn't feel right. Fuck Star.

"What's wrong?" Marta asked me, sensing the tenseness in me.

She reached out and touched my hand again, for the second time, resting on the edge of the glass that held my drink. I thought about tare, the weight of the thing itself, the container and not what was contained within. I thought about the weight of my body, its shell, separate from everything else as if they were not connected, the two worlds, one the casing and the other, the other the what? I felt once again of two wits, of separate parts struggling to make a go of it. And neither part felt like it fared well, as some parts stretched and others contracted, but the end result was the same. Nobody was winning. You could reach the top, get to this finish line and still be the loser.

I looked at her hand resting on mine as some sensation radiated within, that pulse, her pulse. If at first I felt like moving my hand away, the longer that her hand remained, the better it seemed that it should remain. I even felt more calm. Okay, I thought, I can go along with this.

"This is by far the strangest dream I have ever had."

"By far?" she echoed. "Do you have a lot of dreams?"

She caressed my hand very gently, soothingly. I became more relaxed as if the pressure from a few moments ago bottling up dissolved, and I was whole again, one and not separate pieces floating aimlessly about the world, trying to ascertain what each part weighed while at the same time stretching.

"Because this is not one of them," she offered in such a soft, low voice. "Though I might know why you think it is and you feel the way you do and I can help if you want me to."

"Help me? Sure. This is a dream. This has to be. A few moments ago, I felt the separation of the mind and body and probably that third part, the tripartite; at least that's how it seemed to me: mind, body and spirit. I mean, you didn't even know what a Christmas tree was."

"David, there is no such thing as a Christmas tree let alone anything called Christmas. And this is not a dream."

"Christ. What about Jesus Christ?"

"Who's Jesus Christ?"

In this kind of dream, all sense of religion has vanished from the masses, maybe even from the collective. That was interesting. I had to admit that. Just like that John Lennon song. Imagine no religion. Well, here I was in that world, that dream world where there was no religion. And the best part, here was this woman Marta telling me it wasn't a dream as she held my hand. It was all too good to be true. I wonder if you can imagine such a thing I thought as I spoke to her.

"I don't know either," I said. "Just some guy I guess, some jealous guy."

"Jealous?"

It seemed like the best thing to say if she genuinely did not know who Jesus Christ was. I had studied religion, but I had never been that religious, maybe spiritual, but certainly not religious enough for me to explain who Jesus Christ was. I imagined I could have said he was the Son of God. Surely she would know God. But then there's all of that about rising from the dead after being sacrificed on the cross, walking on water, turning it into wine, and all of that would surely make me sound even crazier. So, I just let it go. It took a lot of faith to believe in something and perhaps even more to explain.

"Well, can I at least kiss you?"

"Excuse me?" Marta nearly choked on the rest of her drink. Her eyes darted up in an alarmed fashion. She relinquished the touch of my hand and retreated. That sensation of warmth and being, faded abruptly. This seemed to me to be the part where I would wake up and think to myself that I should have just kissed her, but I didn't, and everything went on as before.

All around us, the conversations continued. Next to us, a joke about what it meant when a network caught a cold. I didn't hear the punchline. Evidently, it was quite funny. Everybody was laughing. Everyone in the whole place. Except Marta and I. What was a network anyway? A connection among things, an organized system. That's all. No more and no less.

"Well, since this is a dream, and you are talking to me and quite attractive by the way, and you don't know who Jesus Christ is or was, I thought I should just kiss you and play along with this charade."

"That makes no sense," she said, half-laughing until she saw I was serious. "Okay, maybe later. If you ask me nicely."

"That's fine. I mean, I could wake up at any moment and probably only remember bits and pieces, but I will surely remember that I didn't kiss you or I asked you and you said no."

"I didn't exactly say no," she clarified.

"So, it's not exactly impossible then," I said smiling. "If I ask you nicely, later. Okay."

She nodded. The bartender came back around. Marta ordered the drink I was having, and because this was a dream, surely, I would have another. It made a little more sense. This seemed like the kind of dream my subconscious would put together. Not that I seemed to have a choice, but the best thing for me to do was to keep playing along and see where it led. Everything was better in a dream, or it was worse; whatever was happening was always magnified. Dreams were seldom, if ever, boring. I even recalled talking to Jeff Tweedy in a recent dream. We both wore masks. Completely normal.

Another round of drinks appeared. We touched our glasses in salute. At least that was still something people did in good cheer, even in a dream. It was nice to know some of the customs lasted forever though so much around us might change, people were clinking glasses for millennia and beyond. What other things might people still do? Well, if I asked her nicely we might kiss. There was still love. No Jesus Christ or Christmas. I could live that. I never liked Christmas, even as a kid.

"So tell me about this place," I said, opening up the conversation.

"This place in particular?" she asked, motioning around the bar. "Or things in general?"

"Let's just talk about things in general." I thought that was an innocent question, but judging by her reaction, something seemed off. She looked hastily around and then took a big swig of her drink, grimacing a little as if all the whiskey was in one part of the glass. I followed suit and likewise took a big gulp. God. Not that that thing was real, but it hit my hard, like a freight train, like this unbearable weight for a moment, but then it was gone and I just breathed and breathed again, then I looked at her, those eyes of hers enchanting me like nothing else.

"I think we should go somewhere else to talk. It's just better."

"Okay," I said, accepting the moment as for what it was in this little dream of mine. "Let me get the tab."

"No need," Marta said. She looked like she wanted to explain something to me but then gave that thought up, so that I knew what she said was an easier explanation. Like Jesus Christ. In a dream, you can easily accept such things, just as I obliged when she suggested we go somewhere else. I figured she just meant another bar. Fine by me. A quiet place, just the two of us, some cozy conversation I only needed to pretend I understood.

"I've got your drinks. Don't worry about them."

It was true as she said that, that I had not noticed anyone pay, though I had seen people come and go around us. And I watched everything. There were no credit cards at the back bar, no tabs exchanging hands, no cash left at a table or put up for a quick round. People simply came and went. Nothing was wrung up. But everything was accounted for. That was a thought that just came to me. *Everything was accounted for.* There was no money in this dream world, at least, in the physical sense. In some form, money had to exist, that intermediary of exchange had always been part of life. Just now, it was invisible, behind the scenes. I supposed that was progress.

I nodded to the bartender as we exited, again, sensing that I knew him, at least part of him and not the composite of people he surely was at this moment in this dream of mine. But who did I know? I tried to think of people I knew. Names came to me, but not so much the faces. And no Marta. The bartender smiled at me and gave me a knowing acknowledgment. Except Star. I had an image of her, a vivacious blond with an irresistible smile, and a figure fine enough to draw in everyone.

A friendly man waited for us in a car that Marta must have arranged, that much I was familiar with. I listened as she so effortlessly chatted him up, filling the void with the emptiness of words, such as they were at times, while I held to my thoughts, letting this dream simply take me where it would, glancing to Marta now and then, half-expecting that she would change shapes and I would find myself sitting next to someone else or something else. That's what happened in dreams. One moment you were talking to your best friend, then all of the sudden they were a gecko and none of that was alarming. And yet, I felt somewhat alarmed, on edge. Probably I was just nervous, for here I was with this stunning woman whom I had just met, in a car, traveling somewhere. Her beauty seemed to increase by the moment, the more I was with her, the more the spell surrounded me.

I looked at her in the darkness of the car, but all I really saw was her face, the side of her face, her delicate lashes, though now and then she did a quick reassuring glance to me as if making sure I was still there. But I was me, so of course I would be there. I checked myself to make sure I hadn't been turned into a gecko. That would have been something, though. I remembered dreams where I wasn't the usual me, like when I was a bird, flying so effortlessly above the world, far removed or even dreams when I looked down and watched myself. What did that even mean? To dream in third person?

We came to a sleek building that curved like a spiral staircase disappearing into the sky. For a moment, I stood mesmerized by its wonderful illusion. She smiled and took my hand for the third time, not that I was counting, and led me out of the car, then into the building, pausing for a second as she was recognized and the door opened. From there, a clean lobby, nicely decorated with a few paintings and a small sculpture that at first glance I thought was Ozymandias or a miniaturized version of the statue of

Ramesses II, sometimes called the colossus, but hardly in this case as it was so diminutive for a king of kings. Still, it made me chuckle that I just pulled that thought out of my head so easily.

Marta looked back to me, noting my preoccupation with the statue and my smile as I thought about the size of things, the absurdity of the small figure versus what it represented, and even that poem about the decay, which triggered that barren world that flashed in and out of me at the beginning of my dream, like breaths, such delicate breaths. For a moment, I felt uneasy, unsteady like those two drinks I had were really starting to hit me. But then her voice brought me back and I remembered where I was, and who I was, no mighty man, per se, but nonetheless somebody. And I just needed to be nice.

"Hey," she said. "Are you coming?"

"Kind of a crude piece, isn't it?" She quickly added. "But everyone has a job to do and everyone gets paid, even artists."

"Even artists," I silently echoed.

I followed her into an elevator. The door quickly closed and before I knew it, we were exiting again into a room, sparsely decorated, but everything of impeccable taste. And clean. Light colored wood-like floors, probably synthetic though, and white walls with black and white prints. One whole wall seemed to be glass, providing an incredibly expansive view of the world outside, the world of lights and irresistible illumination. My gaze was naturally drawn that way, to its glow, like it was heartbeat, a pulse that made all things flow.

She waved her hand and part of the glass wall changed to a screen or covering. That was a neat trick. I wondered what else she could do, or rather, this world could do as I looked around the open floor plan, to the kitchen area and main room. There was a private room in the back, her bedroom I presumed, but only one. She lived alone.

"Nice place," I said. "I really like the view. Some of the buildings are amazing."

"They are," she said, "although, once you get accustomed to them, it's harder to appreciate. Still, I try to look every day and remember how good it is. As you can see, there's something oddly enchanting and beautiful about the city at night."

"It's the lighting," I said.

I looked back to Marta, who now leaned against the stone countertop, hands in the pockets of her dark colored pants. Maybe this was actually my place? That was an interesting thought. I couldn't remember what my flat was like. No surprise there. Not one thing, though. Not a single detail.

"Is this my place?" I asked her, to which she immediately laughed. I followed her gaze and noticed a pair of high heels next to her white couch along with a handbag. Definitely not my place.

"Not unless you have shoes like that at your place."

"Probably not," I said. "But maybe I do. What size are they?"

"You're funny. Funnier that I thought you would be. Hmm?"

"You were expecting me?

"Can I offer you a drink?" she suggested, her hazel eyes seemed to catch the glow of the city like she wore glasses and the image reflected.

"Sure, if you are having one," I said, then added, "Even

if you are not, I suppose I'll have one anyway. Things are just kind of weird. I shouldn't say this, but I am a little nervous being here."

"I know," she said.

"You know? I mean, I didn't think it was that obvious. Is it? It's not you, I mean, maybe partly. It's mostly me."

She nodded in acceptance and moved to the kitchen, rummaging through the cabinet for a pair of glasses, then ice clinked in the glass followed by whiskey, straight, no mixer. I stood in place for a long time, then moved over to the window wall, the part that was not covered, so I could look out.

I saw a vast array of buildings with lights illuminating the night in orange and greenish hues, objects in the sky moving across some imaginary screen, landing on rooftops of various buildings. Bluish lights abetted a waterway, probably where I had first walked. Distances were hard to measure, could have been minutes away or miles.

I don't know how long I looked, but at some point she tapped me on the shoulder and handed me the drink, gazing briefly into my eyes. Her eyes mesmerized me, hazel colored, which meant at different times they looked more golden or brownish green, depending on the light.

"So," she said, still touching me on the shoulder, "Let's talk in general. Isn't that what you wanted?"

I nodded and took a sip of my drink, a real light sip. For whatever reason, the drink tasted stronger than it should. Maybe it wasn't whiskey. I just assumed by the color as she poured the liquid into the tumbler. What was whiskey anyway? An aged spirit in a barrel. If there was no whiskey in this world, there would be no way I would even know how to make it.

"Is this whiskey?" I asked.

"Yes," she nodded. "It's the good stuff."

"Okay," I said as I gingerly took another sip. "What is this place, first of all? Where am I?" And who are you, I wanted to add. Who are you?

"It's the world as you know, as you knew but maybe don't quite remember."

"But it's nothing like I know."

"It is," she said. "You are just adjusting to the changes, the natural disorientation that I imagine comes from relying on something for so long, and now being released from that thing, the network."

"The network?"

"Yes, the network, or the term we use to signify the vast collection of systems that control everything, even us, so that everything we do is known and assisted so that we can lead the perfect life."

"I don't understand."

"We've fused the human brain with technology. Two brains. It compliments what we do."

"So there is a computer inside my brain?"

"Yes," she said. "In a way. Your brain is connected to a whole sequence of computers that interact and compliment what you do, what you think and say, except. . ."

"Except what?"

"Except you are no longer connected to the network," she said, eyeing me cautiously, just like she did in the restaurant when we first met, when she boldly crossed the room and seated herself at the bar stool right next to me.

I couldn't think about what she said. Instead, I thought

about the first time she touched my hand, her smell, was it a smell? In dreams could you notice smells? Women just smelled nice, but she seemed nicer than most. Not that I had a lot of experience.

"Peach hibiscus," she said.

"What?"

"That's the fragrance. I can change it if you like."

"Oh, it's fine." I said. I would have asked how she knew. How did she know? But I didn't. The network. What was this about the network?

"I was connected though?" I asked.

"Yes. You were."

"So you are saying, we, or most everyone lives in a world controlled by a vast computerized grid, a network that knows everything we do, everywhere we go, and not only that, influences our thoughts and actions if they need to be so coerced?"

"More or less. That's a good way of looking at it. The system was designed such that we all ascertain our best selves and are completely happy doing so. There is no have or have not. After all, everything is in abundance. We used to live in a world of scarcity, but scarcity is just another term for the inaccessible. And now, everything is accessible. And if everything is accessible, then nothing is impossible."

"Really? Even love and companionship?" I asked, imagining the network properly matching up people like some ultra-advanced dating service. Given all the network knew, it probably could find the perfect mate for everyone. Such a thing was a mere matter of solving an equation. That was what some people believed, at least, but not at all what I believed. I knew this as my stubborn side, that person not wanting to believe what everyone else seemed to believe.

"Companionship for sure. You can be with anyone you want in the SIM. Love, or the idea of it, has dramatically changed and the way you are asking and thinking about it is not something people consider."

"I don't understand that at all. Love is such a force; what makes the world go around. Love and only love." I said, quoting songs. *Love and only love, it can't be denied.*

"Maybe that was true. Or maybe that was an illusion, something we just liked to believe. Now none of this is what I necessarily might believe. I am just taking the point of view of a program. In that respect, love is inefficient, messy, and complicated. A computer system certainly couldn't model that kind of range of emotions when there exists an easier way to go about things," Marta said so matter-of-factly as if there was nothing odd about any of this.

First no religion and now no love. What kind of world was this that I imagined? I could see where it was complicated, that love in its rapture, the sometimes madness and chaos, led to a lot of unpredictability, but to get rid of it entirely? That seemed absurd. And yet, love could be the most absurd thing too when you loved what was the unattainable.

"And besides, the SIM is better," she added. "Love can be whatever you want or need it to be."

"Better? What's the SIM? What could be better than the real thing?"

"Better? Yes, especially if it feels like the real thing and you don't know otherwise. In some ways it is a lot easier to maintain fiction than a reality. The SIM is a simulated world, what you might think or remember as an advanced form of virtual reality."

"Hmm. I just can't imagine it, that's all. The idea seems so foreign to me that some virtual world can rival this world." I looked at her questioningly, not sure if I could believe or accept what she was saying. She gave every indication she meant what she said.

"Is it really, though? Sure, at first it was a bit crude and unsettling, the earlier versions of what we called virtual reality, but it's come a long way since then. It's like a world of fantasy becoming reality. Just imagine, suppose you wanted to go shopping. You could go to Paris and shop, then ski the alps or sail the ocean. Sex? Later on, you could sleep with whomever you wanted as much as you wanted. Or if that's not your thing, then you could do something else. You could take drugs, experience a great high. Whatever it is people want, it's just a reaction within the brain. All of these things, these pleasures, are merely activations of various brain regions, mesolimbic pathways triggering dopamine. There really is something for everyone. And that something is the SIM."

Again she spoke so matter-of-factly, cold and distant as if it had already been settled and there was no alternative, no Plan B in this. This was how it was and there was nothing else better. I didn't like that about her. It had a visceral effect on me, a kind of repulsion, and yet, I was also drawn to her. It was a terrible place to be, but in a dream, it didn't matter. This was all needless. I felt her beauty slipping away simply because I didn't like what she was saying. I went negative too quickly on things. That was a fault of mine.

I looked back at her leaning against the counter, drink

in hand, in that semi-lit space, partially obscured. I remembered this was just a dream. I could feel any way I wanted, and what I shouldn't feel was negative. More than anything, I needed to maintain an illusion, dream or not, so that I could cope. Otherwise, I was being pulled apart, stretched in too many different directions such that if I didn't retain a shape, any shape, I might get loose and then never come back. So, I kind of lied.

"Wow. That's amazing. I feel like I keep saying that, thinking that. So, I guess that means there are no drug problems or any other kinds of addictions? No other bad behaviors. No bad actors. We're all good."

I watched Marta as she talked. When I moved to the couch, she did not follow, though I expected her to. I took another sip of my drink and listened as best as I could, no matter how crazy it all sounded to me.

"No. There wouldn't be any at all anyway because of the network. You don't ban something. Better just to manage it. Certain people do go to the SIM to get high, for sure, but they do not get addicted per se as that's an issue with how the brain is wired, which is the very thing the network absolves. The deficiencies in the brain. It was just a prototype, anyway, not meant to be perfect."

I thought about the point for a bit, the absolution or suppression of various impulses, the way our brains were wired, all of that internal code that advances in neurotechnology had isolated and made better, with the implication being that this network controlled the brain because it understood each of us, in many cases better than we knew ourselves. Only a computer could do that. But what if it missed something vital? Did she really mean the brain, our human brain, was a mere prototype, a placeholder?

"I see you are still skeptical," she said.

"I am," I said. "I understand it perhaps on a theoretical level, artificial intelligence fused with our brain seems like the best of all possible words, too good to be true, but on a practical level, I don't get it. And as for the SIM, I don't know how real it can possibly be. And if our brains are controlled by the network, then why do we need the SIM?"

"Choice," she said. "Nobody knows they are connected to the network. The brain has been tricked. Part of maintaining that deception is the SIM, a place of perfect illusion and escape, just like we always had in books, movies, video games. You talk about how we are all good, there are no bad actors, well in the SIM, if you wanted, you could exercise those tendencies towards evil, the grotesque. It's a safe place for fantasies."

Marta moved away from the counter and slowly walked to me, dreamily, I thought, in the way she moved, that expression on her face, the calm, reassuring nature in the way she looked at me and then the tenderness when she sat beside me on the couch and took my hand as if she had done this a thousand times, and not maybe only the sixth time.

"But, of course," I said as if I had said the lines before, "like so many things, you can explain all you want, but until that thing is experienced, it is not really known, this SIM."

Though I had known it. I had once known so much. Yet, like a great talent, squandered. When she first mentioned the SIM, something inside me sparked. It wasn't that unfamiliar to me. I seemed to know it without knowing it, but again, for the moment a medium without context.

"Exactly, and it is kind of dreamlike too, so you might feel right at home," Marta teased. Then she added rather brightly and with charm, "If you still want to kiss me, try me in the virtual world. Try it in the SIM. Since it's your fantasy, you won't even have to ask me nicely."

"Really? That would be kind of embarrassing, wouldn't it?"

"Why, are you not attracted to me?" she said, raising her eyebrows, her hazel eyes aglow in a seemingly different shade. She certainly had to know I was drawn to her, felt connected to her merely by the way she looked at me. And from there, it was easy, her eyes, being as they were, truly unique, drawing me in ever so by what I felt was a special look, something just for me.

"It's not that at all," I said. I took a much bigger sip of the whiskey-like drink. It seemed much more palatable now. Even good, quite good. Probably something expensive, whatever that meant in such a world where everything was accessible. Why even drink here when I could drink there in the promise of the SIM?

"And since you think this a dream anyway, what do you have to lose? In the very least, you can use me as a base and make modifications," she offered. She stood up and kicked off her shoes, straightened her posture as if modeling the possibility. And for the first time, I really looked at her, closely, more carefully.

She was petite, wore dark pants and a loose-fitting blouse, bluish purple with some sort of pattern. As she turned, the color seemed more transparent, depending on the light, but maybe that was my imagination. She had lightly bronzed skin and lovely dark, curly hair and hazel eyes. If at first she didn't strike me as beautiful, now she certainly did. In a way, I almost felt like she kept changing, that she was a chameleon. That was impossible.

Then I remembered like she said this was a dream, so maybe this wasn't at all as weird as it seemed. Here I was, considering entering a virtual world referred to as a SIM to be intimate with some variation of the woman in front of me rather than being with her in the flesh, in a sense, a dream within a dream. Rather than stand up and kiss her, I was going to go into some augmented extension of the world to do that very thing. That sounded exactly like something I would create. Had I not once written a play just for the girl I wanted to play the lead? Had I? I wondered. Maybe that had just been a dream too.

"Okay, how do you mean?"

"However you want," she said, as she gazed delectably at me, "make me shorter or taller, change my nose, the color of my eyes."

"Not your eyes," I interjected. They were perfect. "I love your eyes."

"Okay," she said, and paused, "then my skin. Or make me more athletic, taller, give me bigger breasts."

"Or smaller," I said.

She nodded. "Sure, if you want. Whatever you want, you can do in the SIM, with me."

I considered this. How much of this dream would I remember when I awoke, and what would it mean anyway? What sort of symbols would I recall? I would remember Marta and her eyes, those hazel eyes, but maybe not much beyond that. Perhaps that she served me whiskey and told me some crazy tale about this futuristic world where everyone was connected, unknowingly, to a vast computerized network. Sounded both paranoid and delusional, like I was somehow supposed to save everyone, but from what, their own happiness?

"You could even give me a penis if that's what you like?"

I recoiled a bit, not expecting that turn, lost as I was in a mini-reverie about her eyes and a dream, but I didn't show it much. Okay, maybe a little. That definitely wasn't my thing, and even in a dream, I wasn't going to go there. I shook my head as I spoke. Suddenly, she wasn't as beautiful as I thought. Was that her fantasy?

"Has it really become that perverted?"

"It was in the other world too, the one you are thinking about, remembering. People have always had what some might call strange proclivities, fetishes; not all people, but definitely some. And all the things we don't understand in someone can seem strange to us."

"Because they *are* strange."

She nodded. "Yes, they might be strange," she admitted. Her hazel eyes flashed radiantly, in a perpetual state of wonder, in a manner that mesmerized me. What worlds existed inside of her—never mind this other thing she called the SIM. I wanted to know about her. Maybe via the SIM I could learn more. She was beautiful again to me, but it bothered me that she kept changing.

"Good, that's not your fantasy."

"Please," she said.

"Okay, I'll try it, this virtual world."

"SIM," she said again, was what they called it. She added something about how it would be helpful for me to be familiar with it because it was so prevalent in life. Go for a jog in the morning along the beach. Go back in time.

Play a first-person shooter video game. Shoot hoops. All of these things you could utilize the SIM and do. Though you couldn't go back in time and learn about Jesus Christ because apparently the Son of God did not exist. That one really got me. Had I mentioned he was the Son of God to her?

"You know Jesus Christ is the Son of God," I said to her.

She shook her head. "If you say so, then I believe you."

"You believe me."

"Of course, I believe you."

"Even about God?" I asked

"Or Gods," she answered, daringly. "David, I believe in you."

The way she said my name and looked at me, that way she looked at me, then moved away, struck me as magical. I finished the last of my drink and set it on the granite counter in the kitchen, following her as she walked to a doorway that once opened, contained a small, darkened room that lightly lit up as we entered. The room was barely big enough for both of us. Off to the side was a leather chair.

She touched the wall and a panel seemed to light up out of nowhere, like something from nothing. She then explained to me what was going to happen. The system would scan my body and a glove-like sleeve would encase my body like a second layer of skin. A pair of goggles would cover my eyes. From there, this new world would appear

"It's something you have to experience," she said. "I can't really explain it."

I stood in the middle of the room as my body was scanned. I closed my eyes while the red light enveloped me. Like anything that was new, the first time, I could feel my heart beating a little faster and a general uneasiness. Not so much discomfort. A few drinks helped with that.

"Okay," she said. "Let's start with something basic. Like going for a walk with a dog."

"Walking a dog?"

"Yeah, it's quite popular. No one has pets anymore except in the SIM world. Let me know what sort of breed you want. The default is a labrador retriever."

"Why a lab?"

"Because everyone likes labs. They are cute and friendly."

"That's fine."

"Now," she said. "Put on the goggles and headset, and start imagining that dog. At some point, you'll see that very dog and know that it is the right one. We call this customization mode. It doesn't always work with everyone, but it's a good place to start."

"Okay," I said, putting on the contraption and focusing 'til I saw a light colored lab in front of me, just out of reach, wagging its tail like a familiar companion.

"Now, it's a little tricky at first because you'll think too much about it. But try to be as natural as can be. Say the word *begin* and then try to move toward the dog just as you normally would."

"But this is just a dream."

"Indeed," she said. "Just humor me. And sit if you like. Try to be as relaxed as possible. It's kind of weird, but you'll adjust."

I moved awkwardly to the chair and sat down, immediately comforted by the plushness of the leather. I breathed easier and cleared my mind as much as I could of all of the peripheral cluttering, concentrating solely on the black lab in front of me until its coloring changed back to a cream color. Like Shasta.

"Okay," I said then paused. "You'll be right here, right?"

"Yes," she said as she touched my shoulder for a moment.

"Okay, let's begin."

At first there was nothing but the dog, then the playful bark and wag of the tail as the dog approached me with its leash in mouth, ready for a walk. The only thing was, I couldn't move. My feet were so heavy. I knew this dream. When you had to get somewhere but couldn't even move, meanwhile everything was slipping away. I thought about what Marta said then let it slide from my mind. Why was I always having this kind of dream, where I was stuck in place and couldn't move?

I took a step, a little unsteady at first, unsure of where I was and what I was walking on, but after that it was easy and natural as this dog and I walked in a green grass field with blue skies overhead. A light breeze rustled, but the warmth of the sunshine made that sensation pleasant, much like the air, the freshness of the air, so good I wanted to breathe as much as I could.

I let the dog off leash and watched as it ran, as she ran, I should say. Shasta. And I found myself running after her until my lungs were burning inside. It had been a long time since I ran anywhere, maybe not since I was a kid. And why I was running, I didn't know. It just felt good. And where was I now? This must have been some place I was as a kid, some part of my subconscious, a dream within a dream, this lush field, summertime, the buzz of the bees, clover and the faint smell of grain.

First I heard, then above me, saw a bevy of doves in perfect formation. I watched as they soared at high speeds across the bluest skies, but I swore I could still hear their drawn out lament. Up ahead, I was sure there would be a store where I could get something to drink, maybe a coke or something. I just needed to keep walking until I found it, and so I followed Shasta out of that field towards the woods and beyond that, whatever was to be.

I wanted to get a good look at myself, in a pond perhaps, so that I could see how old I was. I know how old I felt, but as Shasta and I came upon a small footbridge bridge spanning a murky looking lagoon, I knew that was unlikely. It felt familiar, though, so we crossed. On the other side a country road raced along the water before winding up into a hillside of trees, and beyond that a protected waterway, like an inlet from the ocean with its seashells and seagulls. As well, I could see my little country store with a single pump gas station and a little shack on the side selling burgers and fish and chips, a line of people waiting for such wares.

Then there was a pause. I heard Marta's voice, distant but distinct, miles away and muffled, moving closer like it was on a motorcycle, until it was clear. Was everything okay? What's happening there? I looked at the dog, my dog, looking back at me in anticipation. Seagulls landed on posts. They sang an aching song, at once anguish and triumph. Perhaps it was just a call and response. Then Marta's voice again as if the motorcycle she had been on had stopped to get gas and she was nearing me.

After that I was back out, a momentary blackness, followed by a cool rush inside my head, and the dim lights of the little room with Marta, sitting in that leather chair as my body returned to itself and I was whole again, if in fact I was not whole before. If I thought about it too much, then I wouldn't be sure, so I left it at that.

"Wow," I said, somewhat stunned as I took off the goggles. "That was something else."

"Where were you?"

"In a field with my dog, the very dog I grew up with. It was kind of weird. Maybe it was not her exactly, but she reminded me of her. Shasta was her name. After the mountain."

I didn't think Marta knew that mountain. I seemed to have knowledge of things that did not exist in this world, but that didn't change a thing, whatever something was named. That thing still existed. And maybe it was called something else. That was fine. There was a mountain somewhere that used to be called Mount Shasta. I was sure of that. She nodded and didn't ask too many questions, but I was excited and ready to talk.

"And this store I remember going to as a kid, that sense of freedom of being allowed to go to the store on my own and buy candy because it was the money I had saved from my paper route."

"Paper route?" Marta asked me. "Candy?"

"You know, sweets? Sugary things."

"Ah," she said. "Crystallized sugar. Confections."

"Yeah," I said, then with disappointment. "But I didn't make it to the store."

"Well, you can go back some other time, but for now, this time, interact with someone else, another person. I'll load myself as a template and then you can go from there."

"It won't be with you?"

"No, just my likeness, which as I mentioned before, you can alter and adjust as you see fit.

"I won't change a thing," I said, quickly. "And I'll be nice. I promise."

She just smiled at me, looking the way she did in that little room where we stood among this amazing contraption she called the SIM, a technology which everyone had access to, a technology which seemed to make anything possible and yet wasn't a Pandora's box. Nothing bad was unleashed from it.

"You seriously have no idea where I am in when I am in this SIM." I was a little suspicious.

She nodded in the affirmative. "Only generally that you were going for a walk with your dog, but I didn't know any of the details, like the store or any of that. That's as much as we know in the custom mode. Some of the other modes are more obvious, I suppose, and we can make assumptions."

I put the headset and goggles back on and took a deep breath. Marta appeared before me. Just because I could, I made some changes, made her taller and then shorter, bigger as she suggested in the bust, before returning to the original rendition. It was magical. And a little bit eerie too. It was kind of fun to make the little tweaks though, I had to admit that. I supposed I could also change me if I wanted. That sort of begged the question, what did it mean to be me? Was my essence primarily body and not mind or soul? I had never liked the way I looked, and yet, given the opportunity, I wouldn't change a thing. I never understood that contradiction.

"Begin," I said, thinking to myself this was a dream and no place for such philosophical discussions.

I found myself walking as I had been before, in that similar place, maybe the very place I had been before, where I was first struck by the shimmering world that seemed to float on air, magically. I saw the shops and little boutiques, felt that rush of life, and of course, I came upon the bar I had been at where I first met Marta.

I went inside, saw all the groups of people, heard the chatter, the laughter, the sound of glasses clinking, speeches being made or perhaps just jokes being told amid the jovial banter. I nodded to the bartender as I sat down at the end of the bar. It wasn't hard to pick Marta out as she was directly across from me on the other side of the bar just like she had been. We locked eyes. Her hazel eyes danced dreamily. She looked at once spectacular. That was different. As she approached, I followed her, noted her slinky black cocktail dress, her short, dark curled hair bobbing slightly as she strode confidently toward me like some runway model.

Things seemed to move faster, at an accelerated pace. Maybe that was just me pushing the moment along, not drawing it out forever like I usually did, so that nothing ever really happened. In a dream, time was different anyhow. Less needed to be explained. Leaps were made that seemed like normal jumps, and cause and effect similarly skewed. Stuff just happened.

"Hey," I said to her. And before I could be smart and say her name, she beat me to it.

"I'm Marta," she said as she sat in the stool next to me, put her right elbow on the bar and turned to me. "Is this seat taken?"

"No. It's been waiting to be claimed by you."

She flashed me a smile, looked at me intently. In that

semi-darkness of the bar, her cocktail dress still sparkled, caught by little wisps of light that trailed like smoke. She smelled sweet, like peaches and cream. She seemed to edge closer to me, teetering on the end of her stool as she put her hand on mine. I had lost track at this point how many times she had touched me, but did it even count in here?

The bartender brought us some drinks, whiskey-like, I presumed. We touched glasses and took a sip. She drew back slightly and watched me closely, so very closely as if all my movements meant something special, though I did not think they did.

"Do you want to kiss me?" she asked as her left hand touched my side.

"Yes, very much so, but not here," I said, even though it was a dream and didn't matter where I was or when we kissed. How I loved her eyes. I felt that she knew everything about me as I looked into them and there was nothing I ever needed to explain. Then I remembered Jesus Christ.

"Do you know who Jesus Christ is?"

"Yes," she said. "He is the Son of God."

"And the Beatles?"

"And the Beatles too. More popular than Jesus Christ. I know these things. I know all these things and more."

"What's your favorite Beatles song?"

"'Happiness is a Warm Gun,'" she said without a pause.

Interesting choice. I smiled to myself, but also a little bit to her too. It was nice that she knew the Beatles were more popular than Jesus Christ. Because at a time long ago, maybe they were. That was the wrong thing for John

Lennon to say. Some things are better thought and not said. That was one of them. In a dream, it was different though. That was the perfect thing to say. In a dream it was okay to let it all loose.

She tilted her chin down then gazed back up at me. She ran her hands through her hair, lifting her curls up before setting them back down, like a dance partner completing a move. She bit her lip then took a sip of her drink. She knew I watched her every move, though I had tried to look away.

"Let's go back to your place," I said. I had no idea where I lived. I took a big taste of my drink then set the glass back down. She seemed to be pausing, considering the proposition, which admittedly was odd. It would have been more normal to suggest my place. But in the last version of Marta, we went to her place. I was merely following precedent. This Marta did not know that. Or did she?

"I was hoping you would say that," Marta said, suddenly rejuvenated. "And don't worry, I got your drink. We're already paid up. There's no cash in this world. It's all just known. Everything is known and accounted for."

"Even what I want?"

"Yes, if you know what you want. Often that's the hardest thing; that's the catch."

"There's always a catch," I said.

"Not always," she said. "You said you wanted to kiss me. There is no catch in that."

"I did say that. And I do."

There was no car this time around. No Uber or Lyft or whatever was the name of the entity that survived that battle. Her flat was close enough to walk, a tall, elegant building that stretched toward the sky like a great, glorious tower, disappearing into the darkness of the night. It was the tallest thing I had ever seen, but nothing resembling a spiral staircase.

She barely paused at the entrance. A doorman greeted us. Nicely dressed, older man with a mustache and a cap. He winked at me. That kind of bothered me. Like he was in on a joke, but this was no joke, so I only smiled and nodded back to him.

There were no miniaturized sculptures of great kings in the lobby. I noted a full-sized pink plaster elephant with painted sides. It seemed out of place next to a pair of plush, oversized chairs.

"Artists!" Marta said offhandedly.

An elevator whisked us up to the top floor in the time it took me to gaze at her legs in that black cocktail dress. I started, noting her black heels, then worked my way up, floor by floor, and then we were there before I got very far.

Her flat was spare, though nicely furnished. Elements of brick, wood and stone coalesced together. Once inside, she closed the door and we kissed immediately, wasting no time, that passionate kind of kiss, that first kiss of unexpected delight and pleasure, and taste too as her tongue touched mine, as her firm body pressed against me, first her breasts then her legs, followed by her hips. Her hands wrapped around me. I moved my hands along the fabric of her cocktail dress, down to her legs and the smoothness of her skin, then retraced up her thighs, higher and higher to the lace of her underwear and the ultimate warmth of her body, its movements that mattered as we kept close, as the rhythm of our hearts sang. But it was all wrong, and I knew it, knew that it was way too fast; even if it was a dream, it just felt wrong.

So I drew away, albeit slowly. All too aware that I was in a virtual world about to make love to a woman who was in the same room with me, not necessarily watching or knowing what was happening, but surely aware on some level. And that felt weird. I had all sorts of questions too, but since this was a dream, maybe those questions didn't matter. Sometimes the things we thought were the most important in a given moment meant virtually nothing.

"Is everything okay," Marta whispered in my ear. Was it the SIM world or the other world, that dream world I came from. It didn't matter. I kissed her delicately on the lips and gazed deeply into her eyes, lost momentarily in that abyss.

"Everything is perfectly fine," I said, but that was not true at all. Nothing was really fine.

I exited the SIM, quickly took the goggles and headset off, and breathed. The rush wasn't as intense as I adjusted to the dim lights from the chair where I sat in that small room with Marta standing nearby. She immediately came over to me and put her hand on my shoulder.

"Is everything okay? Was everything okay?"

"Yes," I said, smiling a little sheepishly. "Everything was fine, perfectly fine. Quite amazing too. I can't really explain how real it was, how it felt, but you probably know all of that anyway. I mean, it was amazing. King Midas would have nothing to wish for."

"King Midas?"

"Yeah, you don't know who he is?"

She shook her head.

"How about the Beatles?"

"Yes. I know them. Old British rock 'n' roll band."

I nodded. At least that was good. She knew the Beatles. This world had the Beatles. And that meant it had music. I thought about asking what her favorite song was, but that would have been too weird if she answered the same. I wondered why some things and not others existed here, what that meant about my subconscious. The Beatles had been important to me, but Christmas and Jesus, not at all.

"And King Midas?" she asked me. "What about him?"

"Well, it's an old story about a King, King Midas, who found one of Dionysus's wandering satyrs," I said then paused, knowing of course, she would not know any of these people. "You don't know Dionysus"

"No, sorry," Marta said almost sadly. "Haven't heard of him either."

"Well, that's okay. Anyway, King Midas entertained and later returned this person to Dionysus, and Dionysus was so overjoyed, he granted King Midas any reward he wanted. Midas asked that everything he touched turned to gold because gold was the most valuable thing there was."

"I know this story. Not as King Midas though," she said, a bit more pleased now.

"Anyway, as you know, if everything you touch turns to gold, then there are some limitations imposed by such a thing, namely trying to eat or drink anything, so such a reward was actually a curse. In fact, too much of anything means that thing is no longer a good thing."

"And so your point is that if you can easily transform any fantasy into a reality like experience, that's too much of a good thing?"

"Yes. The SIM experience was amazing, but at the same time. . . it's just too much. I mean I had a wonderfully intense and real SIM experience with you, but what was happening so quickly seemed to almost take the meaning out of it. If you know what I mean. That such a thing over time would seem to diminish in value."

"You think too much about it. Most people kind of accept the experience as a normal process of life. And so, they are not aware of the same things you are, limitations of having it all. To them, it's the SIM and in the SIM you can get whatever you want."

I nodded to her. And I understood her point. "Still, I suppose, it would have been a little different if I was alone. I mean it was kind of awkward given you were in the room with me."

"Did you kiss me?" Marta asked me with piqued interest.

"Yes," I said sheepishly, then looked away from her. "I met you in a similar bar as earlier, although time was accelerated. Things moved faster. It was interesting, the little details that were different."

"Did you ask nicely?"

"Well, I didn't have a chance. You just seemed to kiss me, and I responded."

"Hmm," she mused.

It had made me think on some level, this very moment now was a SIM experience too. But that only meant that the SIM was very much a dream you could control, where you were in the driver's seat. After all, with Marta, it didn't take much to lure her back to her apartment. And she was right. I did think too much. If I didn't think as much, then I could certainly influence the interaction even more, but I was always more thought than action. And what did she say and mean that most people accept it? Why not at all? I knew why I couldn't completely accept it. Because this was a dream and it was too good to be true.

"There are other modes," she offered as the thin residue of a smile disappeared from her lips as she spoke. "Yours was sort of a customized experience. But you can do a more randomly generated experience. And there are preloaded types of things too. But everything can be changed. Everything can be made exactly as you want it with lots of control or little control. The point is, it's whatever you want, even sometimes if you don't know what you want."

"You said to me in the SIM that knowing what you want is the hardest thing."

"Did I?" Marta said, looking a little surprised, but also pleased. "There's a lot of truth to that. You do need to know what you want in order to get it."

"I suppose so," I said, then continued. "When you told me in the SIM it seemed so profound. I guess it's really pretty straightforward."

"Sometimes the simplest things are the most profound. To reduce an idea to its essence, strip it out of complexity to something so easily grasped. You might say that is true wisdom."

"It's odd. It just seems like something I needed to hear."

She kept her hand on my shoulder. Then she noticed that I had noticed her hand resting there, and it had been there for a long time, but still she kept it there. I thought about that for a moment, then returned to the SIM experience. It would be all too easy to get lost in such a device.

"I can't really understand how it works. It seems to draw from my mind on some level, but how can it know my thoughts?"

"Right now, you are of two brains," she said to me, casually removing her hand from my shoulder and motioning back to the main room. "Let's go back to the main room."

She touched the control panel. I felt the envelope of energy of whatever it was around me, disappear completely. I got up from the chair, literally thinking to myself that I needed to get up from the chair, but of course, such things didn't happen because we willed them to, they just happened because that was how the world was, how we moved and breathed unconsciously.

And no light switch anywhere. I noticed that as I followed Marta back to the main room and sat next to her on the couch. There had to be some other test for lucid dreaming, but if there was, then I was not aware.

"You may not understand a lot of what I am about to tell you. And I think I know what you are thinking. That this is all a dream. But know this, this is not a dream."

The plush leather couch felt so comforting as if I closed my eyes I would simply drift off to sleep, all the same, I focused on Marta, remembered the cocktail dress she wore in the SIM, much different than the dark pants and purplish top she had on now, though such things in no way diminished her. If anything, I felt more attracted to her as time moved on as if she was a different person from earlier, or maybe, it was I who was different, who kept changing.

"Are you with me?" she asked, then repeated her earlier statement. "Maybe not completely. Right now, you are of two brains and both of them remain perplexed by the situation, so some things you remember and others you forget, but mostly what you feel is disorientation. And that will pass."

"I am disoriented. But as to why, I don't understand."

"There was an epidemic many years ago, catastrophic, and at the time, the best known, the best available thing to do was to connect everyone to the network, that way we could understand why some people lived and most people died."

None of this registered with me, yet, it was not surprising to hear in that way you can know things, two completely incompatible ideas and yet believe in the plausibility of either, of knowing or not knowing. I maybe only partially listened as Marta continued, but I grasped everything she said. Like when you've read a book before but don't realize it until you start reading that you've read it before. Something tips you off, a character, a scene, something.

"Once connected to the grid, it made sense for the network to control more and more of our lives, in some ways, to help us cope with the tragedy and in others because we always error too much one way or the other in the beginning, do we not?"

This was turning into some dream. Except Marta said more than once it was not a dream. Not knowing what to believe I looked again to her, knowing only that not long ago I was in a very similar room as this, maybe even the same room, if two things could be the same, and we kissed like the world was ending, and she wore a slinky black cocktail dress, so smooth and wondrous to the touch, or was I now just thinking about her skin, about her body, about the feeling I felt when I was so close to her? Her legs had seemed longer, so much longer then, accentuated by her dress, by the seductive lines from her heels on up. Or maybe, I had made her taller than she was.

"Hey," she said, smiling and then turning to a more serious expression. "You're drifting. I can let you sleep. I just thought you should know."

"Know what exactly? I don't understand how I am part of this?"

She paused before she spoke. In her eyes, a million images flashed upon me, each beckoning a new thought, a new idea, a new direction. And there were so many such things in this infinite world, this endless variation, this SIM I called a dream.

"You were one of the architects of the system."

"I was, was I? Does that mean you were too?" I thought to myself, *I is another*, for this me is not me.

"Indirectly. I am a coder. I wrote a lot of the code. I didn't make the big decisions. I just did what I was supposed to do."

"And I made the big decisions?"

"You were one of eight who decided everything. But you, you were different too," she said, eyeing me rather coolly. It was a look from her I had not yet seen, but it was only briefly there, and I felt so tired I couldn't be sure, though it was partly disgust. Or perhaps, disappointment. Surely, I could explain whatever I had done that was so terrible. I had that dream sense again, of running in place, trying to move, but being unable to do so though all my legs were pumping as fast as they could, cartoon style.

A gloominess overcame me, like that infrared enveloped that engulfed me in the SIM, only this was tighter, less forgiving. I tried my best to picture Marta and me sitting in the bar or in her flat somewhere, but all I could think about was the collapsing walls around me and my inability to move. And all the while I was sinking. Was there really such a thing as quicksand or was that just a device?

"I don't know how you did it, but you altered the code, very slightly, such that after a given length of time you would be disconnected from the network."

She made this statement matter-of-factly but in a hushed tone. And she said it quickly. The longer such words lingered, the greater the weight they carried, the more the implication came to life. That what? I had stolen fire, and like Prometheus, would be punished? I didn't know if that was it. If I had stolen fire, then I didn't know what to do with it.

And strangely, this idea that I disconnected did not seem unfamiliar to me. I thought about the great grid, the wires and connections linked together by the vast network that was underneath everything, and that made sense. Perhaps a part of me remembered doing that very thing, disconnecting myself. Certainly that had to be something I would do. I had never felt wholly part of the world as it was, even when fully and completely connected, nor even before that. Once an outsider, always an outsider. That feeling never left. Not even in a dream.

"You were skeptical, I imagine," Marta said. "As to whether such a thing was worth it."

I nodded. Skeptical, sure, you could call it that. Pessimistic. Definitely not sanguine. But there was more to this story than that. I was terrified too, of being controlled by the network. How would we ever know if we programmed the system well enough or not? And could we? Were we as humans even capable of understanding ourselves enough to design a network to assist us?

"I actually think I remember that," I said after a while. "So, how much time has passed?"

"Fourteen years," she said. "Exactly fourteen years."

That was a long time. And I was suddenly very tired. I looked forward to closing my eyes and waking up, but I was going to miss Marta. I had never met anyone like her, and I had only just met her. I vowed to find her in real life. But I was too tired to think about that. I turned away from her to the great lights of the shimmering city, even at this hour, there was a hum of energy that I could just feel, but not enough to jolt me. I turned back to Marta. I focused on her eyes, her hazel eyes, and in them I saw me—at least, some semblance of me.

"I don't understand," I began because there was one more thing I needed to know. "What I saw at first, at the very beginning then in a glimpse: this horribly, grotesque world."

"You were just adjusting to the change," Marta said patiently. "Imagine if you were almost blind, out at night amid a flood of lights, how terrible that would seem, how distorted and disturbing, but then all of a sudden you could see just fine because. . ."

"Because what?"

"Because you were helped to see what you should see," she said. "Because you had misplaced your glasses and for a moment, you saw a horror like no other, but then everything was fine."

She had a way of making everything seem better, a soothing quality to her voice. Maybe it reminded me of somebody, but I could not be so sure. I couldn't be sure of much of anything as I thought about what she said. And yet, I understood. If our own eyes couldn't see, then that meant they were flawed by design. That was something that could be corrected by glasses in the old world, and here it was just part of life, helping everyone see things just a little bit sharper.

"I'll miss you," I said. My eyes felt heavy but the rest of me felt weightless, so maybe it was just a losing battle.

She put her hands on mine, her touch, almost electric, but if not that then what? Magnetic, I supposed, as it drew me closer to her, both literally and figuratively, as a kind of merging. In my head I pictured being on the other side of a great chasm, below the unfathomable abyss, and here she was, this angel on the other side tossing me a lifeline. That was the last thing I thought as I closed my eyes.

As if this world wasn't enough, I drifted into another strange world, this one more replete with the horrors of a ruined place, whole cities and towns ravaged by the harshness of humanity and its war against nature. Or maybe it was a war against each other as nature didn't set fire to buildings or shoot holes through windows.

In some kind of sport utility vehicle, I drove through such a block, a strange yet familiar woman beside me. I didn't know who she was and yet I knew exactly who she was. That didn't make sense. Who was she? In a dream, things like that don't get explained, no matter when you wake up and crave answers, there are none to be found.

A gas station up ahead had been gutted by an explosion. A smoky residue hung in the air and the ground still smoldered. The cheerful red white and blue colors of what had been a Chevron station were smudged out, blotted out by blackness, half visible and only recognizable by its tattered logo. The attached convenience store looked like it had been someone's last hideout, completely trashed. Racks were knocked over, potato chips bags strewn aimlessly, the doors of the refrigerated beverage cases either wide open or off the hinges. I imagined but could not see spilled milk.

Though the situation was grim, I drove through it all with a placid calmness, almost laughing to myself about the spilled milk, the idea of it, even if it wasn't true. I just thought it should be there like in the movies when there had been a big shootout and the viewer was left with an image of spilled milk streaming across the floor, mixing in with the blood.

"What's so funny?" my companion asked me.

"I don't know," I think I said. I can't remember because this was where things got really weird.

The whole time everything we passed after we had exited the highway looked like a war zone, but not a big war zone, but a localized everyone for themselves all out riot kind of scene, a protest gone awry. Cars with smashed windows, dented sides, upright and upside down, a few black from flames that had since been extinguished. Boarded up windows protected places that once needed protection but were now riddled with graffiti and bullet holes.

A scattering of people milled about in protective gear carrying automatic weapons, sawed off shotguns and some even had knives. It made me think comically of a zombie apocalypse movie. None of them paid us any mind, as if we didn't even exist. Or if someone looked our way, they looked right through us, like they just happened to see something on the other side. Nobody saw us.

An occasional gunshot, some yelling, none of this

seemed to startle us. It was like we were there yet not there. And amidst all of the destruction, one lone building still stood, untouched, so out of place. And that was where I was driving. And that was when I awoke.

Awake. Milk. What was the saying? Don't cry over spilled milk. Because you can't put it back in the bottle. If there were pets, though, then there would be no crying at all. Especially a cat. Why are there no pets? Wouldn't it be simpler to connect with the brain of an animal, like a dog or cat, than a human being? Maybe it wasn't easy or simply not as important at the time.

Milk was weird anyway. When we were born, we nursed and suckled our mother's milk, and yet later we drank milk from a cow, goa,t or even sheep. Baby animals nursed just as humans, only later we drank their milk. Did they drink ours? Of course not. That was absurd. Wasn't it just as absurd to drink their milk, yet I knew humans had been drinking milk for centuries. At least now, all the milk was plant-based, probably soy. Everything was soy now or plant-based, even our meats.

The idea was always to remove the sense of production from anything. We didn't need to know or want to know how things were made, only that they tasted good. And of course, that they were good for us too: healthy, organic, though nothing at all was organic or was it that everything was organic because the term itself at some point had become so ubiquitous that it was meaningless, more of a marketing term than anything else.

Milk. Dairy cows do not constantly produce milk, they

can be kept going if they are regularly milked, though at some point they will dry up, wherein they are freshened up, impregnated via artificial insemination, and thus, the whole process starts again.

It all just starts again. Today was a new day, I thought, though for a moment something wasn't right and I quickly shot from confusion then back again to a placidity, a cool calmness, because I felt everything was as it should be, but then I opened my eyes more fully and found myself sprawled on a leather couch with a shawl half-covering, and that ataraxia faded as the disorientation resumed. So much for spilled milk.

In my mind, I laid the pieces out, remembered the dream I thought was a dream. I remembered Marta. Here I was, I assumed, at Marta's flat, awakened in the early morning hours by not so much as a sound, just an instinct. If Marta was right, I began to think, but of course she was right. I knew it when she said it but didn't want to believe it. I knew as everything was known that could be known that this had been no dream.

My mind raced, so many thoughts at once competing for my attention, but I could only focus on one single thing at a time, one operation followed by the next, not that they needed to be related, for they often weren't, from the dream to Marta, the network, back to Marta, the Ozymandias statue. I couldn't multi-task, though, I could maintain the illusion of such, as anyone could. The thing was, it all depended on the speed in which one thing was performed relative to the other. I exhaled, imagining all those restless thoughts inside of me were being released. In their place was a resolute calm. At least, that was the idea.

I preferred to take it slow. I arose, glancing briefly to the bedroom, its door closed, from behind which presumably Marta slept, continuing to the windows and the view of the world bathed in the early morning light. A delicate orange hue colored the horizon. Closer to me, buildings and structures stuck out from the ground, great and small towers full of people just like me, and yet not like me.

Maybe some of them were awake now. Just as I was, suddenly craving coffee, hoping such a thing really existed, but I knew it did. My thoughts, the images in my head of the world coalesced, went from obscurations to a kind of clarity. Not perfectly clear yet. Just closer.

I knew I would wrestle with this one for a while. So, I extricate myself from the network after a set number of years, but for what purpose? To see what it had made us into? To change something? And supposing I could change something, why did I think I should be the one to make that decision? And maybe the bigger question to me, was about Marta. How did she figure in all of this? Marta, sweet Marta. Met her in a bar twice in the same night. Then here I was in her flat. She was beautiful, wasn't she? She was nice. I knew that was true.

I moved towards the bedroom door, thought about knocking or quietly turning the handle and entering, but something seemed kind of weird about that. For one, it was intrusive. For another, I barely knew Marta. I only met her last night. I thought about how I had kissed her, but not really her, just an image of her, a kind of representation. It had all seemed real enough, though. A lot of things seemed real in the SIM. The SIM?

In the SIM, I even met up with the dog I grew up with.

We walked in a green field then crossed a bridge that spanned a lagoon. I remembered being in a row boat as a kid, on my own, pretending something as I moved about the water, that I was an explorer in a strange land or I was on some special expedition funded by the Queen. I was also pretending something else back then, living in another world, as a different person almost, me but not me.

Coffee. I seemed to know how to work the machine. Or maybe, the machine just seemed to work because it did this every morning. I didn't know if the button I touched did anything or not, anything different than what it might normally do. Still, the coffee was made and that was what mattered most. And beyond that, the fact that it tasted pretty good was a definite bonus, whatever it really was, because it couldn't be coffee? Could it? What was coffee anyway?

And now, to put it all together, at times I felt great, while other times, my head seemed to swirl in a mass of unexplainable things. I thought I would feel more tired as I probably didn't sleep much. The situation though, likely provided some adrenal fluid that kept me going. And coffee would provide the rest. As I sipped the coffee, I continued to gaze out the massive windows to the world outside. The sun rose, slowly from its slumber and as the world came more alight, so did the movements on the street, even motion on the canal not far from Marta's flat. It seemed that was where I was last night.

When I was nearly done with the coffee, the door from Marta's room opened and she emerged appearing as everything I remember, no mere apparition, but the totality, and especially her eyes, which studied me with such a gaze, briefly expressing some surprise, but then like me, as if remembering.

"Good morning," she said, barely missing a step, heading to the coffee machine and quickly dispatching that task with deft efficiency so that she could focus on others. She stood there for a moment, in thought, in black leggings and a loose shirt. Her hair was a bit of a mess, so she rustled her hand through its short locks and coaxed it back to some kind of normalcy.

"It's not a dream just as you told me. I really thought it was." I said, standing there awkwardly, not knowing exactly how to feel, half looking outside then gazing back to her. "But if it is not a dream then, I have some questions."

"I imagine that you have many questions and that they will keep occurring to you until you recall everything."

She seemed only half-ready for an onslaught of queries, her back to me, hovering over the coffee machine. I kept wanting her to turn back to me, flash me some sign that would offer more than a simple reassurance, but a full on gesture.

"I do have lots of questions. So many questions that I don't even know where to begin. Do you really think I'll remember everything?"

"No," she said without a thought. "But maybe at some point those questions will no longer matter."

She poured herself coffee and then glanced at my nearly empty cup. Somehow she had managed to make more than one cup of coffee. That wasn't an important question by any means, still that was something I wondered. And it was just like the mind sometimes to get stuck on the non-essentials. In the morning though, coffee was still an essential thing. Any world where coffee wasn't an essential was no world for me. But what about the milk?

She sensed my confusion to some degree and offered a more soothing explanation, while patting me on the shoulder as she spoke. She hovered next to me. I thought maybe she was looking for signs of something, but I didn't know what. Maybe she just wanted to be close to me. I no doubt didn't mind the proximity. Her natural sweetness mixed with the aromatic, almost nutty smell of coffee.

"There are lots of little things, mechanical things of this world, but don't worry. They'll come back to you. And soon you won't even think twice about making coffee, although I see you figured it out."

"Somehow," I said, not hopefully. "I almost feel like the machine figured me out and not vice versa."

She didn't answer. We looked at each other for a while, sipping our coffee. I do think hers turned out better than mine, but maybe I was just used to the taste, had quickly adjusted to it, just like the whiskey last night. It seemed stupid to ask her about how things tasted, but it made me wonder. There was something a little odd tasting in almost everything I had tasted. Almost everything. But I should have expected that. We all had expectations of taste, and more often than not, they dictated whether we liked them or not, whether they measure up.

"What questions are you thinking about? You can say anything, really."

"Anything?"

"Well, almost anything. I don't know everything. Sometimes I don't think I know all that much."

"Such as," I continued closing my eyes for a moment

and then it hit me, a bitter taste, something that almost made me gag. "Okay, when the dream first started everything was so brilliant, but I had a couple flashes of this terrible thing, this sensation, this vision of decrepit buildings and utter decay, and that sense of devastation was overwhelming. I am almost sick thinking about it again."

"I didn't know the exact moment you would switch over and lose connection to the network," she said as she thoughtfully sipped her coffee as if searching for the right way to put things. "You see, I've been following you for a long time. And not only did I not know the exact moment, I also didn't know if your code had been overwritten somehow. That was certainly a possibility. Such that you wouldn't ever disconnect and all would have been for naught."

"Still, that's what I don't understand."

"I have a parallel version of the network, a copy, so when you went off that grid, I moved you onto my network. There was bound to be a lapse, a little separation."

"Why?"

"For the filter. So that you would see the world the network shows us and not what really is," she said, looking at me very closely, her hazel eyes with glints of radiant sparkles. "And in doing so, I've tricked the network into thinking you are still connected to it, but you are not. It's a bit complicated to explain, but it works for now."

"Won't the system figure it out? I mean, surely the network might suspect such a thing, this all-knowing eye of Providence."

She looked at me with a blank expression, clearly not

following the reference. And in a way, I didn't either. I didn't mean to say such a thing, but after I said it, I knew why I had, but what I didn't know, is why I knew all these things that no one else knew, these expressions, these ideas.

"In time, probably they will," she said, pausing. "I've done my best to make that as difficult as possible to allow you as much time as possible. Until you remember everything, you will need all the help you can get."

"Fourteen years?" I asked and she nodded. "That's a long time. Even if I recall where I was, a lot will have changed. Will I even remember the last fourteen years."

"It's possible. The mind is a unique thing. Difficult to understand and map. But in most cases, the network has been a part of our lives in one way or another for all of our lives. After all, it's always been there to help us be our best self."

"Sounds like an advertising agency jingle."

She looked at me with a fake smile, then sipped some more coffee. I was always drawn back to her eyes, so that some of the time when she talked, I wasn't following because I was too distracted. But more than anything I knew I needed to listen to every word.

"In a way, the network has marketed a version of the world to all of us, so I am not surprised you used that metaphor. The presentation of something is often more important than the very thing itself."

"It's a nightmare," I said. "And I'm part of it."

"Or it's a grand triumph, a historic achievement, uniting the individual brain with a vast network that assists and develops each person, marrying the human mind with artificial intelligence. . ."

As much as I didn't want to think about it, begrudgingly I had to admit, things looked so wonderful, like a kind of paradise. And then there was the SIM world too. No longer was the imagined world simply imagined, but real, as real as something could be, an artist rendering come to life in some sort of collective vision, the very world which I stared out at from the vantage of Marta's flat, to each and everyone accessible from their own home. Was that not a grand achievement? A true marvel, as Marta had said. We had connected what was left of the world, integrated without disintegration.

"Where do I live, by the way? I was kind of wondering that this morning. I suppose I would recognize the place, wouldn't I?"

"Not necessarily," Marta mused. "We live in an age of not a lot of personalization or individuality. You may have already noticed that. Your place will look very much like mine."

"Hmm, not surprising, given that was where we were always heading."

I thought about the trends, the so-called fashion icons and celebs of the bygone era, the influencers of social media, the endless marketing, the need to belong, so that conclusion seemed about right. Given the influence of the network, people would look and dress somewhat similar, and yet still feel unique and individual in doing so. That was actually the most remarkable thing about it. Creating a collective and yet retaining a sense of individuality. There was a media theorist. I couldn't remember his name, but that's what he said would happen when the common mediums became image-based: our ideals would coalesce.

However, although you could standardize something all you wanted, quantify it, there were still some things, which I called quality, that could not as readily be understood. In fact, they could never really be replicated. Just because we said something was beautiful did not make it so. Alternately, on some level, this might be referred to as aesthetics.

"What are you thinking?"

"I'll tell you later. Just trying to put things together. I need to think more," I said.

I was thinking about that very thing, quality vs quantity, one of my own tropes, something I seemed to think endlessly about. I was so sure I would think the same thing again later as Marta filled me in on the world. In fact, I would keep returning to the idea that no matter what: you could not quantify every single thing, condense the stuff of life into a simple formula. The quality of an experience mattered more than the quantity of it. And quality was the one thing that was difficult, hard to define, like love.

She had finished her coffee. She moved towards the kitchen, set her mug down and continued her routine, almost as if I wasn't there. Maybe that was one of her gifts, that natural ability to be so calm, while I felt more and more anxious. I tried to return to my early calmness mantra, but that was easier to do when I was alone.

"Okay, I'll let you think about it. I'm going to go for a morning run," she said, offhandedly, truly stepping into her normal routine, then reconsidered. "Would you like to join me?"

"No thanks," I said, shaking my head. "I don't have my workout gear anyway."

"Very funny. I'm going in the SIM," she said to remind me, almost teasingly. "So that won't matter."

'Really? And it's really a workout?"

"Of course, the mind is a powerful tool. I think I've mentioned that more than once. I can also use the treadmill version too, if I wanted to, but I never do. I like the program as it is."

"And where will you jog?"

"Wherever I want," she said, smiling. "Along the beach, among nature, city streets, country roads, wherever. That's the beauty of it. There are preloaded routes or I can create my own."

"I guess that would be true. The SIM," I said shaking my head in some kind of disbelief, but since I had experienced it twice, I knew that it was all true, that she could jog wherever she wanted to and the experience would be real. I suppose the gym, if there were gyms, probably had some even more complicated and elaborate take on all of that. You could do yoga in the Himalayas. With a class. Maybe it was just one of those things, that sure, it was easier to do at home, but for extra motivation, it was easier to go to the gym and join a SIM group.

"You remember the SIM, right?" she asked me rather jokingly. She knew I hadn't forgotten. How could I forget such an experience?

"Yeah. That was like nothing I had ever experienced. Or it was just a more magical version of anything I have ever experienced. Either way. I see what you mean. Are there still gyms?"

"Of course. They provide both the physical and mental version with custom locations and competition. Plus people like the idea of it, the habitual nature of going to the gym. Kind of like going to get a coffee in the morning."

"Sounds terrible and torturous. The gym, that is, not the coffee."

She laughed. Then she once again gazed at me so thoroughly and completely I felt vulnerable and unworthy of her glance. I wanted to say something about it but didn't as she sized me up. Did I measure up? I spoke just to break the moment.

"I always hated gyms, that's all."

"Okay, well, I always knew that. I never saw you go to one. Not once. . . But I won't be long. Make yourself at home."

"Sure, I'll just think about Jesus Christ and such," I smirked.

"Oh, you do that. Your Son of God, though God is not even a being. You know that, right?"

Hmm. I hadn't recalled that I had told her. Maybe I had. I must have. God not even a being.

But it is a concept, at least. Maybe not flesh and blood. *Deus ex machina.* The God from the machine maybe was more apt for this world. With a half-puzzled look, I watched as Marta went into her SIM room to complete her daily workout. The god in the machine, as it first appeared in Greek tragedy was a way to explain the unexplainable and wrap up the story. I supposed that was always my definition of God too. Everything that we cannot explain we shall call X, and X equals God. At one time long ago, to many, that would not have been an acceptable answer. It would have been blasphemous to suggest a thing. Things were different now. The transformation was complete. We had gone from the God in the sky, the Heavens, to the God within to the God in the machine.

I probably should have been thinking more about why I knew all of the things I did, why I had these thoughts and ideas, at times, for things that did not even exist. I had a lot of questions for Marta. She was right. They would keep coming. Inevitably, some of them I would solve on my own, but others I would not. The next biggest question though, other than why I was here, was why was she? Presumably she was not part of the network either. She had her own version of the network. That made no sense to me. And who was she really?

I didn't consider it snooping, but I did look around. There were not a lot of personal effects as she alluded. Certainly it seemed all things had some sort of purpose. There were no trinkets, no books, no extraneous items. The black and white pictures that hung on her wall were perhaps the only thing somewhat personal. Art. But they were abstracts. For all I knew all of the units could very well be furnished the same way. Maybe even my own flat. I was hoping that was not the case. I was hoping I was somehow different, even when I was part of the network, that I had retained something personal.

I thought I remembered a sculpture in the building lobby. Ozymandias. That was important because it indicated a sense of design about the world. And the Beatles. Marta knew of them. So, art did have a place, as both a function and aesthetic. Maybe that had been my contribution to the world. That was reassuring to note. Aside from that, everything else could be found in the SIM.

From the kitchen, I moved towards Marta's room, again, not really wanting to look too closely, but still curious. I figured I had at least another couple of minutes before Marta emerged from the SIM. And I didn't know if there was anything in particular I was looking for, but if there was something, then I surely would see it. We often don't know what we are looking for until we find it. There was no logic in that, no coherent string and thus nothing a machine could understand, but it was the way us humans sometimes found answers. We followed a hunch or our gut instinct. Sometimes this led us astray.

In Marta's room, I saw her unmade bed, a closet that seemed part of the wall, half-open, full of clothes, dresses and blouses, various kinds of shoes and other accessories. A nearby dresser I assumed contained more clothes, albeit of a different variety. I did not intend to look, although I thought about how in the movies people always kept the most important things in their dresser. I didn't know if that was really true. Nor did I suspect Marta of anything in the first place, yet still I rummaged.

"Hey Mister," I heard a soft voice behind me say. I hadn't heard Marta finish her session. "This would be my bedroom. I suppose I should have given you a tour if I had known you had such interest in my personal things. And especially those things."

"This isn't what it looks like?" I tried to explain.

"Okay," she said simply and for the moment let it go.

I turned towards her. Her face looked flushed from her exercise SIM yet still relaxed and almost playful in her posture as if understanding my curiosity or expecting it in some way, which was good because I felt a little ashamed.

"I'm sorry," I said. "I was just. . ."

"Curious," she offered, playing it off.

I nodded, not really knowing what else to say. I knew how it must have looked. I couldn't even say I was looking for anything specific, and certainly not intending to arouse any sort of suspicion, but I had been looking in a drawer of undergarments, which was plain creepy.

"Well, feel free to continue looking if you must. Pick out something for me to wear if you like. I'm going to take a quick shower. Okay? Nothing too fancy."

I was caught, and here she was, rubbing it in a little, though in a jocose way. I started to say something, but she hushed me up as she went to her dresser and then to the closet, which opened completely when she stood in front of it. I thought she was going to say something more, but she did not. She only looked back at me cheerfully, while I just stood there rather dumbly like a child who had just dropped his ice cream cone and was trying to pick it up off the ground though it was full of rocks and dirt. Or perhaps it was something worse I felt, like I just happened to look over as an attractive woman leaned over and looked at me looking at her. Okay, not quite like that, but surely somewhere in the middle. A child feeling foolish, a little sheepishness crossed with something of a different nature, a clandestine glimpse of the discreet.

Marta raised her eyebrows at me as she walked to the bathroom. A few moments later, I heard the water turn on. By that time I was back in the living room, surely content to just sit still and wait and think about what I had learned, if anything.

Mainly, I presumed that people had very few possessions, at least, if Marta was indicative of the rest, and I figured in some way she was. A highly efficient, modernized society would tend towards a kind of homogeneity by definition. Especially a world where everything was surveilled and a network of machines assisted our everyday life. What was not homogenous, though, I remembered from last night, was the mix of people, of various nationalities, but mostly the same kind of build, that is not overly tall or short, but with a certain relativity to the sexes, and all assembled as a semblance of the beautiful as if cosmeticized.

From the bathroom, Marta stepped out in a dressing gown, a white towel still drying the curls of her dark hair, a slight grin, though timid as she looked at me. Me being here was new to her, I imagined, and not just me but another person. When she stepped out of the bathroom, it was almost like she had momentarily forgotten I was there but didn't want to express that, so she adjusted as best she could. It was the same expression from earlier when she first emerged from the bedroom.

"Government?" I asked her straight out.

"It exists," she said, "but not controversially or even something many people think about."

"How's that? Everybody has some opinion about the government, and usually tends towards the pejorative."

"Pejorative," she mused. "You use words that I don't hear much. But I like it."

"Sorry. It's just what comes to me."

She nodded and continued drying her hair as she went into her bedroom to change clothes, continuing to talk as she did so, keeping the door open probably out of habit more than anything else. It was also easier to hear her. She didn't have an especially loud voice, but it broke through. I remembered the first SIM. I remembered the voice from my dream, my companion, but that wasn't Marta.

"Well, not much unrest among the people when there is no unemployment, no real sense of inequality as those with more money seem to just spend it. Technology acts as the great equalizer. People have a sense of purpose."

"A *raison d'être*," I said without thinking, then corrected the statement so as to be understood. "Latin, darling. A reason for existence."

I don't know why I added the *darling* part. It seemed to be something from a movie. Were they even movies anymore, I wondered. Probably not. The SIM was its own kind of movie, one in which you were the star. What else could you want?

I glanced to her bedroom and saw she had just finished putting on a beige blouse over her dark pants. She adjusted the fit, looking into a mirror I hadn't noticed earlier, probably because it was hidden when not in use, before turning to me, keenly aware I had been watching her.

"So, yes, darling, there is a government but no one has the sense of being ruled."

"It's a ruse then."

She nodded somewhat. I heard her say the word *darling* to herself. Then she was back in the living room with me. I sat on the couch, feeling a bit more relaxed than earlier, but that was a feeling I figured would come and go at great regularity without any kind of announcement or invitation.

"Not a ruse to the people in office, though kind of otherwise, I suppose, but harmless too. Rather, the role of government is simpler. To fix things that need to be fixed, provide that sense of stability, promote a general well-being and happiness. And in a world like this, people are already happy. The mechanisms of the network more or less appeal to most people so the government is more a marketing machine than anything else."

I let it go at that. I needed to understand things a little more before I examined that happiness. I thought about religion as the opiate of the masses, and how words were only what we ascribed to them, and nothing more. And even that quote from Karl Marx was a loose paraphrase, more a summation of the sighs of the oppressed in a world without soul than a singular philosophy.

Maybe after I walked around and contemplated things for myself, I might start to get a sense of where things really were, not the soul of the world per se, but something more than I had. Right then I felt limited, unmoored, and adrift without the benefits of GPS guidance, moving by feel more than anything else.

Everything looked clear and sharp, rather crystalline-like and yet I saw it all through a hazy lens, dreamily as I wandered, a part but not a part, separated by some thin gauzy material that I moved from my eyes from time to time to get a better glimpse. But there was little solace in such glances, those mere mutations of clarity because I couldn't always rely on such sharpness.

I couldn't wait for the sense of disorientation to fade, to feel something more like normal, whatever that would be. I was hoping this wasn't it. Per Marta, I had only been disconnected from the grid for twelve hours at best. Perhaps longer. I had no idea of the time. That was another thing lost on me, especially when I factored in the SIM.

Marta made smoothies for breakfast, which I sucked down despite the taste. I felt ravenous and was at the point that I would eat almost anything, and a good thing, at that, because again I was initially struck by the taste or lack of taste. If I wasn't as hungry, then I might have passed.

"Things are still a bit off," I noted to Marta. "For instance, this smoothie, the way it tastes doesn't seem quite right given what I saw you put in it."

"You are not as off as you think," she remarked, raising her eyebrows for a moment. "And by that, I mean everything tastes kind of funny. The network in many ways acts as a filter to try to make the food more palpable and hopefully the mind picks up the slack."

"So, I didn't really drink a smoothie?"

"Well, you did and you didn't?"

"What do you mean?"

"Certainly not as you might remember it. Food has to change and it always has compared to how it used to taste, how you remember it. I am sure you have fond memories of eating various kinds of foods. More people, more challenging agriculture environments have changed the way we produce food. Crop yield increases don't come without a price. Something has to be sacrificed—usually taste—though it is gradual and not as noticeable that way. Everything in the natural world has limits. And especially now. We are mostly plants, soy mostly."

That part made sense. I did remember how food had become more bland, and yet, in the case of various fruits and vegetables, certainly maintained the look of perfection. Eventually, the mind just accepted that version and filled in what we wanted the taste to be. Not always, but most of the time.

So much had changed over time, even before all of this, whether considering fruits, vegetables or even livestock. Surely a chicken fifty years ago tasted different than one today. It had to, especially when I considered what they looked like then versus how much bigger they were now, how quickly they matured. Of course, that was from the world I remembered, and not necessarily this one. I knew nothing about the modern chicken, but if I had to guess, it was perfect and grown in a lab. And my grandmother wouldn't recognize the taste.

"What about chicken? I suppose everything tastes like chicken."

"Chicken?"

"Touché," I said.

"Bacon. A lot of things taste like bacon."

"Why, especially now?" I said, imagining eating meat that tasted like bacon. I looked at her, and her knowing look suggested I shouldn't have to ask such things, but I was asking them anyway to rejigger my thoughts, for the sake of my own sanity.

"Because we live in a world that is not what it appears to be. Once this world was on the edge of destruction, the pandemic, the virus. Now, that's a distant memory. You might see what looks like rows and rows of lettuce or other vegetation, perfect specimens so to speak, but they likely actually bear more of a resemblance to weeds, scrub brush."

"That's kind of what I first saw."

"Yeah, I imagine so. That's the world without a filter. Hence, my overlapping network to make things seem more normal. My lens."

"What a world," I said, not knowing what else to say. "And where did we go wrong?"

"If we have gone wrong, where do we always go wrong," Marta said, paused for a moment to drink more of her smoothie before continuing. "We think we have the upper hand, that we control things, situations that we really can't. That's the thing."

"Because we thought we knew better, so much better." *Hubris*, I would have said, but it was another one of those words.

"We did, because we always think like that, but we also were out of choices. The sad thing is, long before this we ceded our grand thinking to the network, networks being impartial, that was the thinking, and able to perform so many calculations and computations at once. It's that belief if we feed the network enough data then an answer can be found. You see, we needed the network, but really I just think we lost confidence in our own abilities to solve problems."

"Perhaps," I said, then added, "some of us did. I'm sure others thought that combining the two would produce extraordinary results."

"Yes," she said. "And yet any machine, any system of networks begins somewhere, with an idea that turns into a line of code, something that at least at the beginning was written by a human, from a human brain. So the same kinds of biases can be inherent in these so-called impartial systems."

"Inputs lead to outputs. That's the crux, the catch," I added. "Ironically, the machines or the network, rather, treat humans as mere inputs, all of us, no one distinguishable from the other, which also happens to be how we've fashioned ourselves. So, I suppose that's egalitarian. Long ago, we commoditized some humans as less than human, their labors, called them slaves. And now, we all are."

"Ah," Marta said, "Except we are all happy now. That's the distinct difference."

"Or apathetic. Ignorant."

We didn't say anything for a while. I wondered again about the time and if there was something I was supposed to be doing at this very moment, and me not doing that, would recall some sort of suspicion. Wouldn't the network know I wasn't where I was supposed to be? That I wasn't me? I wouldn't say it was outright paranoia, but the confusion I was feeling did add some disillusion to the mix.

"We could talk about this forever and still not understand," Marta said, clearly ready to move on.

"Yes. That much is true."

"Not that we shouldn't keep talking. I do enjoy talking to you, I really do," Marta emphasized as she looked sympathetically at me, as if she knew something more. "But you have places you are supposed to be. It has just been so nice to talk to someone. I feel like I haven't talked to anyone for years."

She looked far away from me and my general vicinity, to that special world outside, her gaze far away in a thought from some other time and place. And I wished I knew, but I knew that feeling. I knew what it was like to be where she was. I, too, felt like I hadn't talked to anyone for years, that loneliness and longing, the hardening of the outer shell that comes from barriers, blocked points of entry and mighty staircases to the top.

Marta told me where I lived, though she suspected that as I walked to my flat, it would seem familiar, and it was, to a degree. I noticed little details, the color of a sign, even some of the people I knew I had seen because this was somehow part of their daily routine and maybe I was often out walking at this time. Of course, I didn't know these people by name. They were just people I seemed to see all the time. That woman jogging with great form, the lackadaisical biker, a man walking slowly and whistling to himself in something like Italian when he sung. I knew that I knew these people, even if it was only in that way of mere recognition of their faces.

As much as I wanted to walk around and explore things, Marta suggested keeping my curiosity on a tight leash. Still, it was hard not to resist the temptation to look, though I was told, even instructed not to do so, the tantalization remained paramount, so I quickly glanced now and then, committing to memory all that I saw, the people, the familiar places, a little section of shrubbery next to a bench. All of these impressions mattered. I was sure of that. Knowing I wasn't supposed to do something always made me want to do it all the more.

A general cleanliness pervaded everything, from the sidewalks and streets to the various buildings and structures. Seemingly nothing was out of place as if the world was constantly being maintained, all fallen leaves raked up, every bit not meant to be there, quickly gone with devious efficiency. Things were perhaps too clean.

The building where I lived bore little resemblance to Marta's place. Grand columns held up the first few floors and in the middle, an interior garden replete with benches and greenery. It made me think about times I must have sat there, reading a book or maybe just thinking, but not now. There was no time now. I passed through the entryway to the elevators which instinctively took me to a floor near the top, and the instinct was not mine, but the elevator's. Presumably because the elevator knew who I was even if I didn't.

There had been a sculpture in the main lobby just like at Marta's, a female nude with missing arms, perhaps depicting a Greek goddess, like Aphrodite or Amphitrite. It didn't really matter anymore who it was supposed to be. I doubted anyone knew the difference. I hadn't noticed any identifying feature like a fish or a swan, some doves that would have given it away.

The door of my flat opened as I appeared. Not that I was looking, but there were no light switches either, lots of sensors, a world of sensors I thought, as I stepped inside and the lighting adjusted, warming so to speak, to my presence.

Like Marta's flat, black and white abstract art adorned the walls, some stone, others white plaster like sheets. The lay-out was virtually the same, though my furnishings were slightly different. I had a black chesterfield couch that looked terribly uncomfortable, some leather chairs and a table that looked out one of the massive windows to a view of the canal. Much like Marta's, all of the wondrous technology was there in hiding. Screens and panels that masqueraded as walls were the norm. There but not there. That was kind of how I felt too.

I went into the bathroom and looked at myself in the mirror, seeing a *look that at once was so lost that maybe even others didn't notice me.* I didn't know how old I was, how old I was supposed to be, or how I really looked since the person I was seeing was not really me. When my hands neared the sink, warm water gushed out. I wondered how I adjusted the temperature. Maybe the water was always like this. If you wanted cold water, then you went to the kitchen. Maybe the network just knew what you wanted based on your reaction. All of that seemed complicated, but maybe it wasn't when you ceded control to the network.

Here I was, but again, I was not really here, was I? Where was I then? That was the thing. I wondered if I would ever feel a sense of normalcy. Given time, I reassured myself, all of this would seem normal. And as to my purpose, what I hoped to accomplish or even change, I didn't know what that meant or what I really intended when I wrote the code to remove myself from the network. That was among the things I hoped to understand. Maybe I just wasn't meant for these times. I must have left myself some clues, and if so, they were probably all too obvious, yet not obvious at all, either in the SIM or somewhere else.

When I looked in the room to see my SIM, I was surprised to also find bookshelves lined with books, like some secret study. I noted that walls could cover the bookshelves if I wanted, like closets, but these were real books, from fiction writers like Faulkner, Fitzgerald, Kerouac, and Murakami to philosophical texts from Plato, Aristotle, Hume, Nietzsche, and more, as well as whole books on various subjects including music and the arts, sculpture, science, and technology. I noted a book sticking out slightly, as if recently read, by Neil Postman. *Amusing Ourselves to Death.*

I thumbed through a few, noted underlined passages in the writings of William Blake, the poems of William Carlos Williams, and a treatise on government written by John Locke. I had a history of American popular music, of Confucius, including an underlined passage "Your life is what your thoughts make of it." I picked out a book by

Ortega Y. Gasset and read a similar passage: "Man is the novelist of himself."

I paused, put the latest book back in its place—however they were all arranged seemed not to matter—and looked at my own SIM. Recalling Marta's actions, I touched the panel and looked at the settings, in particular the log of previous sessions. Supposedly, this would all come back to me and maybe that was true as I noticed my fingers seemed to know where to go and what to do.

My headset seemed quite comfortable. That envelope of life, the red lights engulfing me as I put on the goggles and came upon the main menu, changing settings with my hands. I explored the options. Not surprisingly, Marta pinged me, and soon I was walking with her in a park. She wore a yellow dress with blue flowers that looked like birds when I looked closer. I reached out to touch her, and she laughed.

"I saw you were online," she said, then added: "This is really me and not a representation of me."

"Cool," I said.

"Cool," she echoed.

"This is strange. So we are both in the SIM, in the comfort of our own little room, in separate space, but together as if we were talking in the real world, in a real park."

"As we are talking, yes," she looked at me with mock amazement as if I was a slow learner. "It feels and seems just like it was, like we were talking earlier in my flat. Is that not so?"

"Yes, it does," I said, "Except I know it's not, so that kind of makes it feel different."

"Because you constantly fight it. As you know, or at

least knew, for the majority of the people it was no big deal to be part of the network. The mind and body naturally adjusted. Other types of people resisted, and some couldn't make the adjustment without lots of work. And others, not at all."

I didn't ask her what that meant. Surely it was some combination of additional coding or drugs. Except we probably didn't call them drugs. That was the thing. A thing was dependent upon how we framed it , whether we named it as such. One could say the SIM was a drug. That thought was not lost on me. For the SIM was the thing everyone was hooked on. Had it been the same for me when I was connected?

"Okay," I said, turning to face her. "Nice dress, by the way. You were not wearing that last time I saw you. It's quite lovely. You look quite lovely in it."

"Thanks," she said. "I changed clothes within the SIM. You did not. It's common for a woman to make alterations when she is in the SIM, different clothes, make-up. . . I am sure you can imagine what else and why."

The thought occurred to me: I hadn't changed clothes since I had been here. That was very much true and unsettling. Not that I expected there to be much variation in my closet. I had the feeling that when I stepped out of the SIM and looked in my closet, I would see a lot of the same stuff, like a uniform. Still, these were the same clothes. Dark pants and white shirt.

"You look the same, though, I think. Your eyes, in particular, are the same. Did you change anything else?" I thought back through what she had said. Yes, there was so much you could change, moving from one world that was not even real to another that was further removed from reality, and yet, all of it was a kind of reality because we experienced it. Something like the SIM could be used in many ways, for ill or well.

"Other than my clothes?" she said. "No. But I do feel better to be out in nature."

"This is a nice park," I remarked, looking around at the so-called natural habitat that we found ourselves a part of. Maybe that was something innate, something within us, this need for nature, and this place was very much nature, the smells, the look, and even Marta.

We walked along a brick, tree-lined path with vintage lamp posts adorned along the edge, interrupted every so often by a park bench. The path stretched far-ahead in the distance before it forked. A few people appeared, but they ignored us as they walked by.

"Here is a simple one. How do I change the temperature of the water?"

She looked at me oddly, those lovely eyes of hers trying to decide if I was being serious or not, then relaxing as if the joke was on me because I was being serious. She gave me a look like the truth was self-evident. I was sure this would not be the first time I would get such a look.

"I was in the bathroom washing my hands, and it just seemed to me there was no way to make the water cold."

She shook her head as she responded.

"Well, your unit should know you quite well. That's the learning aspect. Otherwise, you can say 'colder' or 'warmer' or something to indicate temperature adjustment. Not much has changed there. That technology has been around a while. You seriously didn't think about a voice command?"

"No, I didn't," I said. "I don't know why it didn't occur

to me. I just never had that stuff. I am still missing light switches."

"You are kind of incredible. You know all these things about rather arcane subjects, philosophies, topics. . ."

"Like Jesus Christ."

"Like Jesus Christ," she said, accepting what was now our little joke. "And yet, some of the simple things you seem to have no recollection of. The voice thing was a pretty big deal even. People loved to have these devices in their house they could talk to, even though those early versions were pathetic by current standards, but they made people more comfortable and even accepting of intrusion into their lives for the sake of convenience."

"What about robots?"

"Well, people just preferred to have all of these conveniences hidden, there and not there. And then any human task was reduced to absolute simplicity, like operating the SIM."

I smelled the green as we walked, that sense of being in nature, and though I knew it was not exactly real, so much about it seemed so very real. I considered the reasons as we walked. Marta seemed to know what I was thinking about at some point.

"We fill in the gaps," she said. "Our mind does. This park melds with whatever view we have of a park or various parks, so that if any details are incomplete, we tend not to notice because we've already filled them in."

"How did you know I was thinking about that?"

"Oh, I don't know. I've watched you for a long time, you know. I am used to these kinds of silences too."

"I do know. I can't believe you didn't go crazy. I guess the SIM helps to relieve boredom, tension, fulfill needs and fantasies."

She looked at me as if to say something and then thought better of it. Unlike her special gift, I had no good way of reading her. Sometimes I had the feeling she evaded direct questions and made them into generalities. Or she turned them around on me. That seemed the most likely outcome.

"Which leads me to another question," I said, more to myself than her, knowing that I had asked her before. "What about love? Did I already ask you that?"

"You did. It is a tricky thing for a machine to quantify," she said as she looked at me. "The human attraction, or even love for that matter. It's hard enough for a human."

"So, such a thing does not exist anymore?"

"Love," she said. "Love is complicated."

"Sure," I said, lightly laughing. "But that's the point, it's not something that should be taken lightly."

"Is it? Should it be so difficult?" she asked "Are you one of those people who believe in the one, true love?"

"I wouldn't say that, but I do believe in love. It's complicated what I believe, though" I said, stopping there.

"Hmm. And you chided me for saying love was complicated."

"I didn't chide you, did I?"

"With that look you gave me," she said, smiling, "I would say you did."

"I'm sorry. I didn't mean anything. It's just sometimes the way I think about things, I don't know, it gets complex inside my head."

"Try me. I am curious about those things in your head."

"Well," I said pausing, feeling like I was talking my way

into an opinion, a point of view, which was not what I wanted to do. How did I feel? Why was it always so hard to say what you meant?

"Well?" she goaded me on.

"You get the love you need at the time, if you want it. Nothing is perfect. There is not one true love, but multiple, and I know this sounds crazy, but even though it's not the same person, in some way it is too, like it's just this thing, this otherworldly force, and that binds everything."

"You lost me a little there," she said.

"It's okay, I lose myself too."

We stopped next to a particularly large tree that hung its branches over a bench. I motioned for us to sit down and she did, carefully adjusting her yellow dress as she sat on the bench, dusting off the random bits of the natural world. In spite of myself, I looked for carvings on the bench, the kind of thing young lovers used to do. A pair of initials, D + M = Forever. But there was nothing like that.

"But things are coming back to you, yes?"

"Yes, if you can call it that, all these little thoughts and ideas, clarity and chaos, disillusion and distraction and then at times, real insight. At least, that's what I tell myself."

"That's good," Marta said, patting me on the knee. "I wondered how your brain would react without the help from the network. On its own."

"It's highly adaptable," I said, remembering. "The human mind. We studied it a lot back then. Although, certain people in our group had trouble grasping the 'quality' aspect I was so keen on. They kind of viewed the world as all quantity, known quantities, while I extracted other things. To them, there was no question about what was beautiful or not. Success was all about how rich, how famous. Those were the measures that mattered. More was always better."

I glanced at Marta. She had been listening intently to my words. Sometimes I wondered if the things I said made any sense. I often didn't do a good job explaining things because so much

I took for granted and understood myself so well, I thought everyone knew. The distinction between quality and quantity seemed obvious.

"I suppose if I look more closely in my flat, I will be able to understand more of this, as in my old artifacts—books, for instance. I found my stash of books. That's great. More importantly, I need to find the things I used to write. That's what I need to find. Maybe like a notebook or something. I feel like I used to write."

We were silent for a moment as a group of people passed by. I would have made some remark about how it was interesting they ignored us, but there was really not that much interesting about it. That kind of thing happened outside the SIM too, way before the network. Most of us were always so engrossed in our own lives, head stuck in a device of some kind, so sure our life was of some greater importance as if all these things we did mattered much, when they mostly did not. I was self-absorbed too, albeit in a different way, not in a physical device but the one in my head. I liked to pretend that was different, but I was no better.

"It's possible you might find some of your old writing. And that would certainly be helpful too. Just reading something you wrote will help trigger old thoughts, old connections, old friends."

"This modern world is so clean," I said, looking around us, thinking about all that I had seen. Certainly not much grit or grime. "We don't seem to have notebooks laying around or any extraneous stuff. Not a lot of clutter. There are no messes."

"Yes, we are so very efficient in our little world of maintenance and constant monitoring," Marta joked as we saw a man blowing leaves into a pile to pick up. He paid us no attention as he completed his task. I presumed a lot of the programming in the SIM was easy. All the system had to do was look at old surveillance video to get a sense of the modern world. That was a perfect way to recreate a basic landscape or texture. Not even old surveillance, I supposed, as current would be just fine if not better.

I felt kind of gloomy, and yet, I shouldn't have, given that I was sitting there with Marta in a park in the SIM, leaves rustling around us, the smell of trees, those massive oaks absorbing distant voices, birds, the green and all else so peaceful now that the man blowing leaves had moved on. There were so many things perfect about the moment, and yet, like so much of my life, I didn't get that or grasp that notion fully, at least not until later, when it was too late.

"I suppose we are protected inside this SIM?" I asked Marta, trying to focus on something to get back into the moment.

"Yes. The network believes you to be in a SIM for work purposes, but not this one."

"What sort of work would I be doing?"

"Monitoring—like almost everyone else—except your measurements are more prominent, being an architect of the system."

"Yeah, that's what makes me feel uneasy. Though it is nice to be here with you."

I once again tilted my head to the side, observing her cool profile, the lashes of her eyes, curls of her hair, the curves of her body, the general calmness of her presence. She seemed perfectly relaxed, enjoying the moment. She smiled at me too. It seemed to me this was a place she went often. Maybe even a custom SIM.

"An architect of the system. What does that even mean? Were you not one of the architects?" I asked her.

"No. I was not. I worked under Emrik. You probably knew who I was without knowing me. My name was not Marta then."

She seemed evasive, but that could have been my imagination. In a way though, everything was my imagination, all of that stuff in my head. Still, there was something about that way she said she was not Marta then. But a name is just a name. She was always Marta. Evasive, but flirtatious too. Marta or not Marta, a name was just a name.

"What was it?"

"Does it matter? It's safer for both of us if you don't know."

"I suppose you would know more than I," I responded as I looked at her, and she at me, seeming perhaps a little bit distant in that one moment, both of us, even though we sat so close together the smallest movement by either of us and we would be touching.

"Ander, Mari, Ocie, Cleo, Lando, Emrik, and Siri. Those were the others. Your names spell Damocles, the first letters, each for a specific function. Emrik told me that. Damocles. You would understand the story. Emrik said it was a warning. But you were first, the first name. He told me that was important."

I scoffed a bit, but it was true. All the men five letters, the women four. *Marta* was five letters. So she couldn't have been part of the architect group. And why the number of letters mattered I didn't know, only that it did. Of course, that was the human tendency—and mine in particular—that peculiar proclivity towards finding patterns even in cases where no such patterns really existed. But this one was a real pattern.

"Yes, another Greek story. With great fortune and power also comes great danger, that sense that success might be fleeting for the ground beneath our feet might be retreating."

"A poem?" Marta suggested.

"Perhaps Damocles was that kind of story, though once again one that involved Dionysius. They traded places for a day, Damocles and Dionysius, so that Damocles would be king, but to illustrate the point Dionysius was making about power, it's fickle almost fleeting nature, he dangled a sword above Damocles's head by a single horse's hair. This was maddening to Damocles. He was surrounded by magnificent luxury and opulence that he could scarcely enjoy because he feared for his life. So that in the end, Damocles begged to return to his former life."

"How do you know all these stories?"

"I just do. Part of my purpose, I suppose, if there is such a thing."

"Everyone has a purpose," Marta said.

"So you say."

"Well, it's true," she said. "I know that it's sort of like

the mantra of the network, but I do believe it is true."

"These kinds of stories offer important information about life."

"So this simple life is what we ought to strive for?" Marta asked me. I supposed I was used to such stories as guides, but maybe to Marta, they were just odd little tidbits of useless knowledge. She was a coder, after all.

"Simple life? Perhaps. I expect the real message is that we really don't know what we want, though we think we do, have an idea of what it is when it might not be that at all."

"And do you know what you want?" Marta eyed me, raised her eyebrows a touch perhaps less, so subtly and light as if it could have merely been the breeze.

I was blushing now. And I felt nervous. My hands clammy. Hopefully she wouldn't want to hold hands. And this was the SIM. I wasn't supposed to feel like this, was I? I thought everything was perfect in the SIM.

"Things are not always perfect in the SIM," Marta said as if reading my thoughts. Then she reached for my hand. "It's easier, of course, to interact with a version of me rather than the real me, just like in real life. Maybe you would feel more comfortable if we changed the setting to a bar."

"A bar?" I asked. "Why do you ask that? And what are you alluding to?"

"I could wear a little black cocktail dress and matching lace panties," she offered with a definite raise of her eyebrows as we sat close together on the bench in the park, surrounded by oak trees and the smells of the natural world, our skin prickling on the edge of being cold by a slight breeze, but remaining warm because we remained close enough to almost touch, and maybe even we were at times, our legs, her legs I remembered they were like a series of rooms and I searched in each one, looked and probed in hot pursuit, trying to find the door that led to the top or at least the middle.

I blushed as a rush of embarrassment flooded me, like a door opened that was best left closed, the wrong door, and behind that door was me, naked. How could I not feel that way? This was like having someone look inside my mind and see all those little secrets, those sacred thoughts of mine.

"You saw." I probably shouldn't have been surprised. There was no privacy in this world. Not in the SIM, especially there, but not anywhere else either. And yet, I was under the illusion that this time it was different.

"I was curious," she said, raising her eyebrows for a moment. "As you would have been in the roles were reversed; you who were looking through my stuff when I was in the shower. Am I right?"

"Yes," I said without hesitation. "I would have for sure. Most definitely, but. . ."

"So that's settled," she said, and stood up from the park bench, adjusting her yellow dress with blue flowers in the same moment as she stood.

"What's settled?"

"We're still curious. A very human quality. That's good. Despite everything."

"And full of intrigue and deception," I added, "not knowing for sure, about a moment, but suspicious that you are leading me on."

She smiled at me, then winked. "I don't think so. If anything, *you* are the one leading *me* on. Not that I am turning you down at all."

"I know," I said knowingly, as if knowing and wanting to believe, but these were emotions so that you could never be sure what something meant or didn't mean. "Oh, by the way, do you really have such a dress?"

"See," she said as if to prove a point, poking me in the side. "You want to know."

"I was just curious," I said. "My curiosity is complicated, though."

"No doubt," she said, then added almost sadly. "I don't have such a dress. One could be created, of course, in the SIM."

I thought about such clothes, how they looked to us, how they felt on us and yet what they really were was something more akin to a plain and basic fashion, for even the real world was a filter, its own kind of SIM. It was a weird thought. I pictured Marta so beautifully in a black cocktail dress, sparkling in the light as she turned and changed into Marta in a simple, rugged cloth outfit that she was probably really in. I felt that tension, that pull between two worlds, parallel and overlapping, and in some way, however subtly, I was choosing what no sane person would ever choose. To leave paradise.

As we stood in the park, I touched her yellow dress, felt the softness of the fabric, even the color seemed to flow through it as my fingertips rubbed the surface. She watched me, her eyes once again alive, swaying like the branches of the trees.

"So real. It just feels so real."

"What does it mean for something to be not real?"

"Maybe I don't know the answer to that one anymore. If all of our senses tell us something is real and our brain goes along with it, then it gets hard to argue something is not real. Doesn't it?"

"A conundrum," she smiled. "That's one of your words, I believe."

She whispered it again and again to herself. I liked when she whispered like that, her secret, our secret. Then she nudged me along, back onto the brick pathway in that park. We walked along and came to a sculpture atop a Doric column depicting a man on a horse with a sword. There was no inscription. Not that I would have believed what it said anyway. The man carried a great and mighty sword as all of the heroes used to.

I made up a back story about how this ordinary man saved the republic from ruin, all for a Queen whom he loved but who was set up to marry a noble. In a great battle, our hero saved the nobleman's life when he could have let him perish. The Queen did not love the man she was to marry. She loved our hero. Thus, in his honor, she erected this fabulous statue, larger than life.

"A man and his big sword," Marta exclaimed, pleased with the story. "But why so sad?"

"A lot of fairytales are," I said.

Marta took my arm and led me away from the sculpture, around the roundabout to a botanical garden blooming brightly. Butterflies flitted in and among rose bushes and other florals. The fragrant air felt nice to breathe. Hummingbirds too drew near, such tiny creatures, delicately fluttering in the light with their magic wings. I liked the roses. I almost recalled a memory, something about a rose garden, but I couldn't quite get there.

"Can we get outside the city?" I asked Marta after we

had left the botanicals. She continued holding on to my arm and seemed to wait a while before answering my question.

"Yes, sort of. We can go to the mountains or even the seaside, but there are natural limits. We are in a big enclosure, a sealed off portion that stretches maybe a few hundred square miles. I don't know for sure. You would know for sure if you looked. Luckily this area is water rich."

"You mentioned the seaside. I've got a sense of the mountains and forest region, mostly uninhabited I recall, but something about the seaside strikes me."

"Yes. The seaside remains quite beautiful, Mediterranean climate with a beach, lots of sunshine, old buildings and gelato."

"The frozen stuff."

"Yeah," she said. "'The frozen stuff'? You're funny."

"Well, it is frozen. Isn't it?"

"It 'tis," she said. Then repeated it.

We neared a pond among the colorful flowers and ground cover. Fish swam about, darting amongst each other with an ever-present primordial instinct. If I had a coin in my pocket, then I would have tossed it in. I told Marta about that, about tossing a coin in the pond and making a wish. I handed her an imaginary coin and watched as she ceremoniously tossed it in. I asked her if she made a wish.

"I'm always making wishes," she said quietly as she observed me, then looked off in another direction.

A song played in my head, a soft piano ballad of some kind, somber but not like a dirge, though not too hopeful either and yet, that melody stuck around, echoed off the walls of some distant station, some place I imagined we could be, in time, if we just had time. Speaking of time, I wondered how much time had passed since we were in the SIM. Probably not as much as I thought. I still couldn't get a real sense of time.

"Luckily," Marta was saying, "You are slated to visit the seaside for vacation. That was one thing that worked out well in your timing. You planned to go there right after you got out."

"Thanks," I said, thinking again of the seaside, something about the seaside, but instead of something concrete what I actualized was more postcard than memory. "So what didn't turn out as well?"

"I don't know. Was this what you expected? I know that's not a fair question. You were optimistic about the future, but at the same time unsure too, which is why I assume you programmed an out after fourteen years."

"Well, we often overestimate the immediate and underestimate the long term. And I'm usually more on the pessimistic side."

"That's why I never was part of the grid," Marta said. "I saw how fast the system was evolving, how the network was moving along and the potential of the grid as a negative thing."

Had she told me that earlier? I couldn't recall. I suddenly felt exhausted, overwhelmed by everything. Marta noted this, even recognized it. Perhaps on her own, or perhaps through her version of the network. Did it matter which, I asked myself? Not really. I thought about the seaside as I reached out and touched a flower with orange petals. And if she was never part of the grid, as she said, then why didn't she know about Jesus Christ?

"I often wondered why you kept it secret," Marta said, interrupting my thoughts. "It would be a perfectly normal thing back then to plug into the code a way out for observational purposes. And yet, you told no one. You hid it. That's always puzzled me."

"What if it wasn't me?" I said what I was thinking aloud.

"Someone else?" Marta considered. "Hmm. That's interesting, but another conundrum. We don't need any more of those."

I thought about it, considered how or what I might have been thinking about back then versus where I was now; in a SIM, touching orange flowers, standing beside a woman in a yellow dress who took a strange liking to me, who I was in some way dependent upon. And I didn't think that in a negative way, I was just trying to be objective. This apparition in the bar, across from me, a presence I thought initially was all a dream, was here now with her hazel eyes and calm, her legs like stops on a subway, some out in the open and others hidden by a yellow dress. And here I was, on some part of the track, maybe even on another link, and I was suddenly just overwhelmed.

If I looked at it from where I was now, then surely I kept the information from my colleagues because I wanted to protect them. Who I was really hiding from was the network itself. The fact that the code was in plain sight made it all the more invisible, buried so to speak, in layers upon layers of code as part of the code. That was the best way to hide. As part of it. They called that hidden in plain sight.

"Well, like you said earlier, I am sure I was skeptical, a little suspicious of our endeavor. Any group, no matter how good and skilled they all are, has weaknesses. And usually that weakness is the great human weakness. Believing we know better, that things will be different this time."

I looked to Marta, there as she stood in the garden, surrounded by flowers, bathed in the light of the sun shining against her lightly darkened, almost olive skin, her curled hair expertly dancing in the breeze, while I was losing a step, slipping a little to the song playing because I was a little out of time, off time, out of sync.

"I probably made notes somewhere. I was never the type to divulge much to anyone. I wrote a lot. People knew if they asked for my input, what they would get. The way we always know, I suppose, when we ask someone for advice. Anyway, mostly I kept to myself."

"Well, that's obvious," Marta said. "I've been watching you for a long time you know. You were never quite like the others, even before the network event."

"How so?" I asked, my interest piqued, for she said she knew me before the event, but I did not recall her at all. And it seemed to me I would have remembered someone like Marta. Maybe she looked a lot different then.

"Distant. There but not there, here, but not here. As if two places at once, but never fully present, yet doing the bare minimum to appear so, thus not noticeably absent. Like now. I'm telling you all this, and you are definitely listening, but you are also thinking of something else too. And I wonder what that is?"

"I have been listening."

"I know. I didn't say you weren't listening."

"But I've also been thinking too," I said in agreement. Caught again. Not pants down. But caught all the same.

"Not about anything really specific, just wandering in the passages of my mind, moving from thought to thought, absorbing your words, not consciously, perhaps in a semi-conscious scrawl, something that allows my mind to paint their colors, while all the while I am on this train, in a foreign city, unsure about the stops or whether I should get off."

She nodded, somewhat amused perhaps, and moved a little away from me to smell a golden colored rose. I reached out to touch her hand and looked into her eyes as she looked back to me, still smelling the fragrance of the rose. I didn't detect any change, so if there was one, then it must have been slight.

I wanted to ask her something, but at the same time, I didn't want to say anything. Was I scared of being disappointed? And if so, in whom or what? In myself, in her? Was this not the real her, how she really looked as I looked at her now? Maybe she wasn't being completely honest with me. That would not be a surprise, for it was not an easy task being honest. I surmised that I wasn't even being honest with her. On a conscious level, perhaps on that very surface, I was, wasn't I? But to go deeper, to dig deeper. It was at that point that I didn't know for sure if things were as they seemed. As humans, we needed a little shroud, something of an illusion to give us hope so that we could believe in impossible things. And to be where I was, I must have believed in impossible things too.

"I used to have a place along the seaside, the Adriatic, I believe," I said to her.

Marta smiled at me as if pleased to move along to something else. She stood erect again and motioned to continue our walk, and we did, move out of the botanical gardens to a similar kind of path where in the distance a grand building stood like a marker.

"Yes," she said. "That's where you will be going tomorrow. You haven't been there much in the last couple of years. "

"What did I do there?" I asked, wondering to myself if it was such a magical place, why then had I stopped going there.

"Why does anyone go anywhere?" Marta asked. "To relax. Holiday. The seaside is a nice place, a calm restorative place. I liked it there too."

"Alone?" I asked, though as soon as I asked the question I seemed to know the answer. I pictured things, places and people, certain people.

"No," Marta said, quietly with more than a hint of reluctance, seeming to know or suspect that I knew the answer already, so by asking the question, she was surely pondering what point I was trying to make, but I wasn't trying to make a point.

"Well, Star was sometimes there. And sometimes children."

"Our children?"

"Not really. As I said before, we ceded that kind of thing long before."

The way Marta said it was odd, as if there was something crude and unnatural about the process, when in fact it was basic to our existence, or had been for millennia. What had changed? Everything had changed. I guessed that was the progression. From the birth canal to the C-section to the laboratory, where every stage of the process could be controlled (and the young were equipped with microprocessors as soon as they were able). What *hadn't* changed was a more apt question.

"I forgot about that," I said, suddenly thinking about it all, from the arranged marriages, the forced marriages (because of pregnancy) to the general eroding of the institution to its outright disappearance; huge families, at one time extra hands to smaller families, then on to the broken family unit to the inconvenience of children in general. And maybe some part of it made me sad, wistful for a different time. There was no going back, was there? You can't go home again. That was the point, that you could never step in the same river twice because all things flow.

"You still have feelings for Star?" Marta asked as we approached a large building that looked like maybe at one time it housed a school or a university, but now was just a point on a pathway in a SIM.

"No, not really," I said. "Why? Are you jealous?"

She nodded in deference but offered no corroborating answer. She stopped and looked away, off in the distance at other things the way people do when the issue does not want to be confronted.

"We both know that's not true," I said.

She said my name. I hadn't heard my name in so long. David. Sometimes I forgot that was my name. I really don't know why I should forget such a thing, but names never really stuck with me. The first time I met someone, I knew later I wouldn't remember their name.

"I happen to know that the only SIM you ever really did with any regularity was meeting up with Star at that bar with all of the details constantly being perfected. And it was almost exactly the same thing every time. Now and then you would change something, alter a detail, the music, her dress, the topics of conversation, then you might go back to an earlier version, but you kept this narrative for years and years. That was your normal. You were not interested in variation, in anybody else except Star."

"It was an obsession," I said, more to myself than her. I didn't think it was necessarily about her, but it was still an obsession.

I could have guessed she knew that. And I could also have known that too, if I really thought about, if I wanted to know that. And I further assumed the network viewed such behavior as controllable, as part of my normal pattern, my obsession so to speak. And though maybe everyone had obsessions, not everyone was obsessive, were they? Besides, wasn't the SIM the very place to explore those things?

"It's okay that you have feelings for her," Marta said sternly, but in a resigned kind of way. "It's not okay for you to pretend to me that you don't."

I could tell that she was a little hurt. And I didn't mean to hurt her in any way at all, but wasn't it often the case that the things we did had impacts on lives that we would never know? And still, wasn't it okay to have feelings for someone even though maybe that very person you mostly couldn't stand. That's how I felt about Star.

"So what happened between Star and I?" I asked Marta knowing that it was a risk and strange too, asking someone else about your life, but I needed to know.

"You don't remember," she said, obviously perturbed. Wrong question for me to ask. "Because I'd rather not talk about it. Nothing personal. I am perfectly happy to answer any and all questions you have, but not about her. Nothing about her."

Fair enough. Star. I thought about Star. Blonde. Buxom. Beautiful. Not in need of any enhancements or alterations. Such a natural beauty. Not that that stopped her. She was not satisfied being merely beautiful, when she could be more and more beautiful. I remember that. Constantly changing things. Bigger breasts. Different shapes. More or less curvaceous. It all depended on what she wore, and she was always buying new clothes. And she wanted me to change things too. She wanted to mold me as she liked. But I didn't want that. I had no interest in that at all. I just didn't care.

If she lived on the outside, the surface, that exterior facing element, then I was the polar opposite, inward, tending towards the hidden, unobservable world where thoughts and ideas were championed, the underlying nature of a thing and not it's surface appeal.

"Okay," I said. "Something must have come between us."

"Not something, but someone. Your best friend, Lando" she sternly said in acknowledgement, "He would do anything for her. . . not that relationships really exist anymore in the same way they did."

"So why did he even bother? Or why did it matter?"

"You tell me," she said. "To prove a point? I don't know. Why do men fight over women?"

"I don't know," I admitted. Because I didn't. "But it's a lonely life living in the past."

"For you exactly," Marta said. "And yet you seemed content in a depressing kind of way."

"I suppose so. Though it seems odd for me to think about this part of my life when it exists as something foreign to me, like it is me and it is not me, like I didn't live it but only watched someone live it, so the attachment is tenuous at best. But that's really how I was?

"I believe so. You had an acceptance about you. A resignation to your fate. But that's also the network effect, your mind merging with the network, doing its best to adapt and survive with what limits it has."

"This is complicated," I said half-joking, ignoring the dig, looking not at Marta but the grand building we stood in front of. Complicated indeed, but more so I thought, because of you. Here I am, here with you, your hazel eyes and lovely yellow blue dress, the way you look at me, yet right now, all I can think about is Star. That's ridiculous. Must be residual. I focused on the building. Why had I been so enthralled with Star? Was it just like the raven, forever entranced by shiny objects? And then when Lando won her over, I was left, lonely just looking.

The building looked like an old-style university type building, multi-colored brick with a tower and turrets, rounded archways and rows of square-paned windows. A grand stairway, wide at the bottom and small atop by the entrance as it narrowed to two large doors. I looked away, then was drawn back by a figure in the window, but she was there and not there just like a man who wasn't there, that poem called "Antigonish" and a yesterday upon the stair with a man who wasn't there.

I made up my own version.

Today walking with a woman in yellow, I saw a figure in a window

Oh how I didn't want to stare, she seemed quite content to be there

I too was the man who wasn't there. I keenly felt that.

Even Marta and I being together in the SIM although we were alone in our separate rooms, dreaming this dream as we had never dreamt before, was like being not there. And all I really wanted was to be somewhere, to belong to something, to someone, to something more than the molecules of me which I couldn't understand.

I wondered if we could go into the building or not. I didn't see why it should be locked. And no, I didn't expect to find any figures lurking in the shadows, though I knew very well what I saw: a figure in the window, a woman, faceless and nameless, yet very clear to me in that single instance. In my mind, I was sure I would conflate the moment and come up with an actual face, but the truth was, I didn't know. Yet, this was no mere pareidolia, but a real, perceivable image.

"Hey," Marta said. "What's up? What are you thinking?"

We were at the bottom steps that led to the building entrance. I told her I saw a figure in the window. She asked me a few questions, but stopped after it was clear, I didn't have any answers about what I saw since it was such a momentary thing. She seemed oddly unmoved.

The building was unlocked, so we stepped inside. My eyes quickly adjusted to the change in light, while my mind filled in the gaps. Footsteps, soft but still hard as the flats of the soles slapped against the old wood floor. But there were no steps, were there? No, not except for our own. No figure lounging against the upper bannister, no face like a girl in a painting by some Dutch master long ago. Only our own sounds, our own breath from the beating of our hearts to the subtleties in our movements. That and the musty smell characteristic of old buildings, but a new mustiness, if that was a thing.

For a moment I wondered if Marta and I saw the same building, but before I barely aroused my own suspicions, I had answered them, amazed at the absurdity of my probe. For surely the building was the same, but it would always be perceived differently. I sometimes thought too deeply and too quickly in the submerge that I missed the most basic question. We would always perceive things differently. That was what it meant to be human.

"I'm thinking about dumb stuff. It's really too embarrassing to share because it is nothing insightful."

"Try me," she said, curiously.

"Well, for a moment, I wondered if we were seeing the same building or not in the SIM, then I figured it out. The same but different, just like in the real world. In my perception, I just happened to focus on a figure glimpsed in a window, while you likely keyed in on. . ."

"The stained glass above the entryway."

"Yeah," I said, sheepishly. "I didn't see that."

"Nor I, the figure."

"So that's that. We always see different things, noticed one thing as opposed to the other, and even if we saw the same thing, probably different things would stand out."

"And sometimes nothing at all because we are too lost in our own thoughts."

"No silly, that's just you!"

With that, she gave me a strong nudge, seemingly gentle, yet enough to startle me into momentarily losing my balance. I hadn't expected the contact. I was just about to turn back to see the stained glass when she had pushed me, glancing into my eyes before turning playfully away. I was glad we were back to happier moments.

"See what I mean," she offered somewhat conciliatorily.

"Very funny."

She bumped into me again.

"Let's get out of here. Kind of stuffy in here. It makes me uneasy."

She made the suggestion and I couldn't have agreed more, still, I looked around one last time from the foyer where we stood, an ascending staircase on each side leading up to the second floor. I wasn't necessarily looking for a hidden figure. I was just looking to see what was, to really see. I took it all in while Marta bounded out the door and was half-way down the steps before I stepped out.

"It felt kind of strange in there," she said at the landing. "I couldn't quite place it. I just had a weird feeling like something wasn't quite right."

"I suppose the network can hack into a SIM, change things as might be needed."

"Sure," she offered, but then rather defiantly, qualified her statement. "Not this SIM though. Normally yes as the SIM is just part of the grid, the networked world, all things connected, a web, but not this SIM. This is my separate, parallel network. This one is mine."

I had seen the figure in the window, but now it was Marta who looked as if she'd seen a ghost. Somehow her lightly bronzed skin was paler. Maybe it was just that sense of fear in her eyes and nothing more, but it was something.

"Let's go somewhere else," she said, barely waiting for my nod. A flash of darkness ensued, a brief interruption of the park like setting where we had been, replaced by light, lots of light as I realized the brightness of the sunny day that surrounded us, the soothing sound of the ocean, my gaze directed to that place where the sea met the sky, and then to Marta, who stood beside me.

She wore the same yellow dress as before, but now her eyes were sheltered by a pair of sunglasses. I hadn't noticed her earrings earlier, if they had been there, and probably they had, being just another thing I had not noticed. And now that I wasn't distracted, not drawn in by her eyes, I could notice other things about her, her subtle yet seductive shape, her lovely legs that had taken me places before, whole journeys that only left me breathless.

"Nice," I remarked at nothing in particular did I marvel, as it could have been so many things in that moment. Was this the seaside? I didn't want to ask.

"Amazing, isn't it?"

And truly it was. We stood on a boardwalk, removed from the beach and the roar of the ocean as the swells of surf gave land then greedily took it back, relishing as it rushed over again before relinquishing the sands, then repeating what would be a never-ending process of give and take.

Forever, like a looping program, a tape that played endlessly, finishing what was to be finished then starting again.

On the beach, people sprawled on blankets, stretching their bodies out as if in worship, but it was a primitive posture, defenseless, unlike those who sat in chairs protected by vast umbrellas. I didn't quite know it now, but this scene would later be familiar to me.

"Yes. This could very well be what I now know as the real world, yet it is not yet. And here you are, as am I, like masters of the domain, and yet, we are really just pawns."

Had I said that last bit aloud or not, I couldn't be sure, but since Marta did not immediately respond, I took that to mean that I had not. Maybe she had already become accustomed to me and how I was, prone to these jejune outbursts, not in the least bit interesting, mocking the profound.

"It is a splendid fabrication."

We gazed at such splendor, at the triumph of the age of coding, making a virtual world seem as real as the other world, which I noted, wasn't all that real to begin with. Yes, that was some kind of magic trick, gradually leading us to the precipice before succumbing to the eventuality, but it was too late by then. Because we had already bought in, the set, the performance, and finally the prestige.

"Including you?"

"And you still want to see Star?"

Marta seemed to imply that anything could be created, including Star, which made it absurd that I wanted to see Star, she who would see me anyway, no matter what, no matter what the circumstance. But why did I need to see Star?

"A question with a question. Does that change your answer?"

"Maybe. Although whatever I say will be true."

"Okay," I said, thinking about it.

"Okay," Marta said gazing at me. She may have had a wistful look in her eyes, but the dark frames well hid any indication as such, so I merely presumed

"Yeah. I want to see Star. Talk with her. I don't know why exactly, but I do. Who knows, it might be important."

"The answer is yes then."

"Yes what?" I asked.

"Yes, the me you see now is a fabrication, but you already knew that."

"Can I see the real you?"

"Maybe, but not now."

"Why not?"

"You're not going to see the real Star," she teased. "Nothing even close to the real Star."

"So you think I'll go into a SIM with her, experience an even more fabricated version of her?"

"Oh, I know you'll do that. At least, you want to."

"Maybe. Sometimes you don't know something at all, not even in the moment, though you might act a certain way."

"Hmm," Marta said, unconvinced. "That's just you. Cause and effect. Action and reaction. That's the world."

And for that, to that, I remained unconvinced. For me, that was not the world. For me, it was the interior world and not the exterior, yet paradoxically, I wanted to see Marta as she really was. And not necessarily the same with Star, which was a direct contradiction. Marta knew the hypocrisy of my position. But we were all often hypocrites, clinging to opposing positions without even knowing it, simultaneously for and against something.

We walked along in the sunshine, along the boardwalk, among people that were there, but almost invisible as if we could walk right through them if we wanted. It would have been a strange thing to test out, especially if I was wrong. And I probably was wrong. There was so much I had been wrong about in my life, though I knew one day I would be right about something, and that something was a thing that mattered.

"Remember when you first woke, that dreamlike place

where you kind of saw a little of what the world really looks like and how terrible that made you feel, how vacant and empty."

I couldn't forget that. At various times, the sensation returned to me, visiting like the ghost it was and maybe would always be as if the event itself was transformational, the experience so raw and deep that it would trail me wherever I went, no matter the lengths I went to cut its cord, the link would remain, wireless, beyond the realm of severability.

"Is that it? Does everyone look kind of freakish?"

"No. Not completely. But we don't look like this, none of us. Our diets are different. Food is different."

"And Star?"

I imagined she rolled her eyes. Her head shot back a little. I watched her body move as she breathed in then exhaled. I kind of didn't know why I was hung up on Star. I suspected that Marta was being more than protective of me.

"She looks better than most, actually. Some just have better genes to begin with, no matter how

we try to alter things. But that's not what worries me."

"What are you worried about?"

"That she traps you. That the network uses her as bait knowing she's your weakness."

I considered what she said, the reasonableness, the plausibility versus her jealousy, which seemed to me pretty obvious, not that I was going to mention that. That was never my style to call someone on something like that because the truth often made things worse because one perception of an event, of that truth was very different than another. I wasn't saying there was no truth, rather that the way people felt was often too complicated for someone else to really understand, though we feigned understanding all the time in regard to such matters. The arrogant among us thought otherwise and masqueraded as so-called empaths, proving how easy we could deceive ourselves into magical thinking.

"So you just think I am jealous?" she asked me.

"It's not that," I said. Could she read my thoughts? Or was I just that easy to read.

"I think it is."

"Okay, the thought crossed my mind. And if you look at things from my point of view."

"Yes," she echoed. "Your point of view, as a man, that is."

"And what's that supposed to mean?"

"Well," she said, looking me over, pausing for effect, for a sense of the right words. "It might be a bit of a game to you, playing different people off of each other, but as a woman, that kind of thing doesn't interest me. If you are really interested in Star, that's fine. I don't want to need something that's not there."

"So you don't trust me?"

"No, I do trust you. It's really you who doesn't trust me. You know you need me for your predicament, but you remain suspicious of my motives, yet I've watched and waited for you for fourteen years, waiting for this moment, so please don't doubt me or my intentions.."

I could sense her frustration with me, and whether it was entirely fair or not, I did owe her something. But what was the truth when you yourself didn't know? And that was the thing, I just didn't know. I was still trying to make sense of things, and whether Marta liked it or not, that meant reconnecting somewhat with the past. I couldn't help being skeptical. Even about her.

"Oh, fuck it. Go see her. I can't stop you if that's what you want."

"Marta."

"David," she shot back.

I did what I thought was a first, leaning towards Marta and gently kissing her on the forehead, but then I realized I had kissed her before in the SIM. That was different though. That was not really her. And this was more her because she was the real Marta now, at this moment, standing beside me, before me in her yellow dress with blue birds, her dark sunglasses. Still, it was complicated because we were in the SIM.

"Does what happens in the SIM stay in the SIM?" I joked, trying to lighten the mood. That was sort of a tagline for a place that used to exist. Las Vegas. Or *Lost Wages* as some called it. A mecca for gambling, drinking, and other kinds of excess.

She perked up a little, straightened her posture, moving her hands to my cheek. That I shouldn't be in awe of her, struck me as nothing short of remarkable, she who so diligently kept watch over me. And yet I was too. It was the absolute I struggled with. I seldom accepted things on an absolute basis.

"Okay. Maybe I am a little jealous. Be careful. Remember everything I've said. Remember why you came here in the first place, why you wanted out of the network. You had a purpose. We are not always as smart or clever as we like to think. Even you. Remember your purpose. Let that guide you."

"I will," I said, thinking of the Greek word *telos* and

further of it being a root of teleological, and meaning purpose or goal, but why I should have thought of that, I didn't know. I knew only that I couldn't let her down. Was it a purpose that guides us or passion?

"One can only hope you are not drawn in."

She drew her hand away from my cheek and motioned for me to follow. Come on, she seemed to say. There's something I want to show you. The breeze rustled her dress. She led and I followed in silence until the boardwalk came to a point, at which a modest lighthouse stood of old stone, looking ancient but defiant. She smiled as she turned to me, her hazel eyes smiling too, radiant. And for that moment, she was indomitable, like that old lighthouse, that lost beacon in the night for all the lost ships.

PART TWO

Marta had said I only had to act naturally, as I normally would and things would be fine, that I would fit right in to the flow of the work day. I would know all the people I encountered and could easily pass muster because I wasn't one to say much.

"Just keep my wits," I had said to her, to which she nodded. Everything was always easier said than done, the life imagined much different than the one lived, still we said such things, made assurances because they assuaged our doubts and mollified fears.

She mentioned she would be tracking me. And should I need any assistance, then she would be there to help me. I didn't know quite how that would manifest but was confident that she knew what she was talking about. See, I wanted to say to her, I really do trust you. She, of course, would respond, some of the time.

As a precaution, she showed me a video of my daily routine, pieced together from the infinite, panoptics of the world, sped up and slowed down as necessary. That answered a bunch of my questions, like how I would know where my office was. Occasionally she would stop and ask if I knew who I was talking to. And I did. I had known a lot of these people for a long time, but for how long, I couldn't say for sure. Time was not exactly a thing that made sense to me anymore, if ever it did. Certainly not now.

"So, is everything good?" Marta asked me.

"Yeah," I said, "I got it. But I still feel kind of nervous. Maybe I shouldn't."

"No, it's okay to be a little nervous. Just look for cues. I would say be yourself, but that doesn't really help you, though it is true in all instances."

Marta looked to me in what I termed her surveil mode, as if she was mentally making notes and crossing off the various tags. I know she wasn't doing that. She just had a way of looking at me, of studying me. I remembered when I first saw her, how I thought she certainly had a beauty to her, it just wasn't apparent to me then as it was now.

"Don't overthink it. Most people will think nothing of how you react to them. And I'll know when the network interacts with you. Probably it won't," she added.

She fussed over me, knowing perhaps more than I would ever would. I wasn't that helpless, I told myself. I could function. The key, as she had said, was to not think too much about it, but that was the hardest thing, turning off the normal features of my mind. I felt a little bit like a little boy on his first day of school, and remembered the annual photo, my loving mom reassuring me.

"And where will you be?" I asked her again and again.

"I'll be nearby. I can disappear within the network and make myself not visible to others or the system. Or I can be seen only by you too. Don't worry about me. I'm used to this game. This is my game."

"Very clever," I had said, though it also made me wonder. Maybe Marta wasn't even real. Maybe I had created her as a simulation to appear before me as a means of monitoring, a precaution in case something bad happened. There were lots of things impossible to predict. Could I have created Marta? Was I really that clever? I doubted it. Still, I didn't know for sure. Maybe someone else created her for me? But who? I knew the best explanation was often the simplest.

If Marta was a kind of all-knowing simulation, then she would be akin to God, a concept that didn't even seem to exist here, at least in the same light. Remember, the God was in the machine, *was* the machine. The concept of God always existed, though, just not in the same way it had once been popularized. We just kept changing the definition because we still needed to explain the unexplainable. Network or not, that might not ever change. Or was now everything explained by the network?

I needed Marta, but for what did she need me? She seemed plenty capable without me. Already, more often than not, it did seem like she was reading my mind. Since I wasn't fully immersed in her network, that didn't seem plausible, not that I understood how everything worked anyway, all the advances in cognitive technology and neural connections that made this world possible. Was I or wasn't I?

Still, here was my answer: She had a read on my body conditions from her network, so based on those clues along with having watched me for years, she was able to make certain inferences about what I was thinking or what I would do next. Or maybe I was just all too easy to read. That was the simplest answer. I wasn't as complex as I liked to think.

Another problem: I didn't have a firm grasp on what was real, if anything, ever was real and not just a SIM within a SIM, like a dream within a dream. Maybe the world all along, even the old world, was never what I thought it was? And all those stories I read, the stuff I heard, were never real to begin with. Admittedly, some of it was quite fantastic. Was there a test to prove something was real? I wondered. Absence of evidence was not evidence of absence. Still, that did not help my cause. I wasn't talking about dragons or other fantastical creatures. I was merely wondering about the world before me that I so perceived.

Marta did her best to reassure me she was real, kissing me softly. I suppose I didn't do my best to assure her I was real, for my response was muted. I was too far into my thoughts as we bid our goodbyes from the SIM.

The early part of my life, cherished memories so to speak, were possibly more imagined than I knew, memories I culled into existence rather than experienced. Parts of some originality that were slowly altered, subtly so, so that what I thought I knew now was in fact more fantasy than reality. The brain was not like a computer. That was an important distinction. It did not simply store a memory in perfect condition.

No. It changed things, made tweaks that allowed us to better cope with the world before us. Like the network now. We introduced chips into our bodies so that we could better understand how our bodies really worked so we could trace, track, and monitor changes. And from all of that information learn even more. And after chips, more hardware, more wiring followed by code to do what our brains did naturally only the network knew better because it had that perfect knowledge of where everybody was at all moments in time. *Perfect knowledge.*

That was how it was with driverless cars. When they

were first introduced, while they were not complete chaos, there were errors, seemingly avoidable mistakes, sensors getting caught by a flash of light, by the weather, by someone carrying a surfboard. And then the humans, not just as drivers, but as pedestrians too. There was nothing predictable in their actions, or everything was predictable until it wasn't. That was the problem. The chance that they could be unpredictable. If you could not predict something, then you could not program for it. For strangely enough, driverless cars often tripped up at the simplest things to us. Like a stalled car, that odd stationary object in a place it shouldn't be.

It was only when *all* cars were automated that the driverless cars worked really well, when every driverless car knew exactly where every other vehicle was. That sort of efficiency allowed for greater speeds, less traffic. In fact, *traffic* was a term that was never used, something that was lost, deemed obsolete. And no one missed it when it was gone. It was like that for some things.

In the end, there were still humans in the automated vehicles, but not as drivers, rather as monitors. Everyone had a job. Mostly such jobs consisted of monitoring some part of the network. But everyone had some kind of job. Another perk of the network system. Full employment. Everyone with the sense that they were doing something vital enough. Did it matter that it was all trickery, a mere illusion? Probably not. Even before the network people thought they held jobs of great importance. Why else would they be agonizing over some detail on a phone call everyone could hear. That was the thing about humans, our egos, our sense of the importance of our own life, that cultivation of our identity brand. That remained. We needed to feel unique.

As I saw it, there were at least two different worlds, and within those worlds, subsets via the SIM. There was the filtered world that everyone saw and lived in, effectively snuffing the real world that no one saw or knew of, except for maybe Marta and me, and now that I was not near her, I doubted whether she was real again. I don't know why I thought that, but I couldn't shake it after it took hold of me. Was it crazy? Was I? Sanity and madness seemed clearly linked, separated by a diaphanous layer, transparent at one moment then completely opaque, depending entirely on the angle. How could something be both clothed and naked at the same time?

And if only a few people believed in something, no matter that it might be true, to hold such a belief seemed to be the very definition of crazy. If not crazy, then madness, akin to saying Jesus Christ rose from the dead, which for much of history was commonly accepted. Now such a thing as Jesus Christ was pure lunacy because I was the only one who had heard of him. Well, at least Marta knew of him now. If ever later, in some other world, and we wanted to start up a religion, but I stopped myself there. I was skipping too far ahead, allowing myself to believe all of this would get resolved and we would need religion to trick people because we wouldn't have the network then.

Marta was right. It wasn't so difficult to maneuver around. The streets were familiar, even recognizable, often evoking a memory. I remembered walking with Star along the canal, stopping at that café for a coffee, and over there, that seemed to be the place where Emrik and I first discussed the real possibility of interconnection before the group talked about it. As I thought of that, it was possible, small conversations had been going on all around me, but that was the first time he and I discussed it. And how long ago was that? Here again was that ugly and gross imposition of time, at first just a nudge but then it had you all the way. Time was a blur, a fuzzy object from a distance that didn't focus the nearer it came, speeding through the station stop so that all the figures waiting there blended in like an abstract painting.

I just walked along the street ignoring time, passing boutiques, coffee shops, places to eat. The amazing structures I recalled from the night before were different in the light of day but nonetheless still marvels, varying in size and style, the larger ones likely being housing with their intricate designs on the first few floors, delicate tile work, trusses, curves, arches and points morphing into form following function.

I glanced in windows at dresses on mannequins, at jewels on display, modern age gadgets and other things I was sure no one would ever buy. Yet, people did as they came and went, here then gone, moving past me along their way to the subway with their purchases, where they could take an individual or multi-person pod.

Above me, flying pods hovered in moans and drones of helicopter-like sounds, buzzing down when called to, but otherwise being the birds that were nowhere to be seen. We used to have birds, not just flying objects that made bird-like sounds. Real birds. I was sure of it. We probably killed them all because they were hazards to the drones, a necessary sort of extinction we called something else at the time, something like *planned obsolescence*.

I recalled getting a linen shirt at one of the shops, the

tall thin shop owner making suggestions to the chagrin of Star, who naturally wanted to be the one calling the shots. And perhaps even more, I was listening to the shop owner over Star, intrigued by her knowledge and sense of style, which was quite different from Star's. Quite different. Star thought it was something else and was very pouty after that.

Did that store still exist? I looked for it but didn't see where it was. The place could have been anywhere, on another street, maybe even a different city, yet the thing was, I recalled the experience. That must have meant it really happened. The tall shop owner, her features blurred from my memory, though I certainly conjured some image of a model-esque physique I doubted that was real. I couldn't picture her and yet I did paint a quick depiction. Maybe she wasn't even real and none of it happened, my mind merely confabulating.

Nobody else questioned how real a thing was. Or did they? I observed those everyday movements of people knowing exactly where they were supposed to be going, and here I was, only half knowing until I saw a coffee shop. Something clicked. Before that I was aimless, a wanderer in my thoughts. But now I knew exactly what I needed.

Coffee. I needed some coffee. I stepped inside the crowded shop, looking around, presumably for work colleagues, but it was also something I just did. It felt natural and normal to see tables full of people, some talking, others alone with their screens. Everyone was immersed in something, and me, just in my thoughts. That was about right.

The barista looked to me and nodded, holding up a cup. I then knew his name. Cameron. Though I didn't recognize his co-workers. They were probably new. Or maybe, I didn't have much of a connection to them, but with Cameron, we shared some kind of link. I was sure of that. It seemed deeper than this daily ritual.

"The usual, I presume, on this fine day."

"Yes. And a fine day it is. How are you doing today?"

"I'm great. It's my Friday, and I am looking forward to the weekend, a couple of days off and all of that. Maybe go on a hike or something. You?"

"Me too. I'm going to the seaside for a spell. Looking forward to being away, unplugging so to speak from it all. If that's possible."

Cameron laughed. "If it's possible," he said with a chuckle. "There's a nice coffee shop seaside. Daetslim it's called. Daetslim Coffee. Check it out. I used to work there. It's a nice place."

"Cool. I will. For sure," I said, sure that I would, at least in the moment, but who knew for sure when the time came and the moments presented themselves. I thought about Daetslim but it came to me as thoughts of Daedalus and so I imagined a finely crafted place. Either that or a labyrinth. The labyrinth was more fitting to me at the moment.

Cameron handed me my coffee. Like almost everyone, most of what he did was monitor the machine that made the coffee. Pressed a button if needed, which it was in my case since I didn't order anything officially, he just knew my order. Cameron liked to mess with the system that way. That's why I felt we had some connection. We just didn't go along with things. We added our own little tweak as our way pretending to have some pretense of control. But we knew we didn't, didn't we? We knew we had no control.

Coffee. I tried to picture what it really was, other than just a warm bitter liquid. Coffee plants were difficult to cultivate, and no doubt, did not survive the plague. Maybe this version was some kind of chicory root. A lot of agriculture did not survive the plague according to Marta. And what we ate was less like real food. I would be curious to see what passed for agriculture, except seeing would not be believing, for I knew I would see rows of lettuce, heirloom tomatoes, fields of corn and maybe even avocado trees when Marta said it was all just weeds.

The coffee tasted just fine. I was never one that could taste vanilla hints, cherry, hibiscus (whatever that was) or whatever else was supposed to be in the coffee. Even long ago, I thought all of that was made up. And now, perhaps more so. I knew it was all made up. No one knew what anything really tasted like.

"It's a nice blend," Cameron remarked. "From the upper mountain region. I figured you of all people would appreciate it and get it."

"Thanks," I said, adding that it was really something, though I couldn't taste those subtleties and I was fooling him if I could, and fooling myself by continuing to propagate the fiction. That kind of thing just happened to me so much of the time. I felt like I was faking everything, going through the motions, wandering around in a maze. Maybe that's what Marta meant about me.

"See you later, man!" he said with a smile as the next customer approached, stated a drink for the machine to dutifully make while Cameron made small talk.

I had nodded to him, but maybe he didn't see it. I knew I would be back in less than an hour for another coffee, preferring to leave the office, rather than stay for the local brew. According to Marta I liked coffee. But she didn't need to tell me that.

Some things I just knew. It was odd, though. All these things she knew about me based on my habits. Oh and there was that pesky little question of how much she studied my brain. And if she was real. I had asked her what kind of job she had. She said she had created something especially for herself.

"It's a big network," I recalled her saying, "mostly efficient, but still a massive bureaucracy."

Her use of the word bureaucracy piqued my interest. Some things never change. And her job? It was some kind of obscure post in a building that didn't really exist, reporting to another segment that did, but didn't really know because it was part of a huge trove of endless data that mattered to no one, and the exception was just a fact of the construct.

"How did you manage that?"

"Before the transfer," she had said, "what I created was simply a cog in the machine, just like you. So it's all there if you know where to look. Or should you have a reason to look, which virtually no one would."

Just another cog in the machine. In the face of such insignificance, and yet so many of us felt significant, as if our lives had great meaning and purpose. That was the beauty of the network, of how the system interacted with our brains, which although we felt unique were far from that. It turns out the brain is remarkably adept at assimilation and deception.

Deep in thought, I sipped my coffee and walked to my office on the top floor of a small building, taking the stairs for three flights and emerging in an open office space setting. Or that was how it looked. I knew there were invisible walls, walls made entirely of glass that could darken, walls that seemingly came out of nowhere to make dividers as needed. I should have been struck by something, but I recalled nothing of the building I had just entered, like I had been in overdrive, so-called automatic pilot.

The people I saw looked achingly familiar but were not recognizable to me by name. That did not surprise, for in a glance, the bodies seemed to blend together, to be one, varying little by sex, offering differences that were more subtle except in specific instances, when I looked more closely as I saw secretaries tended to be blond, more curvaceous in their pretty skirts and blouses, while the more powerful women wore pantsuits around low heels. The men looked nearly identical, dressed as I was, in dark slacks and light button-up shirts.

Everyone I saw, though, looked busy, in the midst of something, and yet most of the jobs were so utterly unimportant. Marta had stressed that. No great thing was being created, no problem being solved, at least not by humans, although people likely thought differently about that, which was the crux of the situation.

I had one of the few, somewhat private offices that dotted around the perimeter of the floor, though each space was surrounded by glass and could be enclosed as needed, but otherwise, everything was transparent. I didn't need to count to know I occupied one of the eight private offices, and one would be forever vacant. Emrik's old office.

All workspaces looked relatively the same. There were

no personal effects to be seen. Just spaces full of monitors, adjustable desks to either stand or be seated, no paper to speak of. Tablets too. My desk had yesterday's cup of coffee still there, cold and somewhat oily looking.

I reached for my tablet, unsure for a moment, but thankfully we had gotten rid of all those pesky passwords that had to be changed all too often. The real deal was the fact that everyone was always identifiable. Any tablet anywhere, would open for you.

The bank of monitors came to life as an instantaneous flash of ultraviolet light scanned my features and accepted who I was, that I was in fact a real, living person who went by the moniker David.

"So are you real?" I asked Marta more than once because I became fixated on the idea. *Idee fixe.*

She had calmly laughed and said something like: "Well, yes I am. But I understand why you are questioning everything. Your brain is likely overloaded with so much info that a part of you questions what is real and what is not."

"Are you a female?" I asked, nodding to her response.

"Hmm," she mused, "You question even that despite everything. I would have thought our interactions would have been sufficient."

"They were."

"Or my appearance. I know my breasts are small, but I do have them."

"I know. I haven't not noticed them, it's just that. . ."

"Just that you still have doubts."

"We'll, you've already mentioned the world is not as it seems."

"So my anatomy is not enough nor my emotions. You

indicated I was jealous."

"Yeah," I said. "I know I did."

"You kissed me not once but twice in the SIM and would have made love to me then and there. So some parts of you are obviously not confused."

I had to laugh at that. I don't know why I had even asked her. Perhaps I just wondered if there was some hybrid in the future, more fluidity among gender. Obviously I thought this, since there was no real concept of family or marriage. But such ambiguity, the network would surely never allow, would it? And then, of course, since I wasn't seeing the real her. She could be anyone, even a man. And what made us male or female anyway? And why would the network care unless there was a real difference amongst the sexes.

"That's true. But I didn't really know you knew at the time. And I thought it was all a dream."

"Does that matter or make a difference?"

I thought of the old song by the Kinks. "Lola." And cherry Coca Cola and how the guy in the song met her in a bar, danced all night, had never kissed a woman before and he was a man, and so was she.

"What's so funny?" she asked me, a bit perturbed I was now making a joke of it, but I wasn't. I was just thinking of that song.

"Nothing. Just thinking of something else. And what difference does it make, or does it make a difference? I guess not. I think I framed the question wrong, that's all."

"Okay. There are other things too, that make gender. The existence of various hormones and chromosomes."

"That's abstract, though. I can't readily test that."

"I know, which is why we usually revert to more

obvious things when talking about gender. Like the way someone appears," she said, moving her sunglasses down and raising her eyebrows somewhat provocatively. "Plus, I feel like a woman. It's not like I am secretly Emrik, you know. I am a woman."

"Emrik was gay though," I said, not knowing for sure she if she knew that, but apparently she did because she laughed a little at that.

"Okay, I see your point," she sighed, moved the sunglasses back over her lovely hazel eyes. "This is a pointless conversation. . ."

"I'm sorry. I shouldn't have asked. The thought just crossed my mind, and although I am not usually in the habit of voicing such thoughts, I just did."

"Do I not act like a woman?" Marta asked me.

"Oh, you do for sure. Again, I'm sorry for mentioning it."

"Quit saying that. Anyway, I can be more seductive if that's what you like. In fact, I can change clothes right now."

And she did, right in the SIM, barely so much as a pause. Gone was the yellow dress, which I thought was quite stunning, in its place a more form fitting white ensemble. She flashed an alluring smile as she pranced and paraded in front of me.

"Perhaps that's too formal," she said, and there she was in red capri pants and a white ribbed tank top that fit snugly over her upper body, nicely accentuating her bust. She raised her sunglasses atop her head and winked.

"Do you notice me more now? Is this what you wanted?"

"I haven't not noticed you, Marta."

"Double negative again," she said coyly. "You have a tendency toward them."

"Do I?"

"Yes, you do," she said. "Sometimes you are very difficult."

The thoughts of Marta faded as I glanced at the monitors in front of me. All of that information, endless data seemed to stream from the ultimate machine via video feeds, numbers compiling, tabulations and other monstrosities designed to overwhelm the senses, but it all looked so good due to advanced graphing techniques. Thoughts of Marta returned to me.

Perhaps I was useful to Marta because I had access to things she couldn't hack into, which made me a missing link. In a way, she had been right. I didn't fully trust her. But it wasn't necessarily her or her fault, rather I couldn't see the big picture. Looking at all my monitors only reinforced that sense of overload. That seemed like a double negative too.

I checked what I had most recently been working on, reports of some kind, skimming through data on population, waste, solar energy generation, and food. There was a general report on happiness too based on spending and SIM activity. On an aggregate level, I could even look at the type of SIM activity, which I did, as that was a preemptive clue to wellbeing.

Just then Siri popped up on one of my screens, prompted no doubt because I was looking at one of her reports. Siri monitored the aggregate SIM activity. The network evidently had some preferred algorithm.

"Arts activity is way down," she said. "Let me know if you want some help. I've got some ideas."

"Sure," I said.

"Hemingway," she said. "A whole series. Bull fighting, fishing, and wine tasting. What do you think?"

"Is that really the arts?" I asked, suspicious, and rightly so, not expecting Hemingway to be one to sip wine. He seemed less like a sipper and more a carouser, but it was an interesting idea.

"He was a writer, right? Or am I thinking of someone else?"

"Yeah, okay. I'll think about it. Good ideas."

Not surprisingly, a lot of SIM activity was of the sexual nature, but as Marta said, there were lots of other uses as well, depending on the time of the day. When I looked at those reports, I could see patterns emerge, not that I needed to see them. The network would tell me anything I wanted. I just liked looking for myself, discerning my own sense of what was useful and what was a distraction. I wanted to come to my own conclusions. Maybe that was old-fashioned and out of time, like Jesus and God and Christmas trees.

In the morning, for example, the SIM was used for exercise, followed by meetings and social engagement during the day and finally the excesses of the night. Consistent throughout the day were various role-playing games involving adventures and quests, akin more to what we used to call video games, that is they weren't sexually explicit in nature, though there was some element of that. The network deconstructed every little detail, comparing and contrasting in a myriad of ways. I could have looked up myself but didn't. I didn't want to know. It was bad enough that Marta knew. Yet, she still saw something in me.

And here was the thing that got me. We assumed it was all correct, that all of the info compiled was properly understood and presented accurately. I didn't think that was necessarily the case, so it pleased me when I found multiple versions of the same reports in my archives. But the real thing that bothered me was all the reports of the world outside, how they never changed. I could understand within our enclosed world, everything perfectly managed.

I stood, sipping the last dregs of my coffee, an especially bitter part of the drink, while perusing the endless data stream. New posts from colleagues appeared now and then, flashing to life, and when I looked at them, they were easily answerable by an affirmation, confirmation, or some other determination. Siri was still smiling on a screen at me. I smiled back, then made her go away.

Now and then, I looked up as coworkers passed by, nodding to them, echoing their greeting, be it the simple words or the smile. *Everyone looked familiar, everyone looked the same.* I felt like I was writing a song in my head. *I couldn't be sure whether this was a game.*

I skimmed the reports until I found what I was looking for. When I drilled down to the data, I maybe was not surprised that the faulty readings were coming from some turbines in Seaside, the very place I would be traveling to tomorrow. I sent a quick message to the director, Ander, to let him know.

Ander immediately responded. *Still scrutinizing the old reports*, he said. *Okay. Don't spend too much time on it. We've looked into this before. A failing sensor. No big deal. As you know. Carry on.*

I ran the mod report again. Maybe I shouldn't have been amazed to see all of the information populated, but not out to ten decimals as before. In fact, the mod report now matched the normal report. I had various iterations of the same report, and now, they all mysteriously matched.

Anders sent me another message: *Drop in to see the Twins at Seaside. They can show you the sensors that often fail. . . and tell you how many times they've fixed.*

Okay, thanks, I responded.

Marta was right about how simple so many of these things were. I also kind of just seemed to know my way around the program. I wondered if she knew about the reports being different. She was having a strange effect on me, admittedly, and I was anxious to see her again. I planned to make it up to her, convince her that I trusted her, but I didn't know exactly how to do that.

I thought about reaching out to her but demurred to doing nothing. Often the best thing was to sit still. Now, I didn't know if that was true, but that was what I told myself. She would know better than I.

After a while, I noted my various colleagues breaking for lunch. Ocie dropped in to see if I had plans for lunch. I lied and I said I did. She was in marketing. She coordinated various things related to the SIM. Luckily Marta had shown me what each of us did and that touched on something in my head because I knew all of that.

"Did you see that travel in the SIM is way down?" I asked her.

She nodded as she stood in my doorway, dressed in the professional pantsuit: black pants and a white blouse with a dark jacket. She had short brownish hair and a natural ebullience to her demeanor. Her pointed heels made her seem taller than she was.

"Yes. Siri and I presented a plan to Ander earlier today to boost travel, a kind of awareness campaign, showing off some of the splendors of various areas. We've added a cruise line option and new skiing packages. Of course, we introduced the zipline through the grand canyons, but we didn't promote it just to see what happened. Word of mouth. Now we can easily change that and see what the effect is. You should try the zipline though. It's an amazing experience. Might even change your life."

Now it was my turn to nod and pretend I knew what she was talking about. I did, a little bit. I knew the SIM served many functions, or that was something I was starting to realize and the travel aspect was important because it helped round out our perspective as humans, much the same as the arts, which was apparently my foray. Hiking up a mountain trail to visit a remote monastery was an experience in nature and a window into a way of life. Truly zen. Marta and I should go. Maybe later when we were normal people we could pursue wellness together.

Of course, to the network, how the SIM was used was of vast importance, an additional database into the psyche. It was yet another element of the master profile of all subjects. Even Ocie, I thought as we spoke. What secrets about her did the network know?

Ocie moved on and I did too, heading off to my other plans, which were really nothing more than another cup of coffee. Maybe this time I would taste hints of jasmine. Maybe if Marta and I visited a monastery we could have tea with one of the monks. Jasmine tea. Maybe. *Truly zen,*

I thought to myself and smiled, though it was all wishful thinking and I knew that too, knew that it was pure fantasy mixed with hope. Because I was still human and I could imagine impossible things. Still, as I walked to coffee, I thought about that, pictured her and I in some quiet, serene place sipping tea.

"Any luck on turning on a light switch in your dream?" Cameron asked me as he made pre-ordered coffees for pick up, something I never did. I liked waiting in line and watching all of that magic happen. I thought it was weird he should ask me that question about light switches, though, like he had a window into my mind or I had broadcast some radio signal across the lines his satellite had picked up.

"Not yet," I said, recalling that he and I had talked at various times about lucid dreaming. Still, the timing seemed uncanny. I would mention it to Marta. I was hyper aware, so everything seemed like a clue or of some importance. And I was paranoid too.

"But I did dream I was in another world where everything was the same, like this, yet obviously very different because I didn't understand things," I added.

"Weird," Cameron said, "Was it like a SIM?"

"At first I thought so, but then I seemed to have very little control of anything. Then I realized it was just a dream, and at that moment everything changed, and I woke up."

"That's a drag. Did you search for a light switch?"

"It's odd that we are supposed to search for a light switch in a dream, when there aren't any here, so why would there be one in our dreams? I've always thought it is a strange thing."

"Yeah. I've thought about that too. It's just an old theory. We need to come up with something new."

I listened to the whir and whistle of the machine as it made my coffee. How many coffees had I consumed in my life? Twenty thousand? How many more did I have left? I suppose I could find the stats back to a certain point, the date of the switch. I marveled at the fact that somewhere it was tracked. Under my profile, there was a total amount of coffees and the extrapolated total.

"Have a good one," Cameron said as he handed me my coffee, coffee number twenty thousand and one I jokingly thought. Or maybe even more at this point.

As I turned, I had a sensation, almost like a needle prick in my neck. Then I saw a woman talking with some people, presumably her colleagues. My heart surely dropped a beat and my pulse then thickened to pick up the slack. I knew that woman was Star.

True to form, she looked as stunning as ever. Shoulder length blonde hair, white floral dress, face blushed with color and vigor as she laughed at something, her ample bosom moving buoyantly beneath her dress like it had a life of its own and a yearning to flee.

She must have known someone was staring at her, an innate sense, because she turned to survey the room and found me. Though her expression changed, she gave me a little coquettish wave, dipping her body slightly for the full effect. I sipped my coffee and nodded.

"Why have you been such a stranger?" she asked as she approached me, stretching out her arms to give me a partial hug, which I half accepted, but she made up the difference and our bodies pressed close.

"Sorry," I said. "It's been busy. Work and all of that."

"Oh nonsense. You've just been avoiding me. It's okay. You were a little upset last time. You look at things a little too seriously, hon. I was just trying to loosen things up. Lighten the mood and have some fun."

I didn't exactly know what she was talking about, so I sipped my coffee and watched her. There were generally two types of people in this world when the full network went live. Those who readily embraced the process, some almost too much, so that their natural inclinations had to be tempered down, and those who tended to reject the change, who then had to be nudged along by drugs, small doses of ketamine mainly to help reform brain connections. I suppose it's obvious where I was relative to Star.

And then there were the eight of us who knew what was really going on. Well, there *were* eight, but Emrik didn't make it. Otherwise, myself, Ander (who we all referred to as the Director), Mari, who was yin to Ander as yang, Ocie, Cleo, Lando, Emrik (deceased), and Siri. Emrik *deceased*, I hung onto those words as I made small talk with Star, or rather she talked and I simply prodded the conversation along.

Why had I named Emrik twice? Though he was dead, it was like he was always part of us, as if in a way, he really was the network. Was it possible he became the network? As I stood there with Star, I couldn't help thinking that as I listened to her, a million miles away.

As with the best groups, evenly split, four men and four women. Not all heterosexual. Diverse backgrounds. Not all academics like Emrik, Ander, Mari, and me. Ocie and Simi were marketers. Lando, what to say about him? A man more attune with appetites than attitudes, I suppose. He loved the SIM, especially in proto-type form. He thought it was the greatest thing ever. Maybe he was right and I was wrong. I had reservations on succumbing to a fantasy world as a way to placate the masses. For good reason too. He thought it was the end-all, be-all. I didn't believe in the end-all, be-all grand universal theory of everything.

We were all masters of something, of some aspect of life, at least after the plague, among the survivors. That was the other thing. That utter devastation meant I had to rethink a lot of things. If I ever had an ally, then it was Emrik. And he was gone. Presumed dead. I never quite understood how it happened. Emrik *deceased.*

Star. So perfect in many ways, at least, physically I should say in clarification. A natural embodiment of what was the predominant social collective idea of beauty. Tall, blonde, thin, well-apportioned, athletic, lovely skin, blue eyes, vivacious, and effervescent.

Star embraced the new world as it progressed, as the advances and new technologies took hold offering the sublime and captivating, a simple cosmetic surgery, an alteration here or there, all of which were quick and painless. In some cases, there was a slight pain, added back in like they used to do with smell, in the old days, giving an otherwise odorless compound a scent. Like they did with electric cars too, when they first arrived as silent creatures on the road. Adding something back so that it still seemed real, so you could still hear something.

As a matter of course, all of the procedures were digital, though they had the look and feel as if the operation was physical. That helped make it real. If there was even the slightest imperfection in Star, she erased that. But did you ever feel something was so perfectly embodied that it actually became imperfect?

The network was designed to bring out a person's best self. All miracles then, had to be within reason in order to be believable. Star's starting point was just a little more elevated than all others. In the SIM world there were no limitations, as Marta had said. Anything and everything could be altered. A man could be a superman, presumably lift buildings if so desired, though I liked to think we had passed the marvel of the superhero age that had inflicted earlier elements of society. But maybe that was something all too human we never overcame.

Star's lips moved, her cupid's bow quivering ever so, mesmerizing me in such a way as I allowed because I was so dysfunctional, so lost in her commissures, where her lips joined. What was wrong with me? Could she tell? She was like a drug. And I was the lonely recoverer, the recently redeemed but faltering addict.

From the corner of my eye, I glimpsed something, someone, maybe even Marta as Star suggested we meet for a drink later so that we could catch up. I already had something on the books with Ander, so I supposed afterward would be fine. Wouldn't it?

"A drink?"

"Yes, you still meet people for drinks don't you? I can't imagine that has changed? I can't imagine anything about you has changed."

"Why would you think something has changed?"

"Oh darling, nothing has changed, that's just the thing. That's just what I said. I see you're still not listening."

"Okay, sure."

"Fine. Let's do our happy hour at Drixson. After all,

that's your favorite place, and I'll be happy to see you."

"Okay."

"Perfect. I will see you very soon," Star said, briefly placing her hand on my shoulder before drifting away, giving me a squeeze before she left.

As she moved away, I called after her. And I very rarely used people's names, yet still I found myself calling out "Star." She turned back to me, her body a striking silhouette in that white dress of hers.

"Nice to see you. You look nice."

She smiled with so much knowing and certainty that I felt foolish for my remark. She had that way of making people inferior and small around her. If she knew, she probably thought it gave her great power.

"Thanks, darling. I know."

I watched her walk away, took a deep breath and sipped some more on my coffee, surveying the room as I tasted those bitter fruits. Marta. I was a little surprised to see her looking right at me. I smiled. She shook her head disapprovingly. I felt stupid.

"You look nice too," I said as she approached. She flashed me a look that I hadn't seen before.

"Thanks," she said sarcastically.

"You do, I really do mean it. It's just Star. . ."

She made another face, not a nice one either. But not too mean. Maybe she was just looking for a little reassurance. But she must have known I wasn't the type, although I had complimented Star. I didn't know why though. I was just under her spell. Marta wasn't the type to cast spells, but that didn't mean I wasn't captivated by her too.

"You've looked nice many times today," I said as I

recalled her wardrobe changes within the SIM, but for a moment picturing which was my favorite, though the mind has a way of making a composite, such that I knew nothing. Nothing, except that she looked nice in all of them as all things merged into one, but now her legs were like a grand staircase, innumerable steps to the top of her empire state.

"Marta," I pleaded, but she was having none of that.

"Tell me later," she said. She had a habit of saying that, as if the time was not right, but it felt to me the time was never right, that there would never be time, that this sense of later kept getting pushed farther and farther away until finally disappearing, or if not gone, the way back to the top was so far off.

I tried to say something more, but she shook her head and continued on her way, our brief passing, not quite like ships in the night, but not much more either. And she did look nice, more than nice. I thought she looked fabulous in her off-white blouse and dark pants. I loved her dark hair, short with a bit of curl. And her eyes too. It was different, so very different from Star, who needed to be noticed, who dressed to flaunt. Marta was not defined by that.

By the time I returned to my office, I was almost done with my coffee. Ander had sent me another post, which I had just noticed. I told him I was fine. He had asked how I was. I was probably one of the few that did not emit immediate responses in this age of instantaneous everything. Response, satisfaction, happiness. All of it instant.

Ander knew I often left my hand held at the office when I went for coffee and I didn't wear a watch or any other devices, though in an emergency, he could send me a pulse, which I would feel in my wrist. I could then grab any of the temp phones that seemed to be everywhere and see what was so urgent.

Drink later? Ander suggested, but I already seemed to know we were meeting for a drink. That struck me as strange. A premonition maybe? Or maybe I had already lived all of this and I was just going through the motions. Maybe that was the thing I was supposed to remember, how I actually needed to act and not merely mime the motions.

Meeting Star. 4 p.m.

3 p.m. then. She won't mind if it overlaps. I enjoy her company.

Ander always liked Star. And I suspected he accessed her in the SIM during his personal time, or at least someone a lot like her. I could have certainly found out with my clearance, but then he would have known I had looked. Ultimately, in some way, the network was one massive social network where everyone could know anything about anyone if they looked hard enough. But there was a strange thing about a world being completely transparent. Namely that it was anything but that.

Okay, that was fine by me. 3 p.m. it was. I could already tell it was going to be a busy last day at the office. First with Ander and then with Star. And presumably after that, Marta. I regretted scheduling something with Star, but I needed to.

I would surely feel a bit drunk by then. And suppose if something did happen with Star, and though I knew I shouldn't think that and quite possibly didn't even want that, the idea of it seemed vaguely interesting to me, which sickened me. That was the thrill of the drug. Yet I thought of Marta and how I really longed to be with her, which further confused me. Why would I entertain this Star fantasy? But a fantasy sometimes was just that, nothing more, just a divergence.

I supposed that sometimes we were afraid of the things we really wanted and made poor decisions as a form of self-sabotage. That was where the network was supposed to step in and bring about my best self. Except I couldn't rely on the network to make the right choice. It had to be me. God, I thought, yet there wasn't even that presence either.

I looked around, pondering the so-called dilemma of not trusting myself. Most of my coworkers were back from lunch and mindlessly mesmerized by banks of monitors, obviously not worrying about such things. But what about Emrik. I knew he was still somewhere or in something. Maybe he was worrying about my dilemma, same as Marta. *Wherever he was. Wherever she was.* Worrying about what I would do off the network, not part of the grid. Well, I worried too.

Emrik was the oldest and the most reluctant. He surely could have been saved but didn't want to be. That had puzzled me. That seemed like giving up. I would have to ask Marta, though, because I didn't remember the circumstances under which he died, other than he had the pathogen, which was also maybe not even true. I wasn't convinced he was dead. Maybe that was made up, some collective knowledge we had of an event that never happened.

None of us talked much about Emrik, just as we never spoke of the pre-transition period. The past was the past. It could not be changed. It was no use talking about Emrik and his thoughts on the matter. I had voted to study the matter more, but time was a luxury we didn't have and in the end, the safety of the remainders was secured by sealing off the world and projecting an artificial atmosphere to block out the sun. Outside of the barrier, plenty of solar panels could still generate energy and water easily collected via the aquifers. It really wasn't so hard to create a self-contained biosphere. We had done it ages ago, but what was it like maintaining such a thing I wondered, over the long term. That was what hadn't been done.

"Knock, knock," I heard a voice, instantly recognizable as Lando. He had that kind of voice that rose above all others, even in a loud bar, after a few drinks, his voice was still louder than the rest. In another life, he could have been an auctioneer, calling out the next great lot for sale, but maybe that wouldn't have been prestigious enough.

Lando and Cleo strode into my office, both nicely dressed in what I sensed was the standard uniform. Lando, with his slacks and white shirt, could have picked such things from my closet. Cleo deviated slightly, with a skirt and blouse combination. Not a lot of color though. My mind wandered, for a moment, and I thought about the yellow dress Marta wore in the SIM, how amazing and lovely she looked, that splash of color melding with the sunshine, how a little bit of color enlivened everything, how the city at night seemed alive with color.

"Is this a good time?" Cleo asked me. "If you're busy, then we can do it later."

"Oh, he's not busy," Lando said. "Maybe just busy looking busy."

"Oh, you know," I said. Lando was always interested in what I was doing, what I was working on, but there was often something about the way he pestered me with questions that made me think there was another angle, some other layer he was trying to uncover.

As much as things had changed, meetings seemed not to have, more of a waste of time than anything else. Lando began by explaining the extreme conditions outside. It was reasonable, given computer models, Cleo continued, to expect outside conditions remaining harmful for many years to come.

"It's simply too dangerous," Lando said. "Going outside threatens us all."

It was the way he said it too that surprised me, with such finality. And though I knew the answer, I asked what the network thought, which was the equivalent of asking, no, telling Star, she looked nice. Because she knew, of course, she knew, just as the network knew it was safer to remain as we were.

"The data is incomplete. What little we know indicates extensive damage to the sensors, worn out comm centers with only intermittent signals because of the harsh conditions."

Lando mentioned something about things going bad, how we thought the outside world would hold up better, but it hadn't. All evidence showed deterioration. Perhaps it had been too far gone to begin with. We certainly had pushed the world to the extreme, pursuing growth at all costs, externalities be damned, everything existing just to produce more.

"If things go bad," I said, picturing the conditions, but not knowing. They were harsh, uninhabitable, impossible. That was what we said, that the landscape had been devastated by the cataclysmic event, just as the human race was very nearly eliminated. But surely nature could rebuild itself given time, if we could. And yet no one cared to know.

"Not if," Lando said as if to remind me, "We are no longer speaking in such conditionals. That time has come and gone. Let's not delude ourselves."

"What about drones?" I asked.

"They malfunction almost immediately," Lando said dismissively. "We've crashed at least a dozen now. The network is doing an analysis. They're expensive to build. It's not like we can grow them in labs."

"I know," I said. "Looking forward to the results of the analysis."

"We'll keep you posted," Lando said assuredly, grinning as he often did, because he knew more than all of us, at least that was how he always acted to me. And he never shy away from showing it, giving to me that grin of his, and like Star, those perfect teeth.

"Yes," Cleo said, almost impatiently, as if she had said all of this to me before a thousand times, and she was running out of ways to explain it.

I thought about it for a minute. What did collapsed drones and broken sensors even mean in a world like this? Or even money? It was hard to know. But I didn't trust the network results. Of course, they didn't surprise me. The network had its reasons just as surely as the government never told the truth when the truth mattered. Smoke and mirrors, a mere world of illusion. Maybe not much had ever changed.

Lando and Cleo were simply present to report on the feasibility of exploration outside of the walls, a topic we reviewed annually to see if anything changed. And nothing ever did. To the everyday people, there was no reason to go outside the walls, though the deception was much stronger than that, for they knew not there were even walls or barriers or protective covers in the first place. Filters. Only some of us knew, even could imagine or think about this other world, for the rest, that memory no longer existed, and that was our curse if we chose to accept it.

Only the eight of us knew. Well, seven because Emrik was dead, but then eight again if you counted Marta, which you certainly had to because she knew. Maybe Marta was not Emrik, but she certainly filled in for him nicely except that made the equation out of whack, more females than males. Was it possible Emrik became Marta? Why did I even consider that? Of course not. Because they existed at the same time. And anyway, Emrik couldn't have done it.

Emrik was many things and clearly quite brilliant. But not an amazing coder. Maybe that was something he disguised. But why? Like me, possibly, writing himself out of the code. Possible. That was something to rehash with Marta. Thankfully I was the silent type. It would have been terrible to be thinking these thoughts out loud, much less hint I was even thinking them.

"So, in short, the network concludes it is status quo until the drone analysis is complete and you both concur? I suppose we'll revisit next year."

They both nodded, one after the other. I had known both of them for such a long time. Lando, even longer as he was one of my best friends. And now he was with Star. They didn't know I knew. I didn't actually. I just suspected. Then again, since no one was really with anyone, so what did it matter? Except I was with Marta. So it mattered and it pleased me to think that. Did she think that, though? It seemed to me it was well understood, except then, she would, and rightly so, say I didn't trust her.

"Besides, what could we possibly gain?" Lando asked, typically. "We have everything we need here. I mean, tell me if there's something we don't have, and I'll get it for you. I'll take you on a tour of the best the SIM has to offer. We literally have everything! Everything!"

I had heard Lando so many times tell me this was the best of all possible worlds. *Because of the SIM.* We used to stay up late into the night drinking too much talking about it. We didn't do that anymore. Not that I missed it much. It was just something I recalled. Maybe it was Star that came between us like Marta said.

That idea that this was the best of all possible worlds was Leibniz, and originally it invoked God as the reason. And because only one of these infinitely possible universes can exist and God being good and all-powerful, only God could create such a world. Further, his argument defended the existence of evil. Interestingly enough, there was no conception of God now nor any evil. Did it then follow necessarily that God was the reason for evil? And since there was no evil in this world, thus no place for God. Could God only exist with evil, one balancing out the other? I suppose you could find God in the SIM.

"We know everything worth knowing," Cleo continued as she looked at both of us. "And whatever we don't know, we can find all the answers. Like Lando said, whatever we want, we can have. What else are you looking for?"

"And can we? I suppose we can," I affirmed, a bit resigned to this place I found myself, in a fight against impossible odds. What else was I looking for?

How I wished I was just walking in that park with Marta talking about things, about anything, about why the flowers are all so different, so unique, some fragrant and others not, but for who to decide? And don't tell me it's just the program, the code, some arbitrary form of modeling ascribed at some time, albeit randomly.

"You're never convinced," Lando said finally, looking then to Cleo and toward the direction of the office of Ander. "Ander said you were stubbornly committed to the idea, unreasonably so, in fact were his exact words."

"Did he?" I allowed a slight laugh, a silent sigh.

"Yes. He said that we could present anything and everything and yet you would still remain unconvinced. He called it a strange intuition, unassailable by facts. He likened you to one of those people from long ago who believed in UFOs."

"UFOs," I said. "That's a good one."

"And conspiracy too," Lando added. "Don't forget about that? Like the so-called lunar landings."

The man on the moon I thought. Pure pareidolia, that idea that looking at the moon some kind of face was recognizably depicted. Or that we actually landed someone on the moon. Various cultures, common lore, suggested a man exiled to the moon for a crime, a sheep theft or, as Dante hints, Cain himself. There was a scientific explanation for what looked like the man on the moon, lunar maria, what was once believed to be large bodies of water but were really craters covered by lava.

"All easily explainable," Lando piled on. "It can be dangerous to think otherwise. I told Ander you were just stubborn and unreasonable. You are, you know?"

"David," Cleo added in her soft voice, "The latest

reports are on the shared portal. . ."

"Probably or certainly?" I said more to myself than them.

"A very high probability," Lando exclaimed, "In our view means certainty. It's just like that old mod report you run. You know the numbers always balance out. Let's not kid ourselves and pretend there is much difference between an equation taken out to twenty places versus seventeen."

And to that, I nodded, because that was true, from a certain point of view. I was sure they both thought I was crazy. Everybody liked to joke about my insistence on the old reports. Maybe the whole group thought I was crazy. Well, at least, I was being consistent with my former self. And in that I respect, I felt reassured about who I was, about my sense of curiosity, of not trusting the numbers to mean all things for everything. Because they couldn't, for we all knew, well some of us, that the seeing were blind and all innocence masks fear.

The mood lightened up when Cleo asked about the Seaside. I mentioned the Twins residing in Seaside, the Scandinavians, Evey and Evers. Yin and yang they said in unison, inseparable but contradictory opposites; if one was sad then the other happy, one serious and the other the jokester. Except I wasn't sure that was true. Maybe that was just how they appeared on the screens. I remembered something different. But maybe those were Emrik's recollections and not my own.

"They're programmed that way!" Lando jokingly implied, which was some joke that maybe would have been funnier if we weren't always making it. They were mechanically inclined, in both knowledge and action, as well, they were among the oldest living people. That alone made them an anomaly. Old people in a world full of the young, or at least, everyone looked relatively young except them.

"Are you still coming to dinner tonight?" Lando asked as they were leaving.

"I'll be there," Cleo said. "And Ocie and Siri too. We all want to see you."

"Ander?" I asked.

"No, he's busy."

"Oh well, I am meeting him for a drink in a little bit."

"Fitting," Cleo said, which I ignored. "He never invites me for a drink."

"And I suppose Mari?"

"Of course," Lando said. "If you can't make it, no big deal. I'll enjoy being surrounded by such lovely specimens of the female form."

"Oh Lando," shushed Cleo, aghast and flattered at the same time. "Really, David. It would be nice to see you."

I thought about Marta. Perhaps she knew about this, but probably not. She couldn't know everything. I didn't really want to go and yet I couldn't say no. Not going would be suspicious. After all, what else did I have to do? Besides see Marta. Oh, I just seemed to always find myself in these kinds of situations, stuck doing something I didn't want to do, not knowing how to say no. In the end, all that ever happened, was nothing worked out.

Was I ever going to see Marta? Maybe that was all part of their plan. They all knew I was offline and they were just playing along, joining in on the game because the joke was on me. They probably even knew about Marta. I was going to be ambushed. Or plied with drink such that I would lose my bearings and not be able to think on my own. And all of this, in a world without evil?

"Sure, what time?"

"We're doing cocktails at six. My place," Lando said.

I nodded and they both left, Cleo first and then Lando. I didn't really know about Lando. Sure he was my friend, had been my friend for decades, but that didn't mean as much as he thought it did. I was pretty sure he was with Star, not that I placed that much weight in that kind of thing in this modern world, but it was still a slight, and however light, the tendrils dug in and stuck. I couldn't let it go. The fact that an attractive woman showed interest in me had always bothered him even before all of this. It was like some secret competition where he had to rule. And what lengths would he go to see it out, to win any disagreement we had. That concerned me.

Those old thoughts plagued me. I remembered playing wingman for him many times during our drinking days, hanging out at bars, talking late into the night or until some woman took an interest in him. And maybe the only time it ever happened to me, the reverse, he just wasn't there to help me out because it was somehow unfathomable someone would show an interest in me if he was there. He called it out as he saw it, and he saw himself as better looking than anyone. I kind of went along with it, went along with everything. Was that how it really happened? I couldn't be sure.

That was in another time, a place before this, and unlike the meeting, had not been recorded. Out in the open, no one could hide. And if there was a magic ring that could render invisibility, then none of us had it. Except Marta. She could hide it in the code. Everything kept coming back to Marta. Angel or devil. I felt like that was a song, but maybe not in this world where the was no evil.

She wasn't a devil. I wished I hadn't pictured her as an either or, one or the other. These thoughts of mine. They couldn't be helped. Maybe to doubt was human. To admit you didn't know all of the answers certainly was. And I didn't know all of them, not even some, just a few.

I went over to the window, looking down from my perch at the streets below, the figures that moved about, not hurriedly but with a sense of purpose, alone or in twos, in flow, that constant stream of activity, never stopping, not at all, not even for a moment. There was such a rhythm to their movements, from the overhead drones to the cars, everything in synchronicity.

No matter how big the world ever was, it was also a small world too, the people and places of our daily life, a stop for coffee here, a place to walk there, and at different times, a moment of true significance amid all of the repetition, the organized chaos.

It amazed me how it all worked, not necessarily now, because the network guided everything with its perfect knowledge, but before all that, when we were supposedly left to our own devices. Somehow, we all coexisted. Not perfectly. Not always harmoniously. But it seemed to mostly work, either by hook or crook, or the hand of God.

I glanced to my monitors, to the tables and the rows of calculations, the requisite unending measurability, so neatly encompassing all and explaining the great theory of everything as if reducible to a single integer. Like a forty-two. Or three, that perfect number for the ancient Greeks. I didn't believe the numbers told the whole story and yet I still looked for patterns, for I was convinced the patterns I saw were not easily discernible by the standard algorithm. Apophenia is the tendency to mistake connections between things as meaningful, which was not to be mistaken with pareidolia. Systems, networks, had the former tendency. Human programming was meant to root that out.

I mused for a while, did stuff to appear busy like Lando said I did until it was time. I left my office, pleased that the workday was over, at least the portion in the office. Ander waited for me in an entryway, chatting idly with Mari. They were the co-directors of the firm, inauspiciously called Space Time Ventures, or STV.

We exchanged greetings. Mari looked at me studiously. Perhaps that was the effect of the dark framed glasses she wore. Certainly such things could be fixed. The eyes, that is. Yet, people still wore glasses. Even Ander.

They were distinguishing factors, accessories of success. Ander wore a dark suit with a pink tie. Mari had on a dark plaid skirt and white blouse with a dark jacket, not to mention her high heels, block variety. Her expression was at once a mix of seduction and stern, as if she would tease you one moment and then smash you the next, but no matter what, she would be in control. It was something whenever she and Lando disagreed.

Ander and I left the floor, preferring the soft wind of stairs over the whisk of the elevator, walking silently out of the building, yet briskly towards the direction of Drixson. I supposed he had something on his mind, as did I. In a way, it kind of reminded me of all the times I would leave the office and get a drink with Emrik. We often had long moments of silence, a brooding kind of silence that took longer and longer to break as we neared the point of being unmoored, but we always came to, didn't we?

The quietude allowed me to look around, observe the activity of the day, the people that came and went under such luscious blue skies, barely noticing (I was sure) the beauty all around them because it was easy to no longer be amazed or moved by such splendor. Already, I too, seemed to be getting used to things, to the buildings at first glance I thought so spectacular, so stunning, now somehow appeared normal, and it had only been a day.

Again, I thought of the perfectly maintained world as we walked, the flawless foliage, faultless flowers and the like, with nothing out of place. And yet, the people who cared for such things seemed to be almost invisible. As we walked and neared Drixson's, I looked everywhere until I finally found such a person carefully stooped over a bonsai, precisely pruning.

Unlike some of the other places, the sports bars in particular, Drixson's, was nicer, more upscale with its dark wooded bar and dimmed lights. Often there was a piano player present for happy hour and through the evening dinner. On the weekends, a jazz band floated notes, free flowing. The trumpeter was renowned for his improvisation and versatility.

When we arrived, it was a bit early for music, even happy hour, but nonetheless, a classical piano concerto played in the background. I was probably wrong about who it was. Dare I mention someone who never existed, so I kept the thought to myself.

The bartender, Cash, recognized us as we entered and motioned us over to table well out of the way, not even close to a window, which I would have much preferred. For all I knew, this was probably where Ander and I always sat. The simplest thing, Marta had told me by way of advice, was to just let things happen. I don't think she meant that as literally as she thought.

"Gentleman," Cash said as he approached our table. "Thanks for your continued patronage. I am eternally honored by your presence and ready when you are to attend to your needs."

He laid glasses down and poured bubbly water in them. When he looked at me I just nodded, an indication of the usual. I seemed to have created a world where I could limit my communications with a select group of people, of which, Cash was a member. That was interesting to note. It shouldn't have surprised me I was a creature of habit, alternating between noticing everything to subsisting in autopilot.

Ander ordered a scotch on the rocks. Cash brought me my standard, whiskey with splashes of ginger ale and lime. With rocks. I wondered if we were really drinking the same drink, and the joke was on us for thinking and believing it was all something more.

The taste was exceptional though, that bitter agony of whiskey softened just a little, ever so slightly, delicately by that twinge of ginger ale. It occurred to me that I hadn't eaten much all day, nothing except for the smoothie with Marta, which was also a moment in time that seemed so long ago, far enough away that I couldn't even reach back for it, though I tried, searching in vain in my mind for details, odd details about the moment, about Marta, how she looked at me when I was not looking at her, but I was grasping at straws and climbing staircases in a building with no idea, no idea what floor I needed to find.

Ander and I made small talk through all these

permutations of mind, this and that, the world as we knew it, if it made any sense. Cash entertained us with a joke about being understaffed, how on Fridays everyone flocked to the sports bars to watch the eSports league, which he could never understand. Nor could I.

"It's the playoffs," he said. "People must think we are crazy for not having at least one screen. But I could really care less."

Actual sports had long since vanished, overtaken by eSports, gamers and the world of gaming, precursors in some way to the network. You could watch the games live on screen or go into a special SIM and experience the match anywhere you wanted. Quite a thrill. Or so I had heard from Lando. There was a time he was always pestering me about things like that, but since I had never been good at sports, they didn't interest me much.

"What a world this is," I said as the piano player sat at his bench and flexed his fingers, readying to play some achingly familiar piece, something probably written a half century ago by what we used to call a genius, but that seemed like the wrong term now, in this world full of geniuses, none of whom could write anything like the music the piano player played. Or maybe, he didn't even play. He just pretended to play. But such sounds, the minor chords descending before the major return to allegro were brilliant as if we had some natural inclination to such progressions.

"Yes, this technology is something I never fathomed. When you don't believe something is possible, you sort of dismiss it, but luckily there are innovators, geniuses among us, who believe so many things are possible and with a couple small missteps, we get here."

I listened closely to his technology talk, his musings, as I sipped my drink. When another party arrived, I glanced briefly up at them, another work group, then returned to Ander in time to nod and prod him along. The people in that group seemed familiar to me. If I needed to know them, then I would.

"We have a great responsibility, you and I, the rest of the group. And we shouldn't forget that. With great knowledge comes great power. And power is another name for responsibility. They go hand in hand. And we mustn't forget that. We have an obligation and we must not waste that opportunity."

"That was something Emrik said. Do you ever think of him?" I asked. It was a question I had been meaning to ask the whole time we were together, waiting for the right pause in the conversation, so that it seemed more natural

"Speaking of geniuses," he said with a laugh. "More than you know, I think of him. He was our de-facto leader. Maybe we moved faster than he wanted us to, but I still seek him out for advice. At least in my head. And even today."

I was surprised about his talk of Emrik. For the longest time, and even now, he was the one we never talked about. It was like when the connections were made and the grid went live all existence of Emrik fizzled out. Maybe that was part of the design. The network replaced Emrik as the resident genius.

"I still don't know what really happened?"

"No?" Ander said, polishing off his drink, though he would continue sucking on the ice for some time, clanking that clearly distilled cold around in his glass, like a master over his eminent domain.

"Do you?"

"Not really," Ander said, then paused. "Was it betrayal? Perhaps. Kind of felt like that. We betray the ones we love, and he loved us all. He trained us, recruited us even. Maybe he thought ultimately he could control us, lead us on to certain conclusions, which is almost ironic given where we are and what we built. Perhaps everyone we hold dear will betray us, given the right moment."

I listened but didn't want to hear that as Ander swirled the ice in his glass, a cue for Cash I suppose, though hardly as noticeable above denizens of the bar, which included the piano player doing the thing he did so well, if at all, with those black and white keys, those major notes and the minor ones too.

"Why do you ask about Emrik?" Ander suddenly exclaimed, looking up at me, staring into my eyes. He had such dark eyes, impenetrable. I felt a chill, that kind of *déjà vu* when you stood at the top of a building and looked over the edge.

"No reason. Just curious, as you know, I am inclined to be. Was he a good coder?"

Ander chewed on the remaining ice, cracking the cubes dissonantly clashing with the somber, beautiful piano concerto in the background. I cringed as I awaited his response. He seemed to be waiting for the right moment, for the proper cue from the music.

"Yes," he finally said. "You were always the silent questioner of everything. And though your actions didn't always show it, I could always tell by that skeptical look in your eyes. And you know, that's always made you a bit suspicious to the network, even to others, and especially at the beginning. I've always defended you, but it's been such a long time now, hasn't it? All of that is old news."

"Yes, it is. Time waits for no one."

"But was Emrik a good coder? That's an interesting question," mused Ander. "He was as good as he needed to be, feigning misunderstanding at the very places he understood well. That was his tactic. He knew more than he let on about anything. Maybe even more than all of us combined. But he was also curious about what we knew or thought we knew. He was a deep, complex soul."

The rest of us surely needed the bits of what we knew together with what others knew in order to reach any understanding. That was the great paradox of being an individual against the whole of society. You couldn't do it alone, for alone, we never were quite as good as we thought we were. And that was why I needed Marta, but that wasn't the only reason.

"How do you know all of this?" I asked.

"I know what I'm supposed to know. No more and no less. I may seem all-knowing, but I have my limitations, as do you. Perhaps even the all-knowing Emrik did as well."

I finished off my drink. Cash had waited, but now was delivering us round two. As I allowed the disruption, I wondered whether Ander was secretly warning me or if I was just paranoid. It seemed like he knew more than he let on too. Just like Emrik. And Lando too, for that matter. Maybe all of us, those of us left from the original eight had our secrets.

"Is this about the annual exploration meeting?" Ander asked. "I think it is. You always get a little disconcerted afterwards."

"Probably," I said, knowing that he probably had listened to a condensed version.

Ander laughed, then added, "I told Lando and Cleo you were stubborn. You needed to see the broken drones. You are what I've termed an independent group thinker."

"They mentioned that, kind of like a bet."

"You could call it that."

"So you don't mind if I look at the drones?"

"Not at all. What are we if not human? Curiosity, skepticism—these are the very human qualities that define us. They shouldn't vanish with us just because we have AI assistance."

"Hard to believe sometimes in this age, that such things still exist," I said, thinking about the various geological epochs, from the anthropocene to whatever era we were in now. Some said it was the homogenocene as evidenced by the lack of biodiversity, the loss of ecosystems and ultimately an environment where a devastating pathogen flourished.

"All things change and evolve. Nothing stays stuck in the past for too long before getting rooted out of its position," Ander remarked, sipping thoughtfully on his drink. "Even us. We have to evolve or we risk being overrun."

"And," he continued, "Let the seaside sink in. Breathe in the air. It's a little different there. Relax. And then maybe after a couple of days, maybe then look up the Twins, see what they know, but be careful. Don't discount the network. Sometimes we have to trust the model. It's saved us before, and it will save us again."

I knew what he referenced. It was true, AI and the network had saved us. There were benefits to all of that computing power. But were there not any limits? Without AI, we would probably all be dead. Probably, I thought.

"I think I know how you feel," Ander continued. "Satisfy your curiosity but don't take it too far. You naturally want to push the boundaries, which has been a benefit, to think outside the box, but there's a reason we are inside this box. You of all people should appreciate Aristotle and his idea of maintaining the golden mean."

"Nothing to excess. I know," I said as I looked to Ander. He was smiling at me in a fatherly kind of way. I understood what he was talking about. Stay the course, keep in the middle, otherwise like Icarus flying too close to the sun, your wings of wax will melt.

"Sometimes I feel as if I have no choice about these things. It's like I am compelled to act a certain way, be a certain way."

"And yet, we all believe in free will," Ander remarked, more than a little bit ironically, I imagined, given the circumstances, but then again, I knew more than I was supposed to know. And there were some that thought such a thing worked as an advantage. Then again, there were other schools of thought too, suggesting bliss was merely a state of ignorance. But undeniably, he had warned me, had he not?

Before I could continue that thought, Star strolled in casually with her black polka dotted cocktail dress and high heels, her generous décolleté highlighted by her pearl necklace. She had obviously changed since I had seen her last. She wore red lipstick, and silver bracelets with beaded stones adorned her wrists, changing colors in the light.

Ander greeted her effusively, commenting on the loveliness that she was. As she bowed, he kissed the back of her hand. I smiled at her with a mix of mock affection and mesmerism, for she so easily beguiled us with her spell. And we were all too damn willing.

"Star," I said, softly, not too loud, but loud enough.

"David," she answered, call and response, like a mere song and dance to her, part of the musical medley in the background. "Nice to see you. Thanks for meeting me."

"I hope I am not interrupting," Ander said jokingly, "I didn't realize David was so popular. He never used to be. No offense."

"None taken," I said. "It is a rare thing for me, I think." But they didn't hear me.

"Of course not, he's not that popular anyway, we both know," Star said as she flashed her smile, such white teeth, gleaming. "If anybody is interrupting, then it would be me. And I would hate to be that kind of person."

Ander waved his hand dismissively at the apparent ludicrousness of the suggestion. He got up and pulled a chair out for Star to be seated in. She pecked him softly on the cheek and sat down in between us.

Cash approached, greeting Star like Ander, but also bearing the gift of a drink, a martini of some kind, bright and colorful, reddish pink in color. A toothpick with cucumber and lime hung off to the side, resulting in a dazzling display.

I was already starting to feel the effects of my second drink, though I knew Marta would tell me it was all in my mind. And I tried thinking that for a while as Ander chatted up Star. That was always the thing I struggled with: conversation with more than one person at a time. So I faded into the background, listening to a degree, adding a line now and then as if to show I was still present, though I was really just adrift. Everything changed when Star appeared.

I retraced our brief conversation about free will, one that we never got started because Star arrived. And before that, whether Ander in fact was warning me of something. If he was, then he knew something. Or he was suspicious.

After Ander polished off his third drink, to which I was still nursing my second, he got up to leave. But before doing so, he turned to me to add one last tidbit of advice that seemed to be lurking in his mind the very moment he said we should meet for a drink.

"Remember," he said emphatically, "There's only so far one can go. Call it a line in the sand or a boundary. And we can keep on cutting the distance and yet still never reach absolute zero. So we have to assume we got there."

"'Tis true," I said. Zeno's Paradox. I thought of them, or at least those I could remember, summing them up by thinking that motion was an illusion, that we can't trust what we think we can trust. A single grain of rice makes no sound upon falling, but a thousand of them we can hear. It's not true that the single grain does not make a sound. It is just that we cannot hear it. As such, Ander was alluding to the limitations, was he not, though not in the way he intended. He was also being more direct in case I didn't get the subtlety of his first instance. You never cross that line in the sand.

"Oh, you boys and your big ideas of the world," Star said as if thinking aloud, but Ander didn't seem to hear her.

"In other words," he added lightly. "Enjoy your time away. And remember you can't solve all the problems in the world in a single day."

"Thanks," I said, acknowledging that while I seldom asked for advice, a lot of people certainly had the habit of giving it to me. I was sure when I saw Lando and Cleo later, Lando would offer up his suggestions about a thing or two I would not even have known I needed guidance on. That had always been his way. He knew better than I what I needed.

Star, for her part, eyed us suspiciously as we talked in code. That was what she called such allusiveness, indirect talk and metaphor. Boys will be boys she seemed to say as she twirled her toothpick and looked genuinely beautiful, even if she wasn't.

And then it was Star and I. Cash brought me another drink, which I resolved to drink slower, but here I was with Star, brightly beckoning in her polka dot dress that accentuated her figure, while my apprehension had other ideas about the state of the drink.

"So how are you really?" She asked.

"Fine. And you?"

"I'm well," she said, then paused. "It's been a while, hasn't it?"

"Yes," I said.

"I know you've been busy with work, you'll say, but I don't even think you guys know what you do at that place besides all of that talk and those pretty little notions."

"Work indeed," I agreed. All of us were kept busy with our jobs, whether they were pretty or not, I didn't know, but it was nice to think so.

"I doubt it's anything too terribly important, yet all of you put so much time in it. Oh well. . . I suppose the money is good."

"For some," I offered. "That's part of it. I am sure. Some people just do it for the money."

The present world was mostly egalitarian, even with

jobs, the so-called full employment stature. Everyone had jobs that paid well enough, and for some, just a little bit more, but nothing outrageous, and nothing like part of the twentieth and twenty-first centuries, when it was not uncommon for the boss to make more than three hundred times the average worker.

Perfect equality as expressed by the Gini coefficient would be zero. Today's levels would only be slightly above that. But there was a price for all of that. Nothing is for free. How much was left in all of us?

What is the essence of a human being? I pondered that as I looked across the table at Star. Was this the real Star? Of course, if we only looked at living and breathing, in the flesh, then for sure, this was Star.

"Oh, but not you David. You're different. Aren't you?" she teased. "You don't do it for the money or the power. It's something nobler. But what?"

I couldn't tell if she was mocking me or not. That's not true. I knew she was. She didn't believe there were other reasons to do a thing, if not for money or power. And if I thought otherwise, I was deceiving myself or denying myself. And what was the point of that.

"Anyway," she continued, seductively sipping her martini with all the airs of sophistication.

"So what's new with you?" I engaged Star, unable to hold out much longer. That's all she really wanted, a chance to tell me about what she was doing.

She exuberantly talked about exploring design in the SIM, travelling to older cities, some of them ancient for hints and ideas, places like Hollywood and New York City, Barcelona, Paris. Even a place called Las Vegas. In other words, she could mock me about what I did and yet not see the insignificance in what she did. Perhaps I was just being petty, pretending that one thing was better than another. That was snobbish, I told myself.

"Las Vegas," I remarked with interest. "The gambling place."

"Yes, you've heard of it then." she laughed. "It's much more than gambling. You might have forgotten they had excellent reproductions of Roman Architecture, canals, lost cities. And some great shopping."

"You could go back to Roman times," I said.

"I could, but it's not as glamorous. Shall I put it that way? More barbaric, uncivilized. Besides, Las Vegas is a great place to watch people. You would like it. And, did I mention the shopping?"

I nodded that she had. Was all of this really possible in the SIM? Yes, it was. Anything could be recreated in the SIM. I imagined going back to see Led Zeppelin, a popular British band in the 1970s, at one of their legendary shows. I could even get a concert T-shirt. Not an original T-shirt, for that was impossible. But that didn't matter because people didn't think in those terms, of something being an original or not.

"Such an amazing world David. You should really spend more time in the SIM. So much possibility. You would really like it. We could even go to one of your concerts if you wanted. I would do that with you. You know I would do that, don't you? It will be better than it ever was."

But was it? That was the thing I wondered. I remember being with Marta at the park, at the beach, as she changed outfits. Maybe it was. All of the focus and scrutiny on authenticity in a world that wasn't. That astounded me.

Initially, the SIM was a disappointment to most everyone but the ardent supporters. At its incarnation, the thing was patchy and simplistic, and when it worked, you felt a little sick from the motion. Advances in technology changed that, and people forgot that the so-called cyberspace age had at first failed to live up to the hype too. It took a while to take root, and by then, its sprouts were so deep, we took it for granted as an implicit technology.

Unlike the internal combustion engine or electricity, which transformed the world and underpinned the industrial revolution, the internet age started slowly, was not revolutionary like something such as the toilet and indoor plumbing. Those advances were truly transformative, yet when those technologies advanced, they were more behind the scenes. The modern sewage system evolved over time to a source of energy, but the basic technology on the surface changed very little.

Cyberspace technology advancement was more noticeable, but it took time. As chip sizes decreased, became more complex, the speed and capability of everything increased. An image that once took minutes to load and gain clarity, rendered instantaneously. And then suddenly in a barely discernible speck, there was more computing power than a human brain.

That wasn't a fair comparison though. The human brain was very unlike a computer, more advanced in some ways, and yet less so in others, depending on the task. And yet, combining the two, if you could do that, then you would have a lethal combination. Lethal. And that was what connecting everyone to the grid did. It created a lethal combination.

Everything has a cost. Nothing is for free. The human mind could find patterns in things with no pattern, make connections where there was no logical connection, all because something just seemed to feel right. At least, that's what it used to be able to do. Like any muscle, inactivity weakens ability.

The goal had always been to retain the essence of humanity in such a way that each and every person could be enhanced, made better, able to achieve their best self. The network merely coaxed you along that path, limiting the extremes and the all too fatal human tendency toward destruction, war, and ultimate devastation.

"Hey," Star said, waving her hands at me. "Have you been listening to a word I've said?"

I looked at her. She did her best to reel me back in, changing her position, altering her posture so there was no scant glimpse of the swell of her breasts, but a healthy dose, which I resisted as best I could and returned to my drink. She believed she had power, while I hoped she didn't. We all knew how that often ended up.

"Okay," I said, glancing at the time, because there was time. "Let's go to a concert then."

"Perfect," she said, clasping her hands. "But only if we go to Las Vegas after that."

"Okay," I said, compromising. "I've just got to be at Lando's at 6 p.m. for a cocktail."

She flashed me a strange look and then seductively polished off her drink. For Star, there was a little bit of flirtatiousness in everything. It had always made me a little uncomfortable. And that was still true.

I informed Cash we would use one of their SIM chambers, nearly amazing myself that I knew about them, but things were coming back to me. I asked him for water, but instead he delivered another drink with a wink. My fourth. Though I would scarcely touch.

"Kat will help you get situated," he said.

Kat, a tall, lanky brunette with striking eyes, especially her lashes, led us to a room in the back. Next to Star, she was almost skeletal, and aside from her face and long hair, you wouldn't necessarily have known what she was. I stopped there, once again, noting that pesky question about gender, almost as if there was a third gender, half woman and half man, that had emerged since I had come back. And looking again at Kat, she may very well have been that embodiment.

I watched her as she adjusted controls and handed us headsets. That now familiar laser light enveloped our bodies as a monitor came to life. Star was saying something to Kat, but I didn't hear what it was.

"Bonjour," Kat said to us, and soon thereafter her long gowned body disappeared from the room, or maybe the SIM lenses were in place, so the program was loading and it seemed as if she was gone.

I watched Star from the loading platform as her outfits changed at the blink of an eye, till she was in torn jeans and a faded Blondie T-shirt with medium wedge heels. Her tattooed sleeves extended on one side all the way to her elbow. She was quite a rocker chick, though maybe a bit over the top for the era we would visit. She looked over at me. I was in a dark button-up shirt, blue jeans and black Beatle boots. More to the era. That was the imagination, and what happened in something like this. I was also more modest, an adjective that applied little to Star.

"Are you ready?" she asked, to which I nodded in the

black nothingness where we waited, an eerie silencing settling over us, enveloping us until I felt that momentary sense of drowning before it happened.

"Load." She cooed softly, yet for a moment I imagined being in some lonely desert town about to draw my six shooters and unload all over her. It was such a strange thing to picture, to even think about, but then I didn't have to because that image vanished, replaced by another.

Suddenly we were there, a few rows from the front, among cheering fans as the most recent song had just ended. There on the stage were the Beatles in their matching wool Nehru jackets with mandarin collars and black pants. They looked young and alive and nothing like the people in the place where we came.

"Thank you. Thank you very much," John Lennon said, grinning affectionately at the adoring crowd.

"And now for the next number," Paul McCartney intoned cheerfully.

"Oh, do you really think they want to hear another one?" Lennon said playfully to Paul, before looking at George. "I'm not sure they do."

"I don't know, what do you think, George?"

The crowd roared in response. Even Star was jumping up and down, playing her part. When I glanced back to the band, Paul winked at me. Or maybe it was not me. Maybe he was winking at Star, but it felt like he was looking right at me. And why not?

"Okay."

"A 1-2-3 and 4. . ."

The next song began, which I knew immediately as the song "All You Need is Love" with its asymmetrical time signature. Perfect too. Paul strumming his Hofner Bass,

Lennon playing rhythm on his Rickenbacher and George playing lead on his full-bodied Epiphone. Ringo played drums.

I turned to Star, then glanced back to the rest of the crowd, all dressed more or less like us, though none quite like Star. Perhaps Paul was winking at her after all. I didn't jump and holler like the rest of the crowd though.

The song changed into "She Loves You." I wouldn't say it was natural, it just happened like that. If I closed my eyes, and just listened to the song, I could focus on a single instrument, isolated from the mix, be it Ringo's drums or just John's voice, but all the same, I wasn't prepared for that transition.

When I opened up my eyes, people all around us were holding up phones to get pictures. Some people appeared to be recording the events. Star was no different. She pulled out her phone and grabbed me close and struck a pose for our selfie.

"I'll send this out," she exclaimed above the noise of the song.

The song continued, Star bent over her device typing away on the little screen, much like a host of other people. If the Beatles were annoyed, they certainly didn't show it, happily bouncing along to the song, sharing vocals and laughing like the best of mates, which probably they were at the time. Or maybe in the SIM, the Beatles never broke up.

A couple behind us was making out, groping each other's bodies savagely. I hadn't been to a Beatles SIM in a long time, but this wasn't how I remembered it at all. The stage at Shea Stadium was a lot farther back than it was now, so close I could see the expression on George's face as he soloed. I guessed then I was alone, though, and that probably made a difference. It was different when you were in a SIM solo.

Star nudged me, then tugged on my arm, speaking over the music, but in such a voice that I couldn't hear at all. And then suddenly, everything stopped, was frozen, stuck in that last moment, except for us. I looked to the stage, John and Paul shared the mic so closely their faces almost touched. That made me smile.

"Okay, we've had enough, haven't we?" Star said. "Time to go to Vegas."

"Sure," I said, not arguing, even ready to be out of this strange Beatles concert at a Shea Stadium that seemed more and more like the Cavern Club, a dark din of a music club that had seemed at the last moment to resemble a rage.

"Good," Star said, "I was getting tired of all of that noise. I can't believe you like that stuff."

"Well, I do. And it seemed like you did."

"I know," she added sarcastically as the Beatles and the rest of the set disintegrated and we were left with a new menu. "Fifty years into the future, Las Vegas 2015."

"Sure. You're the expert. Can I get a drink at least?"

"Of course, darling. Of course. You can have whatever you want."

And then, there I was, clad in white linen pants, a light-colored shirt and open-toed sandals. In my right hand, I held a cocktail that sparkled as I turned the glass. Turning to Star, she flaunted a cream-colored skirt and flowery top with high heeled sandals. I noticed her toenails were painted with little palm trees. She had a tiny purse clutched in her hand.

We stood among cobblestone streets lined with shops and terraced outdoor cafés, white stoned buildings with Roman arches. A waiter seemed to be frozen in time, pouring coffee, motionless like Zeno's Paradox, an arrow that never really moves, until it does move and the coffee flows, and the coffee did flow but we had moved away by then as the sounds of life cascaded around us.

This was Las Vegas. Families with ice cream and shopping bags, tour groups led by provocative figures pointed at things, people laughed loudly, if not a bit drunkenly, and then Star, who came alive too and was turning around in the streets.

"Isn't it wonderful?" she radiated. "Isn't it such a dream!"

And maybe it was, the eclectic mix of people, the old and young, light and heavy, the women with baby strollers and khaki clad husbands, the seasoned gamblers, grizzled and groomed for the glitz and glam. I watched as a woman in an elegant dress walked hand in hand with a man in New York Yankees baseball cap and Hawaiian shorts, all the while he talked loudly into his cell phone.

This was a place that it was impossible to look out of place and there were no rules on behavior. Fur coats could walk amid poverty, three-foot long fancy margarita drinks shared alike by frat brothers and nerdy tech convention goers, beside beer drinkers, teetotalers and tourists, men handing out cards for strip joints as superheroes posed for pictures with prepubescent teens. People smoked cigarettes like they were the secret sauce for millionaires.

I avoided eye contact with everyone and nodded to Star. How did they recreate some of these places? Old surveillance footage. We were a world awash in data.

Thank god they perfected DNA storage. And especially the efficient retrieval of info between the synthesis machines and sequencing machines. That had been the hold up. I don't think many people actually grasped the importance of that technology. Some of the most essential things were often missed in favor of what was immediate, what was bright and shiny and the latest must have gadget.

"Where are we?"

"We are in the forum shops. I need to buy a dress for tonight," she said, and I didn't think too much of it at the time, but later I would remember she said that.

At the moment, I had no time to consider, as Star trudged ahead like she knew exactly where to go. I sipped my drink and tried to keep up as she dashed in and out of shops, holding up a dress to gauge its look, its fit, then putting the thing back in place before moving on.

She eventually found a fancy Versace bejeweled baby doll dress. At least, that was what she called it. She grabbed both the pink version and the black, but then settled on the pink, disappearing into a nearby dressing room.

"Wa-lah," she said when she reappeared, asking me how she looked.

"Fabulous," I remarked.

"Okay, I'll try on the other one," she said, reaching back to the black one.

She went back in the fitting room, a little bit of a hop or giddiness in her step, like she was trying on prom dresses, but that was a thing that no longer was, so it couldn't have been that. These were formal dresses, though, and not too cheap as no one else wandered in the shop. Instinctively I knew things were not cheap, but I couldn't say exactly if I understood the currency or the system of money. Things just seemed to happen. Perhaps because everything looked expensive, it was.

"David," Star said. "Can you come here for a moment?"

Without thinking, I went into the fitting room. She hadn't made up her mind yet about the dress and was changing from one into another. She was nearly naked save for her pink undergarments, just looking at me looking at her, which I hadn't meant to do. She stopped for a moment and smiled at me.

"What did you really think of the dress? Not my lingerie, honey, though it looks so lovely, doesn't it?"

"Nice dress," I said. The drinks were really going to my head now. I felt a sudden sense of guilt and shame being where I was. I thought of Marta. We weren't together. No one was really together, but still, she would be disappointed if she knew. And probably she did know, and the mere fact Star stood before me in her pink panties and such, gave off the pretense of something more.

"Do I make you uncomfortable? You seem a little tense. Surely you've seen me like this, though not in a while," Star said, hands unabashedly on her hips as she toyed with the tops of her underwear.

"It's fine," I said. "I'm fine. You look great. Especially in the first dress."

"Thanks," she said, lurching forward to kiss me on the cheek, lingering for a moment close to me so that I felt the fullness of her breasts against me, pushed to me. By design, irresistible design. I felt, oh what did I feel, when I just didn't want to feel anything?

"Sure," I said, and slipped away, out of the dressing

room, out of the shop into the ceaseless din of the place, the cobblestone streets with the fake blue sky and the rustling sounds of water heard, but never quite glimpsed, and the smell, which I hadn't noticed before, fragrant yet chemical.

I breathed a sigh, turning now to watch the people, the endless stream of people, all real enough to me and yet not real at all. Every now and then someone looked at me, but we never made eye contact. Maybe it was not possible to interact with any of them. Yet, I thought the salesgirl in the shop had smiled at me. I've thought so many things, so many useless things. And now here I was, wondering if any of it mattered, if I really could have the effect I thought I could on this world, if I could change anything. And lastly, maybe nobody wanted anything different. Maybe there was no fire to steal because everybody already had it. I thought at one time that I was being heroic. Perhaps that too, was just my imagination.

Star tapped me on the shoulder, bag in hand from the dress she purchased. I was half-surprised she hadn't put the dress on straight away. Like I said, it wouldn't have been out of place in Las Vegas. She would have been the glamorous overdressed woman and I would have been just the inferior guy with her that people wondered about. Why him? Yeah, why me?

"Hey," she said, almost like a different person. "I was wondering where you went. You keep drifting."

"I thought I saw someone I knew, that's all."

"And did you?"

"I don't think so." I felt like I had just awakened from a trance and all of the Las Vegas people had changed. For one, they were more like our time. Everyone looked great as if rendered into the best possible form by the system. That was my last thought as we exited Las Vegas and regained ourselves in the SIM room, but for a moment, probably not even a moment, a flash of a second, I thought I saw the piercing eyes of a dashing man dressed in black.

"What about your dress?" I asked Star.

"You're funny, honey" she said. "Do you like my rhyme? Of course, I'll have it later."

The piano man still played as we left the SIM room and returned to the bar. Cash was entrenched behind the bar talking to patrons. Kat roamed about, tray of drinks in her hand. I stepped uneasily, slightly weary from travel. Maybe it was my imagination, but she seemed to have on some sort of feline dress. She eyed me and smiled rakishly. Perhaps we used to talk.

The Beatles show didn't sit right with me. They played songs they hadn't even written at the time, something I knew for a fact, but probably would not be a fact anymore. At one time, I was right though. I know I was. This thin spool of thread spun away from me, unraveling itself. I chased the lines down and down, flights of stairs, out into winding streets, but I never caught up with the ends.

"Thanks for meeting up with me, David," Star smiled sweetly as she spoke, gleaming teeth, back in her black polka dot cocktail dress. I guessed that's how I knew we were back in real time. Because of her dress, the generous glimpse, her black brassiere. Not pink. Such details.

She hugged me tightly, then looked as if she had something more to say, but nothing more seemed to come from her lips, and when it did, that moment had passed and she was holding up the bag.

"I'm so happy I found this dress."

I should have been a quicker thinker about some things, but maybe she was right, I just drifted. Marta had said that too. Still, imagine my surprise, not more than thirty minutes later as I arrived at Lando's place and there was Star in that pink dress from Vegas.

And maybe that was what she had wanted to tell me after we exited the SIM. She probably thought I already knew. I didn't. I long suspected it but didn't know for sure that they were living together in an age and period of time when no one did that.

Cocktail hour was somewhere in the Adriatic. I wasn't even aware we were in a SIM, but we must have been, because there was a deck that looked out to the water. Off to the side, red roofed houses in white stone scattered about in clusters amid greenery. Quite picturesque, I conceded.

All of us were there, and by that, I meant from the company, except for Ander, of course, who had another engagement, and Star too, who wasn't from the company yet was there, dazzling in her bejeweled dress, almost semi-transparent in parts, or so it seemed, though I did my best to ignore her.

"Hi, David," she said sheepishly then pirouetting as if on display. "I wasn't sure if you knew or not. I wanted to tell you. Maybe this is the best way. You knew, didn't you?"

I nodded and smiled, but my thoughts were elsewhere, in that other world where I roamed, where Emrik was and the Beatles played the right songs, where things were true, yet not true. For nothing anymore could ever be true, could it? But that was a place that I would be, and someday Marta too. I was sure of that. And I was pretty sure we couldn't get fancy party dresses there.

In the background, I heard Lando explaining to the others that the reason I was late had to with the possibility that I was "reading" which was of course something no one else ever did. Well, certainly not for pleasure. That drew some laughs.

"He's the only person on the planet that still reads old books," Lando repeated, some variation of the refrain like the chorus of a song.

"Is that true?" Ocie asked, "I know you probably know that you can experience books visually now, even most of the old classics have been transcribed. I know because I worked on that project."

"Is that so?" I said, pretending that I didn't know, but the sarcasm was lost. "Even the classics, whatever they are now?"

"They are as they have always been," Ocie said matter-of-factly. "Come to think of it, that was your project."

She too wore an interesting dress, though nothing like the razzle dazzle of Star, but beautiful on her nonetheless, periwinkle colored, mid-thigh in length with matching heels. Though what she said was not exactly true. The classics were always changing, even before this period. For whatever reason, each ensuing generation took apart the past from their own perspective, which meant a number of works were no longer acceptable. In small ways, well before all this, the culture was losing. Maybe now it was all the way lost.

"I was actually with Star," I said. "Having an early drink."

"And before that with Ander," Lando remarked. "Quite the lush. I asked him earlier if he still had time to work."

Everyone thought that was funny. And to think these

were my friends. Maybe everyone reaches that point where you look around at those you know and wonder how you ever became so connected. I knew the reasons. But it almost didn't make sense to me. It was all Emrik's doing. He recruited us, each for a set of skills, a perspective, for something.

"Not so much the lush," Star piped in playfully. "We did go to Vegas and a Beatles concert too. I'll send you all a few pics."

Everyone except Lando and I, looked to our devices, for he of course had presumably already seen them. He looked at me and nodded, making some remark, which I couldn't make, but to which I just replied in the affirmative.

"Nice clothes," Mari said. "What year were you?"

"Twentieth century," Lando said before Star, "Circa 1960s for the Beatles. Then early twenty-first century for Vegas."

Lando patted me affectionately on the shoulder and handed me a drink. Something tropical. Clear with a lime, some flavoring like tonic and a twist or two of something else. The cool breeze of the Adriatic filtered through the air as I moved to the balcony to take in the scene. At this point, nothing should have amazed me, for anything seemed possible.

"I'm glad you spent some time with Star. She worries about you, you know? We all do," Lando said to me as we looked off the balcony to the Mediterranean sea. He seemed to want to say something else but didn't. Instead, he continued talking about Star.

"She loves traveling, though. It keeps her busy for all of her design work. She essentially travels for work. She'll spend hours in the SIM."

"I don't doubt it," I said, cordially. "Makes sense. She seemed to really enjoy Vegas."

"And New York, L.A., Hollywood, Paris, all of those old chic cities that for a time enthralled our populace, and for good reason too. They were entertaining cities. And we all loved to be entertained."

I thought again about the old days, when Lando and I spent a lot of time together, meeting for drinks, maybe even too often, debating, inevitably what we always fought over, whether advances in technology were worth the cost. Lando always dismissed that notion as foolish. He insisted that accessibility trumped-all, and the more drinks he had, the louder he made such proclamations, asking anyone near us, and most preferably should there happen to be a young woman beside us, if she wouldn't kill to be forever young and look however she wanted.

His speech was neither as elegant nor as graceful with the ever-present beauty beside us. We didn't necessarily know it, but it was the SIM we talked about, the idea of it, though at that point it didn't have a name. I listened, I always listened as he described in much cruder terms that she could sleep with whomever she wanted, as if such a device was only meant for that, the mere pleasures of the flesh. You can have whatever you want he would say over and over, as if repetition proved the point all the more. Imagine that! It would be incredible.

I argued that the technology would never be good enough to understand the human condition. He passionately disagreed, had more faith in science than I did, but it was as much an art as a science, and that was where I thought things would go awry. While he marveled at the ability of a machine to make calculations, to take pi to the farthest point in a matter of seconds, I spoke of art and music and this whole world of creativity and curiosity that propelled us forward. Naturally, this was really a discussion disguised as something else, as quality vs quantity, and the machines, of course, excelled beyond recognition at quantity. What did taking pi to the millionth place have to do with anything? Not even the best coders could engender AI with aesthetics, or so I argued.

In my mind, I foresaw technology supplementing the human brain, not supplanting it, allowing for the things that it did well, to continue to do so. Plato talked about it in Greek mythology, humans originally having four arms, four legs and a head with two faces, but then Zeus split them in half, condemning one half to look for the other. In this telling, it was really the brain having a missing half. Technology. This was the symposium. The search for the missing half. No one searched for the other in a physical sense, it was the marrying of our brain with technology that all along had been missing. No one searched for the other.

Why was I dwelling on this anyway? There were no real relationships anymore, and all for a number of reasons, beginning with the SIM world, the network and the obviousness of procreation. Women didn't birth children. They were raised in labs where the fertilization process took root. We couldn't possibly be human anymore because of this, could we? That was such a huge transformation, psychologically, which I guess was something the network helped normalize.

And yet, the network would not understand the nurturing process. Maybe those who worked in the lab were particularly adept, but over time, such soft skills, those unquantifiable aspects of existence, would diminish. And so while the network had made a prosperous and harmonious society where everyone had a purpose, a job, stability, at the same time, it was creating its undoing. That was always the folly of quantity.

"Listen, I gotta go back to what you said at the meeting. You don't believe that crap, do you? I thought you were smarter than that."

"What about the moon? You don't believe we landed on the moon?" I asked Lando.

"Fuck no. It's not something you believe or not. It's something I know. We couldn't leave the earth's atmosphere if we tried. That's the truth," Lando stated. "The moon story is actually an apt parable. Imagine a country mired in a terrible war, losing in many respects. And what better way to distract the populace than a so-called moon shot, a pie in the sky endeavor to show off a nation's technological prowess and distract from the real failures, a triumph in space to cover up the defeat on the ground."

"What if the moon is still within the earth's atmosphere?"

"Nonsense. Not a theory I am interested in," Lando said, then proceeded to lay out all the reasons why the landing was faked, but there was really one reason. He was right, the evidence was no longer on my side, but that didn't mean anything. The historical record was missing. It had not been digitized. That had to be it. Because I still believed it happened, that we as humans were capable of great things, once long ago, and even now.

"You still don't get it," Lando said. "You're fucking

impossible."

Not impossible, I thought. I am just complicated. That made me smile, made me think of Marta, I should reach out to her, but she would understand this was important. The reason the moon landing didn't exist was because the network didn't want it to exist, because that was a story of daring, one of courage and astronomical risk. Imagine the probability of failure. The odds of success were so low, and yet that was the human condition, was it not?

Star interrupted our small talk, such that it was, as if she sensed some disunity in the room, sauntering over to Lando in her usual seductive way, and though my drink was sweet, I felt something vulgar as Lando put his arm around her. They pecked and he commented on her dress, which I was sure he had already done, but needed to do so again in my company.

And it hadn't really occurred to me before, but Star and I were never really together. We were just good friends, with one of us wanting something more than the other. It probably was easy to guess which was which and who was who. Because I was that great kind of friend, but not that kind someone like Star would ever be interested in. And sure, we had some moments, times when I was sure that this now meant something, that we were really on track, only to find out all too soon that it was nothing like that. And yet Marta was jealous, jealous of something that never really was. I suppose I couldn't blame her, and being here wasn't helping.

Star and Lando. I surmised they were probably perfect for each other as they allowed for the dalliances of the other, but in the end, all they were doing was keeping up appearances, even in a world that had moved on. And yet

I was still too loyal—to Star, to them—but for reasons I did not understand.

All of the drinks were making me nostalgic for a time that never was. I vowed to drink slower. I wished I could confide in Marta. I wished that for just one moment, I could say how I really felt about everything, instead of keeping it all inside of me. As simple as it was, and as clear as probably seemed to others, the Star thing came to me as a revelation. I would look at everything different from now on. Cue that sad piano music in the background, the soundtrack in my mind played it as I walked, drink in hand, back into Lando (and Star's) expansive flat, away from the balcony that provided a ready window into the Mediterranean.

The dining area seemed to be surrounded by screens on all sides, creating projections such that we were on a rooftop at some steakhouse in Buenos Aires, amid old gothic buildings, churches with red tops and Romanesque towers. I wouldn't have known we were in such a place, but I overheard it being discussed by Siri to Ocie, her twin sister.

Twins are represented in various mythologies in many fashions, some ominous, some auspicious. Apollo and Artemis, for example as sun god and moon goddess, dualities in the universe. Usually there is a sense of a deeper bond, two halves that make a whole, that kind of thing. Castor and Pollux were twin half-brothers in Roman mythology as Leda was their mother from different fathers. In Latin, they are known as the Gemini because after Castor died, Pollux pleaded with Zeus to allow him to share his immortality with his brother. Zeus granted such and they became the constellation Gemini. To sailors, they appeared as St. Elmo's Fire.

Perhaps Siri and Ocie had special powers, like Helen and Clytemnestra except one of them was mortal and the other divine, mother Leda. Sisters of the Dioscuri. Were we immortal within the grid? Or rather, I knew, like so many things, we were immortal until the network decided otherwise.

Spanish waiters in white shirts with red vests, brought out steak atop a bed of arugula for each of us. Matching waitresses, except in skirts, poured red wine from glorious decanters. I hoped none of these drinks were real. I was losing count where I was. I sought Marta's advice, that none of it was real, that my mind made it all real. But we all knew what mind we were talking about. I often had trouble distinguishing reality and fantasy.

Siri and Ocie, as I mentioned, were twins, blonde and tall. They sat side by side. At the head of the table, at each end, Star and Lando as the hosts often sat. I sat across from Mari at Star's end, beside me were Cleo, who was something of an Egyptian goddess, and an empty space, which I supposed was meant to invoke Ander, but I thought of Emrik, as I was inclined to do.

Aside from Star, these were my colleagues. We represented the controllers of the grand experiment, each hand-picked by Emrik based on a particular strength. We were evenly divided, male and female, represented by different colors of skin and even sexual orientation. Emrik had been gay. Mari was widely known to be bisexual. None of these things were secrets. And the twins, of course.

Even though I had known these people for so much of my life, I felt strangely distant from them now, amid all of the small talk. I made some remarks to Cleo as we ate, sipped wine and genuinely enjoyed the impressive meal. She smiled and politely replied to my mentions. We were never that close, I supposed, but then again, maybe I was not that close to anybody.

Towards the end of the meal, Star put her hand on mine and thanked me for coming. Maybe it had been a long time since we all were together outside of work, though even then, it was all of us except Ander. At that moment I wondered if that was by design, so that he could apprehend Marta. But as I smiled passively at Star, I figured Marta could take care of herself. It was me I should worry about.

After dinner, we returned to the balcony, the simulation had faded and the city at night sparkled. I struck up conversations with Cleo and Siri. They were our top coders. At the beginning of the computer age, of course, women had done all of the coding. When men took over coding, it became more prestigious, but the truth was, women tended to be better at it. And I wasn't one who necessarily believed such things, that one sex was better than the other at anything. This just happened to be true.

I asked them some general questions about coding and what they were working on, but I really wasn't interested all that much. Sometimes that's just how you had to play things in order to get the information you needed. I did enjoy talking to them. Siri was someone I used to confide in, which made me wonder, if back then I was the very thing to her that Star was to me, just our roles were reversed. I probably had never even considered it.

"Who was a promising coder in your group? This wouldn't be current, but from much longer ago, pre-network era."

"Pre-network?" Cleo intoned, surprised or caught off guard.

"Why so long ago?" continued Siri with a look of partial concern. Perhaps they both wondered what kind of tangent like task I was dreaming up. Granted, everyone knew about the meetings I had with people and the things I asked. As such, I had something of a reputation for delving into seemingly unimportant things. What concerned people was that they didn't understand, that they were missing something. Lando especially didn't ever want to look like he didn't know something.

We had moved on to cordials. A waitress brought around a tray of drinks, which we all accepted, though both Siri and Cleo intimated they would not be drinking after a quick sniff test, an expression one face echoed off the other.

"What is this stuff?" asked Cleo.

"I think it's an amaro or grape brandy," I said. "Good for digestion."

"Hmm," Siri said dismissively. "It's no good then if you have no need for such an aid."

"Perhaps," I said.

I sipped on the bitter drink, not minding the taste, for there was some sweetness there too, just under the first layer and as I breathed in the cool night air a certain relaxed sense overcame me, masking the obvious fatigue that loomed just across the room, gazing me over like a bird of prey. Maybe even it swooned and circled me, waiting to pick me off once I had fallen.

"So was there," I said, resurrecting my previous thread. "Was there anyone who was promising, potential, yet kind of disappeared?"

"Because of the plague?" asked Cleo. "That was a long time ago."

"Possibly, but I would suspect other reasons," I said, though under the cover of the plague certainly would have been sufficient for anyone to disappear.

"I don't seem to recall anyone," Cleo said, to which Siri simply nodded.

"You weren't thinking of someone in particular," Siri suggested. "It seems as if this query has some purpose, some sort of track."

"No," I said. "It was just a notion I was thinking of that I came about when I talked with Ander earlier over drinks. I was wondering in particular if Emrik was any kind of coder."

"Emirk?" they both said with a chuckle.

Though it was a lie, they accepted it, for Ander always had people doing special little projects outside of the group. Often they were trivial matters, or so they seemed. I was sure there was a deeper purpose to many of them. Ander, in fact, encouraged me to take a look at the broken drones while I was in the Seaside. But he also warned me too. I shouldn't forget that.

"Too much thinking," Cleo laughed, setting her drink down on a high table. She adjusted the straps of her purple dress. "Thankfully you will be spending some time away. Refreshing. Seaside is great this time of year."

I nodded. Though you could go anywhere in the SIM, it was still something of a novelty to actually go somewhere, to the mountains or the desert, the country or the seaside. And yet, sometimes people traveled to those places but still remained embedded to the SIM, out of familiarity perhaps. Go figure. Like traveling halfway across the world to an unknown place only to make it as much like the place you came from.

Cleo was a bit of a marvel, exotic, dark skinned. I likened her to a goddess simply because there was something regal about her, like she descended from royalty. Her manners, the way she carried herself, her genuine demeanor embodied a sense of the refined. There was nothing manufactured about her. She seemed pure, even in this impure world.

When she excused herself from us, I was happy to be alone with Siri as I always felt more comfortable talking with one person. Siri had not taken a drink of her amaro or whatever it was, though from time to time she brought it close to her lips as if she was going to taste. But there was no tasting. She smiled sweetly at me. Once again, I thought about the time we had spent together, how she had always been such a great friend and I thought I had been too, but maybe I hadn't. Maybe from her I always took more than I gave. That was quite a revelation to me, if true.

"How are you?" I asked her, turning from the glimmer of night to the lightness.

Though she had a twin, I could tell them apart fairly easily. I am not sure how. Siri just had a special vibe that always put me at ease, whereas Ocie projected a coldness. And I felt like I could trust Siri. To a point. You can trust a lot of people just to a point. I likened it to how far you could swim out before anyone worried about you. As a kid, I remembered swimming out too far, not even thinking about it, and to this day still not thinking that it had been too far, but it worried some people.

"I'm fine," she said, pleased. "Thanks for asking. It's

you I've been concerned about. You seem a little more preoccupied than usual. Even for you."

I played it off as if it was nothing, remarking only that I had a strange premonition. What do you mean, she had asked, but I didn't know. déjà vu, perhaps. I didn't say that. I didn't say anything and for a moment, we were silent.

"There was a rather brilliant coder. I am not sure why Cleo didn't mention her," Siri said. When I turned back to her, she continued. "I am not sure what happened to her. She went away on holiday and never returned."

"Where did she go?"

"Seaside," she answered. "Things can get a little mixed up there. Broken sensors, the hillside. All kinds of things. We just lost track of her."

"That's strange," I said, amused.

"Yes, it was. She was special, quite brilliant, so if she wanted to disappear, she certainly would have known how."

That sounded a lot like Marta to me. The mere thought of her, warmed me, brought a smile to my face, even as I sipped the remainder of my drink, which I told myself was not real. My mind was just making it real. But what then was reality? And though I knew I couldn't find it, I searched for that building like a spiral staircase, that palace where Marta was.

"What was her name?" I asked as casually as I could.

"Let me think," Siri said.

"Did Ander know her?"

"Of course. He knew everyone that was a coder of any depth."

"Were they together?" I found myself asking, but I didn't want to and felt I should not have.

"So many questions. I wouldn't know." Siri said. "Why are you so interested in this person? Is this why you are going to the Seaside?"

"Probably just spinning my wheels. Just been thinking. Probably too much, like everyone says."

Siri put her hand on my shoulder and rubbed affectionately. It felt nice to be touched by her, even though I usually hated that kind of thing from most people, her presence calmed me. I couldn't deny that. She never cared much for Star. That was probably obvious. They were polar opposites. Siri's dress was simple yet elegant, didn't show too much, but just enough for the curious. She reminded me a little of Marta. Perhaps it was those things we like and admire in someone, we like in all people. She was one of the good ones, like Marta.

Marta. I had so many questions for Marta, too many to remember. I thought again about Ander and how maybe he was with Marta, and that they were in cahoots, conspiring against me, but then I quickly dismissed that and focused on Ander. He had given me the greenlight on exploration in the Seaside, but maybe that was a trap he was luring me into, like a spider and a fly. I didn't like that image. I wasn't a fly. Not even one on a wall. And I hated spiders. It was that movie from my childhood, *Kingdom of the Spiders* or something like that where spiders take over the world. From my childhood, I thought, what else about my childhood I wondered, besides spiders and swimming out too far?

In my mind, I replayed my conversation with Ander, searching for some salient point I had overlooked or simply dismissed. There were clues in the way he spoke. Perhaps I should have pressed him more, but how do you do that without being suspicious? I was never that clever. When I was younger, I surely thought I was in that way we think in our youth, that we are destined for greatness, special and acutely gifted. I was none of that though.

"Just relax," Siri said, still rubbing my shoulder gently, moving in circles like a mini massage.

On the plus side, Marta was real and not something I conjured. That would have made things strange if I had created Marta. Although, it made a lot of sense too, if she was my creation. That explained why she knew so much about me. It wasn't like the days of Frankenstein when things like that were so freakish. Such things were not only plausible, but possible too.

So much had changed, evolved, if that was what you wanted to call it. The system was said to write its own code, but it was also lazy as long as things worked reliably, the network seemed satisfied. Humans sought a level of perfection that was often unattainable. For machines, it was different. Bits of data on a page, ones and zeroes as they always said. What was the purpose of life to a machine? Simply to live and not die, unless dying meant getting rid of some outdated code. Sometimes that was necessary. Creative destruction.

"She must have had a name," I said, not seeming to let it go.

The way Siri looked at me, I wondered what she was thinking. How much control did we have over our thoughts? They seemed so random at times, divorced from what was happening as if triggered by something else, by the tiniest, most insignificant thing. And yet other times, the important details eluded us. It would only happen to occur to us later when we were in the midst of other things, as if the whole time, the mind had been working through it all, unbeknownst to us. That was nothing like the way a machine worked.

Siri was always one to help me, sometimes without me knowing. It was possible she even wrote me out of the code. I didn't want to ask. I knew I wasn't clever enough to do it myself. I had to have assistance from someone. Though I was also not the type to ask for help either. I guess it didn't matter, but I often got hung up on such things. Trivial things, maybe. Did it matter so much how? What was more important was why and what's next.

"I don't remember exactly," she said, rubbing the back of my neck, no longer looking at me, but out into the distance. "But it was something to do with color. Some kind of blue."

Hmm. A kind of blue. I thought of Picasso, Miro, Matisse. Artists and their so-called blue periods. This was the kind of stuff in my head. I wondered how I was ever useful to the group. In my mind, I wasn't good or brilliant at anything. And maybe that was the key. Group dynamics functioned better when there were people of various skill sets and intellects.

"Like Miles Davis," I said jokingly, but I knew that joke was on me, me and my useless knowledge, as music, that ever present soundtrack of my life, propelled me along, but meant almost nothing here.

I often marveled how I could listen to something I hadn't heard in a long time, and yet, recall the lyrics, the tune and melody, the next line. Somehow the grooves embedded themselves in my mind without any sense of time. Could have been yesterday, last year or decades since my last listen and yet I still knew, because some songs sunk in deep and they became one with my thoughts.

Siri stopped and craned her neck around with a confused expression as if to say Miles who? And maybe that was true, if I searched the record, he just might not be there, erased in the digitization process or lost in the transfer. History did not get saved if it wasn't archived properly. First it had to be recorded, but that was not always accurate. Was it possible to get the history of the world in a SIM. Of course. But what history would it be? It would be some history, not necessarily the true history.

"A musician from long ago," I mused, putting all of those other thoughts out of my head, exercising the little control I had, for just as surely as thoughts left, new ones emerged, taking over what had been purged.

And here was the big misconception about the network, that suddenly you had access to this vast trove of information. And while you did, on some level, it was mostly reserved for topics that interested you in the first place, particulars that had been studied. If you had no interest in music, then just like in your brain, there would be little you could recall. You could look it up, though, via a search query, but then you still had to wade through a lot of junk in order to find the pertinent info. The network knew better than to make us all walking encyclopedias.

The network goal was to bring about your best self. Surely that was a lofty yet worthy goal, was it not? But all things had consequences, many of them unintended, for we could never see that far ahead. Such a system created order and arrangement, and when paired with human tendency towards assimilation what resulted was a sameness, a consistent uniformity. And yet, some objects like buildings, retained their own sense of identity. Was it really that? Or were there only so many patterns, scattered about, repeated but in such a way that was less discernible?

It was never going to be that the machines became more like humans, rather that we became more like machines. First it was by metaphor and metaphor alone. We talked about the brain being hard-wired a certain way, about our "bandwidth" to work on so many projects at once. These terms gradually replaced the old metaphors, that we were "firing on all cylinders." That was a reference to the industrial age, and at the time, the wonders of the internal combustion engine. Or "too many irons in the fire" which harkened even further to the age of blacksmiths. Although, some said the expression related to surgeons on the battlefield who needed to keep a fire going to warm the iron needed to cauterize a wound.

"That explains that," Siri said, smiling. "You always did have a thing for music. I never got that myself."

Siri was older, but I am not sure how much older. It was so hard to tell now. On some level, perhaps she would have been reluctant to embrace the network, but as a coder, it was a preternatural instinct to do so, to explain the world in little bits, which was something music was not. It was also imperative to embrace the new order. Decisions could no longer afford to be made in isolation.

Penicillin was a good example, an antibiotic that was innocently over prescribed thereby eliminating its effectiveness against bacterial infections, gutting the versatility of the human ecosystem, and eventually contributing to the decimation of the planet. That was an over-statement. It is never one thing, but generally an accumulation. Still, it is a telling tale when a miracle of science disappears, a remarkable tendency that humans exacerbated. No need to talk about climate change here. That was another one, maybe the biggest one. But couldn't nature rebuild itself? I thought momentarily about that as I looked back to Siri, that nature was another code written at one time or another, a code that had become obsolete.

Because we now depended so much on the network and not nature. Babies once born through the birth canal were exposed to essential bacteria. With the rise of the C-section in the late twentieth century, the birthing process was fundamentally changed, and when increases in infertility first appeared, such changes were irreversible.

Thankfully, babies were grown in labs now, with the network carefully monitoring the progress of every newborn, making all necessary adjustments so that the task was perfectly efficient. These babies were not clones as science fiction would have you believe, though there was certainly some gene editing to rid out imperfections and irregularities. Sperm samples were readily taken from all men and stored. No surprise, the SIM made this process rather easy. A new birth was simply a matter of pushing a button.

If I had forgotten any of this, Marta surely had reminded me. Not that I really had forgotten. It was just something I seldom thought of. It was all in there somewhere, in storage, but a different kind of memory, not as exacting or precise. There were no such things in the human mind, both a source of great strength and inherent weakness. The strength, I figured, was partially its ability to shield us from the truth, but that too was its weakness because sometimes we needed a stronger dose.

"Hey, what are you thinking about?" Siri had stopped

rubbing my shoulder and now stood beside me, lightly pressed against me. Why had I never noticed how much affection Siri had toward me. Too caught up in Star's web. There I was, once again, just a fly, a poor misguided insect with a single pair of wings slipping too close to the sun.

"Oh, maybe I'm just amazed at this world, at how much things have changed, full of all kinds of people, coexisting. All of these separate lives, hopes and dreams, separate yet connected. And all of it works. Here we are. Here I am, and you too."

"Truly a wonder," Siri agreed. "Humanity has evolved at a tremendous rate. And because of the network, we are finally a harmonious society."

I would remember that phrase and tell Marta, as something about it in particular struck me as

strange. And as Siri moved away to go to Ocie, I should have chosen that moment to leave too, but I didn't. Something kept me there. All of the uncertainty? There was a kind of certainty in doing nothing, staying rooted in the same spot, so maybe that was what I embraced as I stood there, outside on the balcony, gazing out to the wondrous world around me.

By now, everyone had left. Lando wandered out. I knew he was pretty drunk at this point, and so was I. I could say I didn't know how it happened, but I had been counting my drinks all night long until I lost track. And that was how it happened. There was no mystery. Things were okay until they weren't.

"You're still here, huh?" he said to me. "I figured you might be the first to leave, but here you are the last. What's that mean? It must mean something."

"It doesn't mean anything," I said quietly.

"Everything means something with you," he said. "Tell me, David, what do you expect? Is it Star? Do you think she wants you? Or do you want to talk about UFOs?"

"I don't expect anything," I said. "And I should be going."

"No. Let's have another drink. Just like old times," he said as he disappeared still talking about another drink.

He found a bottle of something and pushed it towards me. I took a sip, then looked away into the night. I should have said something. I should have left long ago. All the things I should have done in my life.

"Whatever you think is going to happen, it's not going to happen," Lando gushed.

"I don't think anything is going to happen," I responded as casually as I could.

"Bullshit, I know you. You're planning something. That's bullshit."

"Is it?" I asked him. In the background, I could hear Star asking if things were okay, and never before had I felt so relieved to hear Star's voice.

"And here's the thing. In case you don't know. Sometimes I think you forget or think you're special," Lando said. "It's not for one, but for the many, for all. One for all, all for one. We are the keepers of the network. That's what we do. We built it. Now we maintain it. We maintain it. We make sure things are on course. We steer the fucking ship."

I let Lando's words sink in until they sunk me, that Latin phrase *unus pro omnibus, omnes pro uno*. And as I drifted lower and lower, I knew there was no treasure at the bottom, that even if there was, someone else likely held the claim. When Star came out to retrieve him, I resurfaced. She looked at me like it was my fault, waving me away, and I didn't linger.

As I walked unsteadily from Lando's, exhausted, images flashed through my head at a brutish pace, exploding from one scene to the next, the whole day in disparate sketches, unordered, the SIM, coffee, Marta, another SIM, Star and along the way, all of those drinks, too many of them as the words of Lando trailed out of me and things blurred. If I could, I wanted to start again.

I guessed without the filter, I would have felt even worse. Still, the sheen of the world, even at night, conjured a luminescence as I walked home past the brightness of street-side cafés, and that light lifted my spirits as I moved toward the more sparse LED street lamps near my flat, characteristic of the more residential sections, though the buildings themselves lit up like they were on display.

I took to looking inside them as I walked, the city to myself, me and the shadows, the sculptures inside the buildings that surely rushed to life as I passed. I would know my building by the woman with the missing arms, not the one with wings who could fly anywhere nor the art deco horse who could surely gallop off into the sunset. No, mine could see everything and yet touch nothing.

A voice in the shadows awakened me from slumbering steps, maybe even I heard it twice, since the first time, I was still stuck in my thoughts, plugged into them not unlike all the others, distracted, no doubt, by something. We were always so distracted.

"Remember me?"

"Marta, I. . ."

She just looked at me as if in astonishment, that there was anything I thought I could say to remedy the situation.

I wobbled towards her, not meaning to grope her, but I did, and she pushed me away. All I wanted to do was touch her, feel her close so that I could close my eyes and fall asleep in her arms.

"Watch your hands, please."

"I'm sorry, it's just. . ."

"I get it," she interrupted, "You are disoriented, this is all new, all of that. But the thing is, just because you are not connected to the grid does not give you a free pass. You are still accountable."

"I know," I said. "And I can explain."

"Well, maybe you think you can, but you can't and not now. You're pretty drunk."

"Am I? I'm sorry," I said. "I really am sorry. I didn't mean, I mean I am sorry."

"I know, you've said that a lot."

"I'm really glad to see you. I've missed you, and I've wanted to see you," I said. "And I'm sorry it happened like this. Now I don't feel good."

"The drinking does that," she replied. "The mind, as I said, is a powerful tool. Perhaps we all need a network to control it."

"What can I do to make this better?"

She gave me a glance as if to say there was nothing that could be done and that I should have known better. And I probably should have. I had momentarily thought at various times of reaching out to her, and I certainly could have before I met up with everyone for dinner, but I got lost along the way because of Star and what happened in the SIM. And so I didn't. But the whole time I meant to. I know that didn't really count for anything because I didn't.

"Yeah, I know. I get it," she resounded gloomily. "Time

for one more drink with Lando. And yet. . ."

I did feel guilty, for though I was thinking so much of getting back to see her, I stayed later than I should have, had a drink with Lando on the balcony, which was only supposed to be a quick drink, but it evolved into something a little more. He wanted to be just like it was, and I was just trying to be cordial. Sometimes when you tried to please people, you pleased no one. And Star was there too, at the end, so it was complicated.

She made no effort to elaborate further, and I didn't feel like pushing it. She had a point. I lost track of time a little bit. It was a damned interesting though. This world I had come back to. And I felt conflicted, full of a range of emotions that were hard to sort out. I just needed more time for everything I experienced. At least, she wasn't in partnership with Ander. That much seemed to be true and that relieved me. And she was real, too, though I should have known that.

We walked slowly back to my place. I did my best to walk as straight as I could, to appear more in control than I was, but I was tired—too tired and probably even my speech was slurred—so I resisted saying anything more so that I wouldn't give myself away.

I followed her into my place and collapsed on my couch. She brought me a glass of water and dropped something into it, which immediately became effervescent before calming to an off color.

"Drink this," she commanded me sternly.

I did as I was told and watched as she moved across the room, first from the window and then to the edge of the couch. I finished off the glass of modified water and handed it back to her when she reached for it.

"I'm sorry," I said.

"I know." she said. "You're kind of pathetic. You keep saying that. And it doesn't help."

"You're beautiful, really beautiful. Have I ever told you that? Can I kiss you? Am I asking nicely."

"Tell me later," she said then added, "if you remember."

She said nothing about the kiss. Beautiful didn't seem like an apt word to describe Marta. I didn't know what was. The language hobbled me, and not just because of my condition, rather we were stuck with words even when words alone remained inadequate.

Sprawled on my side on the couch, my head throbbing like heartbeats, pulsing in perfect rhythm, I closed my eyes and massaged my temples. When I opened my eyes, I saw a pair of heels. I turned back to the kitchen towards Marta, but she wasn't there. I saw her over by the window, looking out at the city of lights.

"I'm not staying," she said, like she had been mulling it over and there was something I could have done to make it better, but I doubted that was the case.

She looked back at me. I wondered what she saw, what she ever saw in me to even want to be part of this assignment. Did she choose? Or was she chosen? Of course, maybe it was bigger than me and I was just collateral damage, a mere means to an end.

My heart sank. I tried not to show it or feel it or do much of anything. Some say you get what you deserve. Maybe, some of the time, but not all the time. I probably deserved this. No, I did absolutely, and I hated absolutes, but this was a case when it applied.

And then Marta was gone. I missed her almost

immediately and suddenly felt unsure of myself. An intense desire filled me then quickly deflated, its vacancy as potent as its obverse. If a moment ago I was light, then now it was all too heavy. I imagined myself being the caretaker of a roadside motel on a Monday morning, wandering from room to empty room, no guests to be seen, no other bodies present. I don't know why I thought of that image, the loneliness of the solitary wanderer. Existing only to take care of the needs of others. No recognition or special dispensation. Just this thankless task.

That was my brain. Off the network. Imagining such things. Not even wanting to clean any of the rooms as if I knew there would be no more guests for days, maybe even weeks, depending on the season. I consoled myself that this was somehow better than losing the filter and walking alone in the world no one could see, dared to see, seeing it for what it was, as it was, what it used to be and never would be.

I supposed that was like my endless Star SIM. Kind of creepy. It really was. No wonder it bothered Marta. It bothered me thinking about it. She spent years watching me, observing the details of my life. That was probably the one thing she couldn't stand, the futility of it all. And yet, apparently, it had not phased me thanks to the network. I was resigned to the simulation, and whatever it provided was enough to sustain me. I thought about how *simulation* and *stimulation* were similar words and how the SIM was really a stimulation.

Was I ever really part of this world? Even when I was connected, it seemed I was still disconnected. Not even able to enjoy paradise. It's as if I was listening to the same album over and over, not really getting that there was other stuff out there. Content, in some way, to stick with that familiar grove. And maybe that was just what it knew, the part of me that existed when reduced to the core.

I tried not to think about Marta being gone, believing she would come back and not because I was irresistible because I knew I was not. Rather, we wanted the same things. But what was that? At the moment, I wanted lots of things, some relatively short term, like just to feel better. On a deeper level, she wanted a way out, out of this network world.

I put on some music, toned down the volume and tried not to think about all the spinning in my mind, endless webs, but none of them connected because they were too weak, because I was too tired to secure the lines. I didn't know how to tie proper knots. I didn't know much. And I certainly didn't know anything about love.

It's like that sometimes. I felt as if I couldn't sleep and wouldn't sleep. I rolled over, changed positions, sat up, looked outside then went back to the couch, the floor, but not my bed. And at some point, fell asleep.

There I was again, in a truck on the highway with a female companion. Half of the landscape was in ruins, but the road we were on was untouched. Whole sections of the land looked like they had been hit by a combination of wildfire and massive unrest, cars blackened and busted out, still burning by the side of the road, fragments and debris blowing in the breeze, but on the opposite side, everything was eerily fine.

A signpost for an exit, a few bullet holes cut through so the middle number was empty, but even with it wholly there, we still would have exited. She looked at me, but there was no alarm in that glance, more just recognition, a little bit of a smile.

"I thought maybe we could get a snack," I said to which she nodded, looking at the window as we listened to Dylan's record called Desire. It was half-way through the album, a song about another cup of coffee had just ended, and now it was on to "Oh, Sister."

"I always like this one," she said to me. "It's kind that juxtaposition of brother and sister, lover, death and rebirth."

"There's a lot going on in that song. I've always felt it was just about soul mates, you know, that idea of two people meant to be together, but time and place, circumstance. I don't know, just kept them apart. He sings that one well."

We had exited the highway and now drove on a street lined with various shops and buildings on each side, some of which were perfectly fine, while others were mere shells, make-to shelters with boarded up windows and graffiti scribbled walls. A shutter hung from its frame, tilting back and forth, at any moment threatening to fall. That really struck me, its teetering, the scratchy sound it made.

A few people milled about, all covered up with face masks and goggles, carrying various kinds of guns, ready to shoot anything, but not us. The street wasn't at all like the highway. Obstacles, from smashed up cars to shopping carts and big green dumpsters littered about. Slowly, I drove around them as Dylan fittingly sang in the background about the gangster Joey Gallo and a Con Edison explosion. This was kind of the aftermath, and everyone ensured their building still stood.

Up ahead there was an outlet mall full of retail stores

and beyond that a park with a shimmery lake, seeming so serene and cerulean from far off, but maybe not as good close up. As the sun blazed through the windshield, the thought of a swim enticed me.

"We could swim," I suggested. "Buy suits from one of the outlet stores."

"We could," she said, glancing toward the lake. "But this place is strange. Let's just get some french fries and get out of here."

I agreed, though I had some thought from however long ago, a hot summer day and the cold water of the lake as I jumped in, moved around through its coldness, warmed now and then by mysterious pockets of warmth. It was such a wonderful memory, the crispness of the water, the blue sky, the feeling that anything was possible. I wondered if it had been that way at all, or if it was just a polished apple.

We got out of the truck and went into a right out of the box burger joint, she moved first, in her jeans and Dylan shirt. I remembered we were on our way to a Dylan show. Hopefully, the theatre would still be standing. It seemed like every place we needed to go still existed, but I knew, or seemed to know, that at some point things wouldn't work out so swimmingly.

I watched as she went right up to the counter and ordered french fries and a soft serve ice cream cone. They both sounded good, but I didn't want to order the same thing, so I asked for fries and coffee. The woman behind the counter looked at me strangely.

"Hmm, Anna," she said to herself, "Maybe I should remind him that it is warm outside. Some would even say iced."

"It's okay," I said.

"Iced coffee?" she blurted out, then added. "I think you mean an iced coffee."

"Hot is fine,"

"He's weird," my companion added, glancing at me with a sly smile. "I'm used to it by now."

I liked how she said she was used to it. I didn't know if that was true or if she was just saying that, but either way, the sentiment mattered. The way she said it was so sweet and even our server Anna acquiesced.

"Well, that explains a lot," she said, resigned. "How about super fries?"

"Yes," we both said at the same time, looking at each other after it happened.

I wanted to say something more, even taste my fries or coffee, but as I looked outside, the skies darkened like a storm or some unknown event loomed, and when I looked back at her, she was gone and where we were was gone too, and I was left standing in the middle of nowhere, one foot on an empty highway, as a swath of darkness swooped down like a vulture.

I awoke, alone and disoriented, a gnawing at my head like the beating of an expressionless drum, unvarying and unwavering, while in the background that same Dylan record kept on playing, like it had been on repeat the whole night. The lines of the song were:

One more cup of coffee for the road. One more cup of coffee before I go. . . to the valley below.

I felt I had been in that valley below as I looked at myself in the mirror, after I had showered and stood there half-dressed, gazing at the image before me, the man that I was, wondering if I was really there or if I was the man who wasn't there who I happened to see on the stair? I remember mentioning the lines of that poem to Marta. When? Seemed like a lifetime ago, so long ago that maybe it never happened. She seemed amused then, interested in my little bits of nonsense. Now she was probably just annoyed.

Closing my eyes, I opened them again, then again. I always figured out things. I just needed time to think my way through. I believed that. And this time was going to be no different. I just needed time.

I rummaged around through the little belongings I had. There wasn't much to choose from. I had a daily uniform that seemed to vary only slightly, mostly dark pants and light button-up shirts. I had several pairs of the same shoes, all with varied signs of wear. My socks and underwear were the same, black colored. I finished dressing. A pair of gray pants and a dark polo shirt. Though the seaside would undoubtedly be warm, I could change later.

Seaside. What did Seaside mean to me? It must have been something. Here I was, freshly disconnected, grasping for straws and what little I had to go on was Marta, who at the moment seemed to hate me, and my destination, Seaside. Both the name of the place and what it was.

My head hummed along. I supposed I could go into the SIM and that would cure my headache, at least while I was in there. Maybe if I went to a spa or yoga, that would relax me enough so that I felt better. Perhaps, it was deceptively simple, though, and I just needed to drink water, but I also needed to know things were okay with Marta. It wasn't enough that she was helping me, I wanted to know that she *wanted* to help me. I retraced my steps, thought about the things I said, how I acted, if I had done something especially mean. It seemed to me my lack of communication frustrated her. And anything with Star didn't help. Did she know about the Vegas thing? I could explain how I ended up alone with Star in a fitting room. She wanted my opinion on a dress. That didn't sound like a good explanation.

I thought about my companion in the dream, the only secret I seemed to have, as all the other secrets were kept from me. The second dream of its kind. I didn't want to say recurring, but there was a pattern starting. And who was that woman? It didn't seem like Marta or anyone I knew. She had dirty blond hair; Marta's was dark, curly and so beautiful, like her eyes. But the woman in the dream had special eyes too.

I thought about getting in touch with Marta, either in the SIM or a call, but decided to just give her space. And while she had space, I still wanted her to think about me in a more positive way. Listening to Dylan gave me an idea. I would make her a mix tape. A dozen or so songs from artists I liked. It was a thing people used to do. Mix tapes, so named when there used to be magnetic tapes, and after that compact discs. Artifacts of the past like me. Even music, in a way, was a thing from the past, but such a remarkable thing too.

That gave me some hope, so I moved on, leaving that solitary caretaker behind to tend to his ghost like retreat. The idea of the mix tape was to convey some sort of message, but not really, or not truly. That was for the person who listened to them to decide. Subtlety was an especially capricious art form. I picked a light Dylan song called "'Cept You," as the opener followed by Tom Waits and "Hope I Don't Fall in Love With You." That was a good start.

As I thought about the rest of the songs, I moved into my room with the SIM. The books. They were the most personal things I owned. For a moment, I thought about Seaside, being on the beach reading a book. That had been a thing. There used to be a whole genre of fiction called beach reads, but books now were relics, at least in the printed form. Siri had talked about "reading" the classics in the SIM, which was a quick way to experience a story. Audio books, too. That was another way.

I reached for *The Great Gatsby* but saw something else instead. An odd cover for a book, at least the visible spine, which looked wooden, and when I pulled it out, it was not a book but a vintage cigar box, the name *Punch* embossed on the cover.

Inside the box was a pair of small flashlights with lithium batteries, a skeleton key and old coin dated 1881 and inscribed *E Pluribus Unum* above a crowned woman. On the obverse, an eagle with outstretched arms, United States of America, In God We Trust. Wow, Marta would get a kick out of that. Here was my God inscribed on an ancient coin. The inside of the box had a slip of paper taped to the bottom with the word *seaside* written out. I recognized my own handwriting.

I packed my bags for the Seaside trip, including the cigar box. The slip of paper had the stationary from a hotel in Seaside called Hotel Piran, which I quickly booked. And just because it seemed quaint, I hauled out that Fitzgerald book to read just in case I happened to lounge on the beach, no lake, but an actual beach. And eventually everything made me think of Marta. I set about finishing her mix tape.

Most of my favorite songs seemed to be sad, so that kind of made it a challenge. I added "Dear Prudence" by the Beatles over "Happiness is a Warm Gun," then Leonard Cohen's "Hallelujah." No. Too much. I changed it to "I'm Your Man." Prince. "Nothing Compares 2 U" and then "Wish You Were Here" by Pink Floyd. I broke it up from there with an instrumental song from M. Ward called "Outro (AKA: I'm a Fool to Want You)." He was a more obscure artist, which was always a good addition to a proper mix tape, and even more so, that he still existed.

Songs just came to me. There was no rhyme or reason. "As Tears Go By" by the Rolling Stones was next, but I changed it out for "Angie." That was eight songs. Not necessarily my favorite songs. That would be a hard list to compose and would depend a lot on how I was feeling. And for the moment I was somewhere between two points of hopelessness.

U2 and "With or Without You." That was a good one to follow the Stones, nice build and drive. Then some Bowie to keep up the momentum. I picked "Heroes" and then "Common People" by Pulp. After that, I chose a real downer, and I don't know why. Probably the way I was feeling, sneaking back in, that lost caretaker wandering through the rooms again, finding things, little mementos left behind from various guests, some of whom he talked to, sharing some brief moment of humanity.

I didn't want to change the song. Jesus and Mary Chain's "Feeling Lucky." The sentiment was nice, but the music seemed sad and since I didn't want to end so downbeat, I added "Wishful Thinking" by Wilco, which was more hopeful, though still a tad sad but it seemed to connect lucky and wishful. Okay. wait. One more song. I wanted to end on a different note, with a real closer, something to really reach out to her and bring her back. "Into My Arms" by Nick Cave & The Bad Seeds. That seemed like a better close. Even the mention of God. Beginnings and endings could make the whole thing. Like a book, the middle just had to carry the weight for a while.

I sent the mix tape along with a short note, careful not to say sorry as I had used up the term:

Marta, You and only you in my thoughts. I hope to be seeing you soon. —David

I pictured Marta going into the SIM for a walk while listening to the songs. I thought a little about where she would go, even what she would wear, though all of that would depend on where she decided to go. If I remembered, then I would ask her. Maybe she would go to that same place we went. I should have done an Oasis song. Every mix tape had some misgivings, though when I looked up the band, I found they didn't exist, which was too bad because I really liked them.

Again, I thought of the songs, but it was too late. I had already sent them. I left little chance to second guess my selections. I had wanted a variety, a mix, but I also didn't want to overthink the whole thing. I had a tendency to do that.

I chose shorter songs, when some of my favorite songs were actually quite long. Naturally, there were artists I really liked that missed the cut, or in some cases, songs from artists that were in no way representative of their body of work.

Marta had said there would be time to listen to more

music, but yet the way she said it, made me think just the opposite. Or was it the other way around? Had I said there would be time and then she flashed me that strange look? Maybe there was no time, or not enough time. INXS. Yes. I tended to think in song lyrics. That was my normal brain functioning. I should have put that song in the mix.

The hyperloop station was not far, though when I left my building, I had no idea where it was, and yet I still found my way. Coffee sounded nice, but I told myself I would wait till Seaside for coffee, if for nothing else than something to look forward to. Maybe at Daetslim if I could find it.

I liked to imagine there was a weakness in the network, some secret capacitor that only needed to be destroyed and the whole system would falter, but that was hardly true. Any network, any system worth its mettle, had numerous redundancies. Marta and I couldn't fly our spaceship in some narrow passage with a target at the end, but if we could, if we could fly anywhere, then with Marta I would, but first I conceded that I needed to find her station, get to the place, that special place where she was.

However, even if there was a magic bullet to destroy the network, something would have to take its place. You can't overthrow the government without a viable plan. There was no going back to the world that once was. Maybe Marta's backup was the plan. The only advantage that I had, and maybe it was not an advantage, was that we were small in number, Marta and I, and thus nimble. That was the parable of David and Goliath. That's also the story of Dylan: the individual versus the whole of humankind, I thought.

I had read a lot about Dylan at one time in my life. In

a life full of obsessions, he was one of my early ones. Although, you could never be too sure of the sources. Just like the Shakespeare debates that were popular at one time. But did it matter? Here was a phenomenal body of work. Enjoy it. In Dylan's case, though, it was difficult to imagine this output was all from the same person, beginning with his initial foray and prominence in the folk scene, which he shunned to go electric, protest songs to hallucinations, then recluse, religion, gospel, radio rock and blues before returning to the old standards, which was the very music he rebelled against at the start, like it was all just one big circle.

As I walked, the people around me went about their day, surely they did not think as I did, about the system, the network, this whole interconnected grid. They just lived the life they knew, what they always knew. And that was something I could no longer just do. For once you've seen behind the curtain, once the veneer has been lifted and you see the guy pulling the strings, the magic disappears.

If a tree falls in a forest and there's no one there to hear it, does that tree really exist? Well, no tree falls in the forest. That's the thing, the network thing. And besides that, no one ever wandered into a forest when you could hike in the SIM. Besides, it was a better workout overall. At least, that was what the network would say since the whole thing would be based on perceived ability. A trio of people on the same "hike" would experience a different hike based on that, though it would seem like the same hike with the same sights and sounds.

Imagine never picking up a golf club, yet being able to step on a golf course and be somewhat competitive? That was the idea. The obverse, though, meant that the old adage of ten thousand hours of practice in order to be good at something no longer applied, if ever it did. *If it ever did.* That was a ruse too, as maybe so much was always smokescreen.

And that changed everything. And that was the trade-off, too. As the old saying used to go, you can't have your cake and eat it too. Because once you've eaten your cake, the cake is gone. Marta probably didn't know that one. No one knew of such idioms. They had virtually disappeared from language.

At the hyperloop station, I entered, conscious of my entry being scanned, my every movement tracked and surveilled, plotted on a point among the other points. And it was all so good and seemingly unobtrusive, that no one noticed. That was the beauty of chips and the smallest of sensors, this secret, hidden world. And yet, being at the station, about to get on a train like thing and shoot off somewhere, I felt all too visible and all too lost.

I entered my solitary pod, which was all glass, small yet comfortable, fitted with a plush chair and of course, the SIM. What else would one do for the trip to the Seaside? One hour and change, Marta had said.

I felt the initial motion, but after that initial jerkiness, everything smoothed out and I was lulled into lazy thoughts as the pod effortlessly glided. Marta had explained to me how she patched me into the network, and especially to the SIM, so that I was part and yet not part. That sounded familiar.

In the loading program, my various SIM logs appeared by day, by session, by subject, by whatever method I wished to know like they had all been examined and the metadata recorded. I could look at various Star entries, music, walks, sessions either solo or joined by others, which happened a lot for work and with Star too. The Marta session did not appear. That was interesting, but not unexpected. It happened off the record. Or did it? I glanced through a recent entry and saw that it was Marta and I in the park labeled as something else, not keyworded properly.

I chose the mode where I simply watched, like it was a movie, and I could skip ahead if I wanted or rewind, even pause. There we were in the park, on the path among the trees and the flowers, the rose bushes, even the butterflies that I had not noticed.

And yet none of this was real. We experienced things, bought all this stuff, and yet, what we really bought were representations. I thought again of the horror of seeing the world, what the real world had been like, but what was really real? Was that even real? How could you argue with what you see as being anything other than real?

"It's real and not real," Marta said as we stood in the park, seemingly reading my thoughts. "But has it ever occurred to you that maybe that's not any different than what our own eyes used to show, a representation of a world. Even if you stop and take a picture of it, it was never the same, never could be the same thing visible by the eye. Why was that?"

"Because the eye, as developed, was truly amazing."

"As developed. Interesting choice of words. As developed," she mused, repeated. "Sometimes I think that maybe, this new paradigm, is still kind of like the old but just a more advanced version. So seeing the world without the filter, as we call it, would be like it must have been to be blind in the old days."

"What it means to be a human has always been changing," I said, more or less in agreement. "Technology has a way of accelerating some of those changes."

"Well, at first, it is just subtle things. By making the world quantifiable, we change the world and the way we fit into it. Instead of just being in the process of becoming, being is about numbers, codes, boxes to check. Being is about order. Suddenly there is a massive amount of data to analyze and from that analysis, solutions can be seen. And just because something is better in terms of it being more quantifiable, that does not make it better. But the network does think it can make us into better humans."

"Ah," I said, "the story of Procrustes."

She looked at me blankly, so I briefly explained the cruelties Procrustes imposed on his fellow travelers, feeding them a sumptuous meal before inviting them to a special bed, which they were forced to fit into by removing limbs and other extremities, though ultimately, his own fate was met the same way.

"Another metaphor," Marta said. "You and your stories. From the Greeks? I get it, forcing us to be a certain way, which is like the network, I suppose, making us into better humans."

"Yes, the Greeks," I said, watching as I looked far off into the distance at a building.

"Your quantity vs quality," she said. "Is what I look at as analog versus digital."

"What did you mean?" I asked. "I don't understand."

"Well, the world used to be analog. That's the human world. Full of an infinite number of possibilities. But a digital world, the world we live in now by nature is finite, defined. To me, that's where the quantity arises in being able to define things, create order whether needed or not."

"And so we get solutions to problems we didn't even know existed because we only look at one thing. In a world of quantity, we get more because more is better. Because it is measurable. What does that all mean? We think we can answer all the questions, but we cannot," I said in finishing what she had started.

"That's the beauty of it, I suppose," she said, "that we don't even know of our possibilities as limited. Subtleties over time became huge. No one knows how we used to be able to see the world and we ate real food and we interacted with people in a more real way.

"Things always evolve. Nothing abides. And you are right. Especially food. One could argue that for some time, the realness of the food we ate diminished. It was necessary. Food production could never have fed the planet. We needed a very long time ago to mess with crop yields."

"Now who is defending the network?" she asked as she bent down to smell a rose so named Liverpool Remembers.

"I am, on some level," I said, resigned to the point. "But we've always had some kind of network. It just gives me fits. I love and hate it."

"But it is maybe too good of a thing. Because the network makes assumptions, makes things fit into the box, your Procrustean box, rounds numbers, rejects what is not quantifiable so that something gets quantified and calculated that maybe shouldn't. Like you said. Meanwhile, us humans become less capable, less up to the challenge of truly solving any real problem should be put into that position. And we may never be in that position again anyway."

I watched myself, feeling like one of those dreams in third person, as I stood there with Marta, looking intently at her as she spoke. I also studied my movements and mannerisms, in awe at how surreal the experience was to actually re-live a conversation rather than the remembrance of it. And then I focused on her eyes, her lovely eyes right after she made the point about the ability of humans.

"Some might say that the eyes are windows to the soul, but I think more and more, they are windows to the brain," she said to me, knowing that I gazed deep into her eyes.

"Or at least they were," I said.

"Maybe they still are. Or they still can be. When all of this started, there was a lot of talk about the self, how the self would respond. And we looked at the self back then in three ways: as the actual self; the self you thought others wanted you to be, like society, family, or other influences; and then the idealized self, what we might think of as hopes and dreams."

I paused the SIM, made it freeze on Marta in her yellow dress, that little bit of a smile having just drifted away as she looked at me. In the background was that building, that old, eerie and musty place that Marta said felt like death. I moved the frames ahead until I caught a glimpse of the figure in the window, a sad distinct face of a woman, not so much like a ghost for she seemed real enough. And then she was gone and I felt heavy and uneasy and I didn't want to think about her anymore.

I needed something simpler, so I glanced over a few

Star sessions and used one of them, a walk along the canal, as a starting point. I made no modifications, allowing the network to do as it was inclined to do. Afterall, it knew me better than I knew myself. And who was I really, but the summation of my SIM?

"Know thyself," I found myself saying as the momentary darkness became light and I found myself walking under a bridge along a waterway, trees interspersed on the border among various shrubbery, some flowering. I moved close, felt the leaves in my fingers before drawing them close enough to smell their sweet, wondrous fragrance.

On the water, a few pleasure boats cruised on by. People stood on the bow, some in the rear. A black dog on one of them playfully barked at seagulls. I couldn't be sure, but I didn't remember ever being on a boat. And suddenly, I wanted to be on a boat. Maybe that was something we could do, Marta and I. If there was still such a thing. If nothing else, then in the SIM I could always pretend.

Oh, Marta, hopefully listening to my songs. Was I foolish to have done that sort of thing? It felt a bit childish, like I was a teenager and she was some girl I liked but was too afraid to say anything to her. I didn't believe in fate, yet I found myself thinking, if it happens then it happens, then it must be so.

I made a modification to the program. More dogs. Suddenly a man appeared walking a pair of terriers, one black and the other white, but both well-behaved and not stubbornly pulling to one side or the other to sniff something out.

A woman jogged by in spandex, then a shirtless man, slightly taller and with a little bit better form, moved by me with a retriever, tongue happily out. Both of them smiled, one after the other. And then, there was Star, walking along in a blue summer dress with white flowers filled out by her shapely figure. Our eyes met, and she too smiled, hurrying her pace as I slowed mine down.

As she neared me, I felt a bit nervous, though I shouldn't have been nervous at all. There was no reason to be so, yet I was. My hands even felt clammy. I hoped she didn't want to hold my hand, which was ridiculous to think about.

"Hi, David," she exclaimed when she was upon me, pressing her body against mine and embracing me warmly, holding on for just that extra second or two so I could feel the entire sensation of her body against mine.

Hi," I said as we separated. "It's been a long time."

"Too long of a time," she said. "You've been quite the stranger lately. Busy at work, I am so sure you'll say. Won't you?"

"But that's all true."

"Of course," she pooh-poohed. "There is always so much going on up in that top floor office where you just sit all day and look at screens. Time, of course, to step out a few times a day for coffee, but no time to meet up with me. Seems a bit suspicious."

I felt slightly guilty, like I had been caught, which was now a recurring feeling for me, that thing that kept happening, with Marta and now Star, like everyone was on to me and I was the clueless one, oblivious to the obvious.

"I'm sorry. I wanted to meet up with you and I also didn't, and in the end it was the latter sentiment that won out."

"Fair enough," Star said, bemused, then winked at me like it was not possible to deny her and it was a ploy, a playful game we played. "No time like the present."

No time like the present. That's what Marta had said. I know, nothing that original, yet Marta had said that very same thing. Was that just a coincidence? Perhaps that was the network's way of showing it was on to me. That feeling returned and resonated, that I had been had, taken for a ride for a fabulous ruse.

Star, though, for her part, kept on with the game. She just smiled, that luscious smile, her full lips slightly parted, her posture tilted for the maximum effect as she ran her hands through her blonde hair.

"Indeed. The moment is now. There's a little café ahead. Let's go get a drink."

"I was hoping you would say that," she said, though a bit too excitedly I thought.

But then, you weren't supposed to think of any of that. You were supposed to just go with the flow, for all things flow. Nothing abides. And so, this was my endless torture? Somehow it was okay. Apparently the network thought I operated well with a little doom and gloom, a precariousness above melancholy, however slightly, as like Sisyphus I pushed my boulder up the hill like it was some gift to Star she would never receive, seemingly content to let it fall back down so I could do it all again, pretending as if this time it might be different.

There was a little café with chairs and tables, some with umbrellas, astride the pathway, overlooking the water. A tall, impeccably dressed waiter in the classic black and white combo, quickly strode over to us as we sat down, as if his only purpose was to serve us, though there were a few others seated. Not many. And none close. It was my SIM though.

I ordered a cappuccino. Star ordered some complicated coffee like drink that I lost track of with its myriad iterations, from temperature to flavor. I was sure it was some exotic thing. I was sure I would never order anything like that.

I waited and thought about what to say. And that was the worst thing when things didn't just occur to you, when you had to think of things to say. At best, the conversation was forced, intentional.

"What do you remember about childhood?" I asked Star.

"What are you, my guidance counselor?" she playfully responded. "Is that really what you want to talk about?"

And yes, therapists still existed, even in the network age, people still liked talking about themselves to someone. If anything, they were more common. Such trained professionals often helped create specialized SIMs as a form of treatment. That was a job that no one would have imagined a hundred years ago. Custom SIM environment designer.

"Oh," Star said as she considered the thought, seeing I was serious, for just a second or two. "The usual things, the good things, all the good things, like summer days and swimming by the lake, popsicles, how I love popsicles and riding horses too."

"You rode horses?" I exclaimed, taken aback.

"Yeah. I used to ride horses when I was a little girl. Little ponies. They were sweet. I called them my little ponies. I made a whole game out of them."

"Hmm. I didn't know that. And I thought I knew a lot

about you."

"Well, David, this may surprise you, but you don't know everything. There are still parts of me that are a mystery. I am a lot deeper than you think. Besides, you never asked me either. It's not something I would hide."

"Yeah," I agreed, not suspecting Star would hide anything at all. Not that I really believed the thing about the ponies.

The waiter dropped off our drinks. We thanked him for his prompt service. He bowed ceremoniously and then skittered off. I looked back to Star. She blew on her drink, pursing her lips to cool it down.

"Family vacations. I know that seems so strange. Road trips too. I remember being a little girl and slowly changing into a woman, too slowly for me. I wished and wished it would happen sooner. Seems silly now. Everything worked out fine."

Star. Not one for modesty. Of course, that would be something Star would say, any little thing, however small, to draw attention to herself, to her body and its endowments. And this was the SIM too. How many SIM sessions were purely sexual? And even the ones that were not overtly so, they still had that element, whether they were the computer-generated version or the simulated version of the real thing, a simulacrum.

I wondered why I thought of that word. Before it was stimulation, now simulacrum, a representation of a thing, in this case, of Star. The actual likeness was uncanny. There was virtually no distinction between them. Physically, emotionally, right down to that voice of hers that could always be heard in a crowd. Much like Lando.

Certainly this encounter would be different if Star was

playing herself and not the network playing her, and yet, I couldn't escape the fact that the network too also played the real Star because it was so much a part of our existence and it knew enough about everyone to create the perfect replica.

I couldn't help thinking too, that the anonymous network was watching all of this, creating it and cataloging it for the archive, for its endless stream of information. And maybe too, Marta was watching this as she listened to the tape I made. Or monitoring it. Normal people, I thought, did not consider such things. They had no reason for such paranoia.

The truth was probably that there was too much information all of the time, at every moment of life, so the network sifted through it and only made connections as needed, as necessary. A lot of it was meaningless data, more quantity than quality. Maybe that's why no one cared about privacy. It was not like you could spy on a fellow citizen. Or could you? Not likely. Except at the top. Even in the so-called equal societies, things were different at the top. Humans, like machines, had ingrained biases, though in the machines case, it wasn't their fault. They were programmed like that.

"I'm happy with the way I developed," Star continued on that thread.

I realized she was trying to be provocative, but when I didn't respond, she changed. That was the beauty of the SIM. The ability to adapt, to try a new tact. I sipped on my cappuccino, my mind wandered, marveled at the simple, yet completely civilized beauty in the world, the crystalline blue of the water, the sunlight sparkling and the colors of the leaves, the flowers, the people that passed so carelessly by.

"It's a beautiful day, isn't it?" she stated. "What's wrong?"

"Nothing. I am just thinking."

"Well, I can see that. That would be all of those moments of silence layering on another, building the impenetrable."

That struck me as a very un-Star like thing to say, that expression, that use of words. But they suited me, did they not? They soothed me, such opaque language mixed among metaphor, almost like I was speaking to myself, but that other self was Star.

"It's just strange to me that we used to spend a lot of time together. That's all. We are not so much alike."

"Maybe not in some ways, but in others we are. And we could spend more time together if you wanted," she said, lighting up, beaming and boasting too in a not at all bashful way as the sunlight reflected off of her hair, the sparkle of her diamond like necklace, shimmery yet sedate, relaxed as she breathed.

"I know you are still attracted to me," she continued.

"It's complicated," I said softly, barely audible, borrowing a phrase, but she heard it anyway because this was the SIM world, and everything said was meant to be heard, especially in solo mode. And I took another drink of my cappuccino, though all that was left was foam, and even then, hardly any of it.

"Ah, but it is so simple," she implored, ever so confident in every way that it was and begging me to agree. "Even if you've met someone else. I don't mind. I am willing to share. Or compete, if that is how you want it to be. I know I'll win."

And for Star, that much was true. For her, it would be a competition, though on a level she would not comprehend because it would be different criteria than what she was used to. In a world where virtually anything was within the realm of possibility, there were other kinds of limits, weren't there?

Star was certainly a representative of an ideal, a paragon to the female form, a *ne plus ultra*, and yet that was also the thing that bothered me. When something became too perfect, it ceased to embody perfection, and in a way, rendered itself to a certain kind of grotesqueness

By that, I didn't mean to say Star was ugly or anything close to that. I watched as she shifted her body, parted her lips, posed, and preened in an invisible parade for the passersby. Far from it. There was just something when it was all too much. Why didn't I see it before? Maybe I just liked the *idea* of Star.

"Such lovely boats," I said as I looked at the water. Maybe it was what you might call a yacht. Sleek in its design, multiple levels, wood paneling. Extravagantly elegant. "I've always wanted a boat. Yet not really. I've liked the idea of having a boat available, of just being on the water."

Star twisted her body around to get a better look at the boat. A couple, not unlike us, a man and a woman, were onboard. The woman had on shorts and a bikini top. She seemed to be looking our way. Maybe, at that moment, she longed to be ashore, sipping a coffee, but instead she was at sea.

"We could go for a boat ride if you like. What fun it would be! I've loved to get some sun. I've even brought along a bikini I could change into."

Star fished around in her purse as if I didn't believe her. And of course she did. It was true. She showed me the black stringy bits, for all was true and possible and attainable within the SIM. If this was a music SIM, then I would get to meet the band, get invited backstage and find some real connection with the musicians. Because I was special, because I was, oh, I don't know. It was too much. That's what it was. I wasn't special. If I was so special, then Marta would be here, wouldn't she, because she would see all that specialness. And if I was special, then I wouldn't be in a SIM with Star.

"I'm not sure I have time for a boat trip."

"Oh, come on, that's nonsense. It doesn't have to be long. Besides, there's always time."

Time enough for a million decisions and revisions, I thought, time enough for you and time enough for me. But it was all an illusion, this sense of time. Wasn't it? And I swear, the SIM was making Star more attractive by the moment, but I didn't know how. A minute ago, I was telling myself she wasn't all that, that I was over her, but now something had changed. Was that all there was to her, the way she looked? Maybe to the network that was all that mattered, how everyone looked and not what it was, or what we were. But what exactly were we? Mere bits of data, stretched and strained, made to be or not to be.

The essence of a thing, its soul, could not so easily be discerned. And this sentiment was nothing new. The world had been like this for a long time, measuring out such things as appearance and wealth, its quantity, the have and have nots ever since the dawn of the media age.

Once, a long time ago, a person's voice might have meant something. Or the way they wrote. Or their ideas.

All of this was just my useless quality vs quantity debate. I could see it in everything. It was the lens I used to look the world over. If there were no deformities of note, if people looked all so very similar aside from differences in skin color, height, then did that mean Star was quality? I was confusing myself now. The answer was no. No. Emphatically, no.

I could feel the pull of the boat. I didn't have to imagine Star in her bikini, because suddenly she would just be there, aboard the boat, sauntering across the deck. I had to have a good reason why she was not quality, and quick, why she represented quantity on my interpretive scale because my mind was wandering again.

We were there in the boat. Star stood before me, sipping champagne, offering more coverage than her tiny bikini top in that simple gesture, then her arms were back by her side. She looked at me hopefully, resplendent with effervescent charm. The champagne in my glass sparkled, bubbled, effused the moment. Was there a minimum amount of covering that constituted a bikini top to begin with? I looked away. Star was nothing. I didn't want to look back at her. Star was everything.

Once, long ago, I had been transfixed by her, that much was true, cast upon her spell, but something broke and now nothing would be the same. Looking at Star, I thought of Marta, how different they were. And the thing about Marta was that special thing she had remained invisible, in hiding, and that secret was hers and hers alone, was sacred. And she had let me in on that sub rosa, just a little bit of that mystery and now I wanted more, for I recognized in her a secrecy I shared and not silence.

My SIM warned me of the looming destination point, the Seaside. I left Star, standing in the boat by the harbor, scantily clad and dreamy, returning to the surroundings of my pod, which seemed sterile in comparison and was a jarring return. A world outside passed by, but at such a speed that was not clear enough to focus, though the world was slowing down and in the distance I glimpsed the station, knowing it was not the station I wanted at all, but it was nonetheless the station I would take the next step on, a pathway, a simple way forward. A rolling stone gathers no moss. This was Seaside.

PART THREE

The SIM was how we passed time. There was no time for idle thoughts, yet idle thoughts were what I craved, and so I let my mind wander for the few moments that remained. Somehow, all of this worked. We built it, became inextricably linked to it and now all that was left was maintenance. I had the feeling nothing would ever be more advanced than this moment, quite simply because we had reached the peak of our interest and desire for anything more. I don't know why I thought that. Thoughts came and went as I looked out to where I was, and only some of them made sense.

How neatly we had gone about, removed the inefficiencies of the world from our daily lives. Was it even possible to be bored? I didn't see a lot of people sitting around thinking much. People always seemed to be engaged with something, a device, another person, just something other than being alone as I was now. It was constant, entertainment on demand.

I thought of Star, lounging on the boat. Like a green screen. A glimpse of the ruined world flashed before me. I saw Star lounging in a wasteland, the sun burned out and smoky, collapsed buildings, decay and yet, a golden skinned goddess amidst it all, gleaming in the disintegration, a long drink of perfection among the starkness. I saw her again, for just a moment, as a skeleton. It could have been anyone though, couldn't it?

How long would all of this infrastructure last? Long enough. As long as it could. That was possible. The old space missions from the late twentieth century relied on technology decades old to get to the moon. It took a long time to plan those epic explorations, so everything built needed to last. Of course, the whole moon thing was a hoax. There was that.

But nothing was written for certain. Not the future. Not even the past, apparently. It was complacency. We had constructed too good of a world, though a lot was destroyed in the process. But nothing was written. No matter how the network calculated such things, the results were not inevitable.

Suddenly the brightness of Seaside emerged, the sun sparkling off the water, shooting diamonds of light, glistening so that there was a sheen to everything, even the boardwalk. I felt at once that I had seen this place before and various memories stirred, a mishmash of sights and sounds, sidewalk cafes and curio shops, beach beauties and their muscled admirers, cool ice cream treats and cotton candy. There was a ferris wheel and merry go-round music played, horses danced and bobbed, throngs of people wandered everywhere, children shrieked and ran towards roadside attractions, carnival games, and whatever else caught their fancy.

This was childhood as retold like a scene from a movie, where I would win prizes, huge stuffed toys, but I never did. I had asked Marta what she remembered, but she was cagey in her response, saying something like the way we framed things as a kid was way different than an adult, and while that was true, it seemed to me, on some level, childhood had a lot to do with the development of our brains. It made me wonder what the modern-day kids were like, what they would be like. But that was a little too simplistic. This change had been happening all along as each ensuing generation was closer and closer to technology, more exposed to it, such that, for some this technology became a part of their life, like living and breathing so that was all they knew, a world with all of these things. It was wonderfully seamless.

This was well before everyone was implanted with a chip at birth. Nothing happens overnight. Nothing except the sun rises anew. Maybe that doesn't even happen anymore. So truly, perhaps, nothing happens overnight at all. But a long time ago, things were different. Children grew up in an environment full of imagination, of games to be made up and played, a whole world outside, and that was the world of my Seaside, this carnival-like amusement park of a place.

My pod docked, gliding into place with a smoothness that defied the task, then the gull wing doors opened. Though I smelt the sea, I felt gloomy as I departed, alone in a passageway, no other people there, no voices or the controlled chaos of crowds, just the silence save for any sound I created. And instead of being a caretaker, I now saw that ever-invisible station agent reigning over a desolate and abandoned but ever so clean realm.

Saw was a strange word. The station agent, not real, not even there, greeted me with a perfunctory grin, asked how my trip was and sent me along with a customary welcome. He surveyed his station with a gaze that knew at once all of the regulars and all the transients. He knew who I was, even if I didn't.

I stepped out and walked along the passageway with my bag, the white walls unscathed, neither marked nor marred as if no one had ever passed this way, but I knew that wasn't true. That was just how it appeared. I glanced back at my pod as its engine came to life and it whisked away, hoping for a moment that I would catch a glimpse of the real station agent, that if we waited there long enough, then I would see him, see him and others, new arrivals. But there was no we, was there?

The good sea, though, as savior, nestled close, nudged against me like a loyal dog as I walked down the steps to the street, pushing me so that if I stretched closer, close to the sandy expanse of shoreline, I was close to a paradise I could almost touch, but still was none closer and so far from a station called Marta.

I followed along, a sheer glance away from sun worshippers with sultry bodies to the sidewalk gawkers and gazers, gelato holders, to the point, first the marina and beyond that the hotel. If I could see farther, then I too would have seen the next jut and the skeletal remains of the lighthouse, a beacon for its time, for the lost ships sailing on the high seas. But I could not see that far. I saw other buildings, hotels and inns and restaurants, coffee shops and boutiques, mostly white stoned structures with reddish roofs, renditions of Venetian Gothic Architecture.

Gone was the silence of the imaginary station agent, on the platform upon exiting my pod. Here was the sudden noise, the voices, the sounds of waves and even seagulls squawking. I didn't remember any birds in the city. Maybe they snuck in here, flew under the radar, under the cover of the great dome that seemed to cover all. Or maybe they were designed to be part and parcel for the picturesque town on the sea. This was not the Seaside I remembered.

At the Hotel Piran, I took a room with a view, overlooking the boardwalk and the area just beyond that offered beach access next to a small marina. I could gaze down a long stretch of the boardwalk. It reminded me back home, of the canal where I liked to walk, but it too was different. There was no beach there and the people here seemed different, more relaxed, less inclined to hurry.

Downstairs, I set about to get a cappuccino. And from there, move along to see the Twins, Evers and Evey. With everything I had heard about them, I wasn't sure what to expect. My contact with them, although somewhat limited, never gave anything away.

"Hmm, Anna thinks the gentleman wishes for something. Anna can sense he has a real need," the woman, presumably Anna, said in greeting me at the counter where she stood. At night, this would double as the bar, but it was mid-day at best.

"Cappuccino," I said, taken a little aback by her directness.

"And for your lovely girl?" she asked, raised her dark eyebrows just so. "What would she like?"

As there was no one with me, I paused for a moment, had that kind of déjà vu sensation, and seeing my deliberation, Anna too paused to study me. She did look familiar to me, in both words and action, her very presence too was striking.

"Ah, perhaps Anna has mistaken you for someone else," she said as he handed me a small cup and saucer. "And you have no one?"

"Do I know you?" I said. "I feel like we've met."

"In the Seaside, yes?" she queried. "Perhaps you've seen me before here or is it now you who has been mistaken?"

"In a dream," I found myself saying as I remembered the burger joint I stopped at. And I was with someone then, somewhere, who I both knew and didn't know, but the woman at the counter was right here, right now.

"Anna in your dreams," she mulled over it. "That's possible. I am popular, yes?"

"Or someone that looked a lot like you," I clarified. "But her name was Anna too."

This news seemed to thrill her. A giddiness ensued as she moved unsteadily then recovered. I simply smiled and stepped back to enjoy my delicious cappuccino. Something about the proximity of water, the light breeze, the flow of people and hum of leisure activity made everything better. The sunshine too, it was somehow different here.

"Hmm, I am Anna One," she jokingly said, so I turned my attention back to her, and maybe it was my expression, because her tone became serious. "I sense something is wrong. Is it your cappuccino?"

"I'm okay," I said. "It's just fine."

"Now I know something is wrong. Let Anna guess. Oh, it is the girl? Something happened between you and the girl."

"It's nothing," I said, but I couldn't hide so well. I was not a good liar. Like all skills. They needed to be mastered, but that was not one I ever wanted to be good at. And I almost felt like she knew something. Maybe Marta was right. I was too easy to read.

"Anna can show you nothing if you like. This is not

nothing. I can see it in your eyes. Let Anna help."

"I'm okay," I said again.

"Hmm. What's your name?"

"David."

"Meet me here, David, at three o'clock when I am off. Anna will help you. Yes, she will."

She seemed serious about it and convinced. I didn't know what to think or how she could even help me. Maybe she thought I was lonely and she could help me in that way, as a companion. I wasn't going to lie to myself and say she wasn't attractive because she certainly was in a coquettish yet innocent way. Anyone would have been attracted to her, her full lips, her little accent that seemed Eastern European, but I wasn't into her that way, and I didn't want to be.

I finished my coffee and set it on the counter. She promptly took away the dish and busied herself with other things, half-talking to herself, little mutterings that I couldn't make out and didn't want to, and yet she fascinated me.

"Don't forget," she called out after me as I left. "Anna will track you down."

I thought about that as I went back up to my room. In my absence, a trunk had been dropped off. Inside were clothes and other mementos, things I had left last time I stayed at the hotel so many years ago. My clothes were invariably representations of what I normally wore, only more suited to a beach town. Linen pants, light shirts. Not much color.

There was a notebook on my desk. A book. *The Great Gatsby*. That was funny, since I already packed a copy with me, although this one had a different cover. Instead of the eyes, there was a cocktail glass. I picked it up and thumbed through it, looked at my notebook, and read some passages—lines that meant nothing to me, even occurred to me as foreign. Maybe in time I would understand from whence they came because they didn't seem like me.

So enough with the relics
Good riddance to the specimens
It's rough being among the derelicts
Lost and alone with no friends
The bitter dance takes hold
Envelopes me with cold
I lose a step in the song
And I know it's wrong

I skimmed some more pages, coming across stories, little things I had written about the myths of the Amazons, Persephone, Theseus, Pygmalion and others. No wonder I remembered such things. I came upon a section full of various symbols and their meanings. What did these things mean to me, I wondered as I read them. Curiously, a few were set off from the rest.

- Flower of life is said to contain vital secrets about the universe and all living things. The first known reference was said to be on the alabaster steps of the palace of King Ashurbanipal, 645 BC.
- The word *labyrinth* comes from the Greek *labrys* meaning "double-edged axe." Symbol of the long path towards communion with God.
- Caduceus, a short rod with two serpents coiled around it, the messenger.
- Ouroboros, serpent eating its own tail.
- The Gorgon, Medusa. Sisters.
- Anubis, Egyptian god of dead; depicted as stylized

jackal head.

I set the notebook down and moved to the juliet balcony, stepping out to get a view of the water, the people on the beach, glancing to those who walked by, looking for Marta, if by chance I could bring her into existence by thoughts alone. Alas, I couldn't.

Outside the hotel, I glanced once more to the beach, slightly envious of the bodies there, the leisure, the tanned skin, so much darker than mine, not that such a thing mattered anymore, but at one time, it was a big deal, this whole talk of race and the color of your skin. Now it was just a feature of one's appearance, signifying nothing more than that.

Race, though, had always been a human construct, a way to categorize people. At its best, implying some sort of shared physical and genetic traits, while at its worst a form of discrimination. In the end, biology won as there were more genetic variations within a so-called race than between them. In other words, the people of the world comprised a single species, that is humans or *homo sapiens*, members of opposite sex who could mate and produce offspring. Distinctions beyond that were not important except the ones not discernible by the human eye. The network age had shown that skin color was but an arbitrary grouping.

That older world, I considered, was inevitably constructed by a similar network that grew obsolete over time, much like the current one would prove, although, I am sure we all thought it would last forever. But we never learned. This world, that world, while different, were still the same. The so-called perfection was anything but that.

As I walked to see the Twins on that dirt road, the

sounds and swells of the great sea came to me and had a way of making everything pleasant. I turned to the surf, saw a small wave, then another, form and reform, endlessly in some cycle that I would not necessarily understand. Except that life had always been a repeating cycle, even before all of this.

Perhaps the air was warmer here. I had seen hillsides like this, mighty, jutting rocks and harsh cliffs, sparse vegetation disguised as bits of greenery, violent yet inviting, depending on the angle, beautiful or desperate. This kind of landscape was everywhere, had been everywhere, was repeated in some surely patented pattern all across the known world. Or what used to be the known world.

The Twins, Evey and Evers, lived in a nondescript two story structure that could have been an electrical outpost or some storage center, but like other buildings, had the dirty white stone walls and the red-tiled roof because all materials were local.

Inside, I pictured a spartan-like place, and I was not wrong in its simplicity: the fireplace, stove, the desks and the bunk bed against the far wall. Other than that, a long wooden table was oddly placed in the center of the room, on which scatterings of paper seemed to depict various drawings. I couldn't tell what at first glance. Schematics of some kind? Perhaps. They certainly were not recipes or romantic poetry.

In a world predominantly young and youthful, Evey and Evers also stood out because they were so much older than the rest of us. I was struck that maybe Evey and Evers were the last of the people who knew how to fix things, who knew how systems actually worked. I certainly couldn't pretend my understanding was anything more than running a diagnostics and clicking Okay to repair or reset or reboot if something went really wrong.

Out on the fringes, it certainly should have occurred to me that they fixed things, but I never thought why. It was just what they did. And who they were, was a bit of a mystery. They eyed me with suspicion as they stood in the doorway, tall and angular and a bit androgynous.

We referred to them as the Twins, but were they really? Brother and sister, some said but that made no sense unless they were among the gods. Then anything was possible. But so was anything here.

They let me in. One of them tidied up the table, drawing all of the papers into a neat pile, while the other awkwardly watched, not sure if I should be offered a chair or not. Eventually I was. And then some coffee too, though the heat would have suggested something colder. The coffee was black. No cream or sugar offered.

"We make it strong," Evers said.

Evey echoed, "We like it strong."

"And so we make it strong," Evers repeated.

We sat in near silence, sipping hot, black coffee, soundless except for the drinking sound then the mug set upon the table. This was repeated as we looked at each other, wondering who would begin, but I got the feeling they didn't care to start and were content to remain in stalemate forever.

"I'm David, by the way, if you don't know."

"Evers and Evey."

All stuff we knew, but at least something was said. There would be no small talk and that was fine by me. I continued to study them as they studied me. We had communicated before and sometimes via the vid screen, but something about that process was less real than this moment. Plus, I couldn't even be sure they were the same people on the vid screen. I don't know why I thought that.

That was the thing, these degrees of reality, like the SIM, I supposed. All of our life tended to blend into one almost interchangeable thing, so that moments were less distinguishable, and yet sitting in this room with them was like nothing I had ever experienced. Maybe it was all in my head and without the help of the network, I simply wasn't as capable.

When I looked around the room, I swear new things had appeared since my first reckoning. The black coffee was really, *really* strong and still quite hot, almost burning, though it should have cooled some by now. I focused on an old rotary phone, an object way before my time that I never believed really existed and was just something from the old films. It was black and dusty. In fact, there were more than a few of them and there were lots of clocks, too, the kind you wound up. Why hadn't I noticed the ticking sounds I now heard? They were now everywhere as if suddenly brought to life.

Evey and Evers were no longer sitting. They were fiddling with something, working in unison, keenly aware of my presence, and yet, at the same time disinterested to the point that maybe I didn't exist. What they were working on, I didn't know. A machine of some kind, but that explained little. They added lubricant, then slowly turned some wheels, sparking a blue current that seemed to glow like a candle.

Evey and Evers, siblings, sister and brother, although they looked uncannily alike, as if they *were* twins. Similar builds too, that tall, lanky, ruggedness. If there ever was a theory that man and woman were originally connected, as Plato said, then surely they were the living embodiment.

They seemed to communicate with each other by mere glances, by gestures and mild gesticulations. If one started the sentence, then the other could surely finish it, if he or she wanted, or else they would let it linger. I finally spoke and afterwards, I wondered if I had spoken because it took so long to elicit a response.

"What's out there?" Evers repeated my question. And he gazed right through me, to some point, not fixed, but not ever varying, yet still indeterminate. Evey echoed the same phrase, but lower and lighter in such a way I was scarcely aware she spoke or if it was merely the ticking of the clocks tricking me in my thoughts with its sing song tock.

They lived on a border wall, maybe even the very separation of what we all knew and what we no longer knew. Every day they walked into the seaside paradise, and what a sight they were, I surmised, imagining if I saw them while seated at an outdoor café. One after another, as if following, yet not at all like they were following as they traversed those same steps, eyes fixed to the distance, seeing everything and yet, seeing nothing, slowly making their way to the lighthouse.

Some speculated privately that they were in fact, robots, or alternates as they were often called. There was no way of knowing for sure. Not without testing. Surely, there were alternates among us. That was the grand speculation. No one, of course, suggested that we were alternates too, in a way, altered forever, inextricably no longer human.

"The sensors are old," Evey said

"We used to go out and repair them," Evers added.

"But at some point," Evey continued, "We stopped because they always reported the same thing."

"You see, they always reported the same thing." Evers said. "Even after we fixed them."

"When was the last time they were repaired?" I asked.

"A decade"

"A decade, perhaps."

In a way it was two against one with Evey and Evers. And at the moment, I wasn't feeling clever enough. They didn't trust me, and I didn't trust them. We all knew that. As for common ground, that was something I didn't know.

I don't know why this troubled me so, but it did. Surely if I was properly connected to the network, I would not press the point. I would simply be here, talking to Evey and Evers as part of a promised inspection that was years, decades in the making, and I would acknowledge that everything was okay. But nothing was okay.

I wanted to ask them about Emrik, but instead I watched as they worked, sipped on my coffee and considered my next move. They looked like they belonged in another time with their old faded dungarees and flannel, and while the temperature remained mostly warm, too warm for their working class fashion, they likely never changed into anything else.

I should probably just have left. I had pictured such grand things, some sort of keys to the kingdom kind of moment with them, but alas, there was nothing like that. I had made too much of the moment, hoped for something that wasn't ever going to be there.

"Did anyone else ever ask you about the readings?"

Self-doubt crept in, nearly startling me. And I couldn't tell anyone why, but at that moment, I felt so alone, again like the joke was all on me, that even off in the distance wherever she was, Marta was laughing at me too. And most of all, the network. I half expected to feel its claws upon me, hear its drones coming to get me. Thankfully, there was nothing like that, but I still felt Marta smirking. That hurt.

And I hated feeling that sort of dig, that I could handle the rest of the world, the network so to speak, being in on it, because they were ultimately, but not Marta. Please, not her. In the old days, one would have prayed to God, even if you didn't believe in God. There was that whole sense of precarious faith, only when you needed it, like so much in a throw-away society. No one believed in God anymore. God was just a concept from long ago by which we measured our pain. At least, that was what John Lennon said. And his band was once bigger than Jesus.

"The sensors are broken," I said, but I really meant everything was broken, no matter how much it all looked together, how confident the presentation seemed, it was still all a front.

They both looked blankly at me, right through me, like they were merely talking to themselves, which was fine. I felt a little distant too as my mind drifted to other things. I reached into my pocket, like I was searching for my keys and I was going to drive away from this place forever, when I felt that coin. I fished it out and set it on the table.

"Morgan Silver Dollar," Evers said, noticing immediately. Then he examined the coin and added. "Carson City, low mintage, very rare. Two hundred ninety-six thousand minted and few, if any, remain. Very valuable."

To whom I wondered. He was clearly impressed. Evey had stopped what she was doing and even smiled. This was their language. Old stuff. Older ways. Evers opened a cigar box full of coins and showed them to me. Now I was getting somewhere. Valuable at one time, but now not worth anything.

After what seemed like a long time, I excused myself from the Twins and their coin collection, pleased I had made some inroads, not wanting to push my luck. Outside, the air was warm and the sun hot, beating down on me in a way that I wasn't used to.

I walked briskly past the shops, the cafés where people sat and talked and watched the world go by. The boardwalk was not crowded, but there were groups of people here and there, some with ice cream or gelato, others with shopping bags. I passed by one section of beach where glorious bodies stretched out on towels in the sand. Very few people swam. Only young kids played in the water. Everyone else looked at their devices as they soaked up the sun, basking in brilliance.

The beach gave way as a small marina emerged, full of various sized boats, and on the other side, the beach returned so I knew that I was near the hotel, and as I neared the hotel a knot formed in the pit of my stomach, an uneasy kind of fatalism, that it suddenly didn't matter what I did or tried to do, for nothing would ever change. This was all how it was meant to happen. And not me nor even Marta, as magical as she was, could change that because all of this had happened before.

Marta. She hadn't called me. She hadn't made any kind of contact. She must have opened my message. I was thinking of her, didn't she know that? Was she thinking of me too? I used to think that people were connected by some secret thing, this was before the network and all that, and it was this special force that bound you to someone else. They would know when you were thinking of them. I know that was perhaps wishful thinking, serendipity, maybe even pure coincidence, that some things just happened, yet that was how I was thinking about Marta, as if she would just know.

I had forgotten about Anna. Yet, there she was, outside the hotel, near the boardwalk, fanning herself and looking impatient, but beautiful. She nicely filled out a summery dress and wore strappy sandals. As soon as she saw me, she came bounding over. She looked spectacular beyond belief. I nervously wondered what she had in mind because it couldn't be what I had in mind.

"I thought you stood me up. Anna was starting to get very upset," she said. "I was thinking to myself, no wonder David has trouble with the ladies."

I started to try to explain myself, but she was having none of that. She reached into her handbag and put on a pair of sunglasses. She gestured excitedly and then spun herself around. I had no idea what to make of her.

"David," she said, spinning, "This is Anna when she is not at work."

"Are you always so full of energy?"

"Only when I know I am about to do something good. Yes, Anna will help you David. Us women can be delicate in matters of the heart. You will return with a gift and this will please her."

"Should I?" I asked, not knowing what to make of it. I didn't really remember the last time I bought a gift for anyone. That was an old custom. What was it? People used to celebrate one day as year as being the day they were born. And gifts were meant to be supplied. Seems a contrived convention now. Why was one day so special over all others?

"Yes, Anna knows what you should bring. She knows the very thing."

And with that, she took hold of my hand and guided me away from the hotel to the historic town square. We stopped for a minute—so I could get a good look, she said—then I followed as she led me out of the square to the narrow streets that composed the inner part of the city. She had surprising strength, or a kind of force about her, and eventually she let go of my hand and we walked side by side. She walked fast, though, as if time was everything, and so maybe it was. I didn't know for sure how time played into anything, whether time was running out or if this was just going to be how it always was, for the rest of my life, searching for something but not quite knowing what, unable to distinguish between diversion or substance. And all the while that dark cloud of time hung over me, followed me, encircled me like the SIM, like a venue of vultures.

"What about flowers?" I suggested to Anna as the temperature dropped when we moved out of the sunlight and into the shadows. She rolled her eyes and stared directly at me, for a moment, searching for something, while I felt a bit of a shiver inside. Then she brightened and took pity on me.

"Oh, David. That is a thoughtful idea but not a good one. Anna will say that while flowers are nice, jewelry is what a woman really wants."

I wouldn't say I was reluctant, but I moved with trepidation as Anna guided me, and as the sudden sense of cold really hit, I shivered even more as the narrow cobblestone streets contracted further. She seemed unfazed by that change in temperature, smiling cheerfully as she spoke in her usual, self-referential manner. None of her words seemed to register with me, they floated by as if I was in some kind of dead zone, mere spectral. When she spoke, I strained to focus so that I could understand what she was saying just in case her words were important.

"David, it's that sudden change of temperature. Anna grew up here. She is very familiar with it, the sunlight to the semi-dark, as if it could be any other time of day. The key is just to keep breathing. It's easy. Just like this."

And she stopped, demonstrably breathing so that her whole upper body moved in that shimmery summer dress, in then out, expansion and contraction. She paused and then repeated the exercise. If Marta could see me now, I thought, as I watched her.

"You're mocking me," I said to which she said nothing, spinning playfully away from me, turning back to the task at hand.

As we continued on, the last of the storefronts faded and the streets narrowed so we could barely walk abreast without touching. The uneven, patchwork of stones we walked on augmented the challenge. Anna relished the opportunity, freely bumping against me like it was all a game, like those sidewalk etchings you were supposed to hop, skip, and jump through.

The buildings we came upon were thoroughly residential, though they remained eerily quiet. We saw no one else, no figures in the shadows, movement behind curtains. Nothing. When I looked at Anna, she seemed to glow almost incandescently, but not continuously, but rather in one moment then not the next.

Finally, we came to a door. She knocked and then almost immediately entered, as if the knock was purely informal. We passed through a layer of beads suspended from the doorway into a general living space, with an old couch and some chairs, a table full of various artifacts stood beyond that. In the center of the room, a nice woven rug stretched out and a dead rose hung from the ceiling.

The smell, I couldn't trace. Perhaps some kind of eucalyptus root. Or licorice. I didn't know. That was never my strength. Definitely something medicinal. The air, again, felt very different, light and, dare I say, airy. Then again, maybe I was just making all this up, imagining it, and everything was actually normal, hanging out with Anna in some stranger's apartment like we were old friends, but Anna herself was little more than a stranger.

"This is a special place," Anna said. "Very special."

"And why are we here?" I asked.

And before Anna could answer, and not that she planned to answer, came another voice out of nowhere, projecting from all around me. Anna didn't seem to be bothered. Maybe she hadn't heard and it was just something more in my head, but there it was again.

"Why indeed? David, why indeed?"

I turned and searched for that voice that was at once familiar, and yet also entirely foreign. The lighting in the room was such that I could scarcely make out Anna, much less the general shapes of the furniture. Had it all changed since I entered? I reached for her, for where I thought she was, but she was not there. I touched the worn leather top of an easy chair, rough grooves and fissures, my hands sunk in.

"Anna is here," she said, gently touching me on the arm, appearing as if suddenly, but maybe she had always been by my side.

She was right next to me. I could feel her close proximity, her breathing. There no longer was a chair. And another woman was also there, much older, darker skinned than any of us, with braided hair. My eyes adjusted to the light. Her face was kind, but tired, or weary might be a better take. A bit weathered, worse for wear, but her eyes were lustrous. She was the voice.

"I don't know why I am here. Anna brought me."

Anna was no longer beside me. The world no longer seemed to exist in real time. Maybe I was in a SIM and didn't even notice, crossed some threshold to arrive here. Anna sat on the couch with her legs crossed, staring across the room at a picture on the wall. She breathed like she did before, as if in some kind of meditation, her upper body moving up and down. The picture depicted a church on a hill with a steep cliff on the opposite side. I blinked my eyes, looked to Anna and then again to the picture that now showed a nondescript home in the middle of nowhere, surrounded by the emptiness of rolling hills and patches of trees. Anna didn't seem to be breathing. She was so still. Then the desert, the eternal dread of a beaten down and barren place, a landscape on fire, opened up before me and breathed heavy breaths.

"Yes, she did, didn't she, bring you here?"

I thought she would say more, but she didn't. The ever-lingering thought came back to me that I was in a SIM.

That meant I could do anything, right? Like in a waking dream. That meant I had control of the situation, and while that would have explained a lot, I still felt powerless. All remained silent. Anna had no clothes on. Her dress was neatly folded beside her. She still gazed at the picture, which was now a windmill. And it was spinning. I found myself looking at her body, the silhouette, but at the same time I was looking at the woman. Anna's prominent nipples were pierced with little greenish jewels in each. They shone. They projected light, a spectacular lightness. The woman's nose was pierced too, with a diamond like stud that alternated colors as she breathed, as her nostrils moved. It was greenish too, then it wasn't. But it was. And it too shone like Anna's extraordinary jewels.

"The city was once fortified. When you arrived, you might have noticed its remnants, though I suspect not. The walls are there, but we can't always see them, can we? Nor the gates. Seven of them. The eighth one crumbled a while ago."

I nodded. Maybe I had noticed. Maybe I had remembered them. Certainly, the sea was a natural barrier. And yes, I recalled a church on the hill was inset against the steep slope. A robust wall to block the main access points would be sufficient protection given the nature of the city. I didn't know if I really remembered the walls or not.

"When you leave here, you will suddenly start noticing these things. While they are not necessarily important, they are in context, in and as a symbol. We see what we need to see and when we need to see it. No sooner, no later. All in time."

"Context? A symbol?"

She paused, then poured tea that I knew not where it came from, neither the tea kettle nor the cups, but alas, there they were in front of us. She motioned for me to take a sip. I no longer saw Anna in the chair. Where had she gone? I waited for the woman to take a sip, but I already tasted it, such bitterness that suddenly turned sweet as for a moment I was kissing Anna and felt her tongue lapping against mine, that supple sweetness, and then, the tangy, bitterness of the tea.

"The church?" she asked.

"Yes," I said, "the church?"

"You are getting ahead of yourself. First the fortified city. There is a system of tunnels underneath the city that lead out beyond the walls. The gates above exist as checkpoints. Some of these tunnels have tracks. Some don't. Nonetheless they are emblematic."

"So, I gain access to the tunnels via the church?" I said not knowing the symbolism and what it had to do with anything.

She nodded. And we drank more tea. God, it was awful. Why had that word come to mind—at the mention of the church perhaps. God didn't even exist. We all knew that now. It was just a concept by which people once used to measure their pain. Once it was such a powerful concept that people willingly died for entry into its domain, that domain of the afterlife. And when things could not be explained, they said the lord worked in mysterious ways.

"Some say the tunnels are a labyrinth, others a maze." She seemed to say it, but her lips did not move. I glanced a moment around the room, but we seemed to be alone. "But they may be both."

"And what lies beyond?"

"What lies beyond," she echoed, "everything that is not here is beyond just as everything that is beyond is not here."

I had to get a hold of my thoughts. Too many questions. Emrik. Marta. Even Anna? How did they all connect? Or *did* they even connect? What lies beyond? Whatever is there, is what's there, and it is not what is here. That wasn't much to go on.

"So many questions and so little time," she said. She motioned to Anna, who now stood, still naked, but lost in her dreamscape. "Don't ask Anna. She doesn't know. She's just a messenger. She certainly has your attention."

I gazed back to Anna, her glistening silhouette, perfectly still, body erect, the richness of her skin, the brownish color, the jewels as they shone, as they seemed to reach out and entreat me, imploring me to be. She turned and faced me, arms relaxed by her side, her full breasts and expressionless gaze, firm yet entrancing, pierced but not piercing. A greenish stone protruding from her navel held my gaze. I felt she was near me again, but she wasn't, like I could touch her and feel her, but I could not. Yet her skin was cool and smooth and like an ocean. That was easily my imagination. I had to think of something else.

"Marta?"

"Yes, Marta. That's a little more delicate. She's harder to read, for she is after all, another. Luckily, we have a remedy. A gift."

She produced a green stone, calling it moldavite, an extraterrestrial gemstone. She said it was sacred and only meant for some people, and for others, it would have absolutely no effect. Marta should have it. She handed the stone to me. For her, it might work.

"Emrik? My dreams, my companion. . . "

Anna, I was close to Anna again, close enough to smell a sweet fragrance as she stretched her body out, lifted her hair off her neck so I could see the small, double axe tattoo, but that was not what stood out. The whole of her back was covered with markings that resembled a labyrinth. I ran my hands along her body, traced the curve of her hips to the pits of her arm then around to the small of her back, all the while she spoke in tongue and smelled so nice.

"So many questions," the woman said again, "but you already know the answers, don't you? And yet you keep asking me the question. It's almost as if you don't like the answers and you want new ones. Or perhaps, you don't believe them. Or perhaps you are not focused on the right things. Time will tell, this time that waits for no one. And it won't wait, not even for you."

She got up. And was distinctively cold to me, suddenly ever distant as if a spell had been broken or the time she spoke of, was no longer there waiting. Its station, I kept thinking in stations, or whatever it was, all the same I didn't like the feeling of being left there, left out, left over.

"You can pay at my booth."

At that moment, Anna tapped on my shoulder. Again, she wore her dress. The woman was gone. The only trace that remained was that recurring medicinal smell. The room was almost completely empty, aside from a shabby couch and chair. There was no picture on the wall. I felt an emptiness inside and turned to Anna, wanting to touch her to see if she was real, to see how she smelled, but when I reached for her she was already moving.

"Hey," she said. "Let's get out of here."

We passed through the layer of beads out into the cool, semi-dark streets, from one gauzy milieu into another slightly more transparent one, but before doing so I took one last glance back at the room we were leaving, stepping halfway through the beads. And I saw nothing. I felt the green stone in my pocket like a pulse, though. Like a little piece of life balanced against the void. I felt its energy, its vitality. And that was comforting.

"Anna helped you," she said to me. And I felt she was different. I thought about what happened in that room and wondered if it really happened, or if it was in my subconscious. I didn't know the best way to bring it up. Perhaps not at all, and certainly nothing of this to Marta. Maybe she already knew the way she seemed to know so many things? I hoped not. I wasn't in control at all.

"Did she?" That question I asked was two-fold. And maybe I hadn't meant to say it aloud, but I did.

She eyed me rather intently, then nodded as if there was no question. In her eyes, I felt the eyes of that woman piercing me and wanted to recoil, but then they relaxed and happily shone. She grabbed my hand and led me briskly back along the narrow, cobblestone streets. As if in reassurance, she squeezed my hand. That seemed to be what comforted her. She squeezed my hand a few times, and then she was almost skipping along the streets.

The street widened, and up ahead, I glimpsed shops and storefronts, and beyond that I could see the brightness of the square, which made me breathe a little easier. I was still a little shaken from the experience, as if things were still not quite right. I felt the weight of the stone in my pocket. That made it all real. And again, its energy.

"Here," Anna said as we stopped in front of a store

with a table outside full of various kinds of gemstones and jewelry.

That woman appeared, the same but different; her presence, that is. It was hard to explain. She just wasn't the same woman, though she looked exactly the same. She was even dressed the same, wasn't she? But I didn't really remember what she had been wearing. She certainly wasn't naked. That was Anna. Temporarily. I really only remembered the woman's face. Maybe her hands as we drank tea, but mostly her face, her eyes, the piercing in her nose that changed colors. God, how unreliable our impressions were.

"Three-fifty for the moldavite," she said, knowing that I had it in my pocket

I nodded in acceptance and the deal was done. Nothing else in her eyes suggested there would be anything more to our conversation. But I wanted there to be. I wanted to talk to her again, though I had just talked to her.

"Thank you," was all she said in the matter.

As we walked away, Anna asked to see the stone. There was something about the gemstone, I didn't know what it was, but Anna was clearly taken by it, taking it from my hands and holding it against her chest for a few moments, looking especially radiant and ever vibrant during those scant seconds as it touched her. Was it the same stone? I thought but didn't want to think of the picture in my mind.

"So beautiful," she said, "So very beautiful I can almost feel it hum. Anna thinks the lovely girl desires such a thing."

At that moment, I felt a buzz in my pocket from my device. It was Marta calling. And what a time for her to call. I had been waiting, hoping, wanting, wishing for her call, except at that very moment, I didn't want to talk to her because of the Anna thing, because of all that had just happened. Did she know? She must have known.

"Aren't you going to answer? Anna wants to know," she said, holding up the stone. "See the power this stone has. It's magical."

"David," Marta's voice, her once sweet voice, desperate and troubled. "David, are you there? Is that really you?"

"Marta," I said, relieved and not knowing where to begin, what to say. It was a lie, all of that acting naturally. Life often called for something more, something beyond the normal call of duty, the mere walking of the line. It asked instead for us to walk across fire, steal it if necessary, and scale walls and jump across huge ravines on something akin to faith.

"I didn't know where you were. I thought I lost you. I thought you were gone," she said, talking as fast as I had ever heard her talk, words rushing out of her mouth. "You disappeared. What happened? Are you okay?"

"I'm okay," I said, uneasily, but all too happy hearing her voice. "How are you?"

"David, I'm fine. It's you I'm worried about. You disappeared. I don't understand it. Where were you?"

"I was with Anna," I said.

"Hold on," she said.

I waited as she found my coordinates and tapped into a camera. I tried to imagine what she saw, from what angle. Anna was off to the side, doing her thing, whatever that was, waiting for me to finish mine.

"Who's Anna?" she asked.

"It's complicated," I said. "But I can really explain. Please trust me."

I had told Marta to trust me. She did trust me, it's just that she wasn't sure the kind of man she was trusting. I suspected she had an idea of who I was, what I was, and maybe I wasn't living up to that. Or maybe I was, all too well, and she just hoped for something more, for something better. I can't say I didn't share that belief, if that's what she was thinking. I too wanted to be better than this.

Of course, I apologized again, but she was having none of that. Whatever had happened to me, the concern she felt when I disappeared changed all of that. My sins of the past, at least temporarily, were absolved. I knew that fully when I saw her exiting the pod.

I waited for her there, imagining myself again cast in the role of a station agent, there to watch the trains arrive and depart, assisting passengers as needed, but otherwise, keeping up appearances of my station. I did all of this in my head to pass the time, waiting for her arrival, for the moment of uncertainty, apprehensive beyond belief in the absence of any other activity. Finally, in the distance, I glimpsed an approaching pod.

Marta looked luminescent in a shimmery black cocktail dress, light and almost gauze like, half diaphanous like nothing I had ever seen depending on the way that she moved. She dashed quickly towards me and maybe that was the first time we really kissed, and the first time we held each other close for so long. In those moments, I felt like I learned something about her, something I had never known, all in the way we touched and what it felt like to feel her so close. When we moved apart, we moved back in again and kissed once more, pulled by the flow between us, propelled by its force.

"David," she said. "Oh, David. I'm sorry."

I was speechless. She had told me several times that I just disappeared, right off the screen from her network. She had not even been thinking about me at all, which I hoped was a lie, when she heard the alert. She immediately thought the worst and hated herself for being too harsh on me. I let that part slide, her apology, though it was nice to hear her concede her position a little, but I didn't think I deserved being fully let off the hook.

Now she was the one touching me to see if I was real. She was saying so much at once, more than I had ever heard her say in such a short span of time. Normally, she was calm, measured and not easily rattled. I didn't initially have time to compliment her on her dress.

"Marta," I said. "I'm really okay. And you look just fabulous."

"Thanks. It seemed right for the occasion. A dress like this, would have been something I would never have worn. I don't know why. No reason, I guess. I am glad you like it."

"It is beautiful, but so are you too. I would like you in anything."

She writhed for a moment as if feeling the dress with her body, the way it enveloped her. And then looking at me, there was a moment, beyond words, nestling up close to us, some secret that meant everything.

I reached to grab her small bag, then with my other hand, took hold of her hand. Leading her out of the station, down the steps to the boardwalk, we walked aside the water that shimmered with the last remnants of sunset. Dusk closed in, and her dress sparkled so in the razzle dazzle of lights from the restaurants and bars.

"It's so beautiful here," she mused, raising her head to take in the atmosphere.

"Like many things are," I added. "I'm so happy you are here too."

She turned and smiled, for it was a moment together like no other, as if we had lived lifetimes apart and now were returning, long lost lovers reunited, knowing full well everything that had been lost was all in the past.

"I'm happy too," she replied. "But you are not completely off the hook, you know. I want to know about Anna, and I want to see where you went."

"Scot- free," I said. "That was an expression people used to use."

"Well, you still have some explaining to do," she said, playfully poking me in the sides. "And don't tell me it's complicated."

"It is, though, complicated," I retorted with a sly smile. "Cavorting and gallivanting with beautiful women can be."

"Cavorting?"

"Yeah, I thought I would throw in some of those big words you like."

"I was doing neither of those things," I said.

"Is that so?" she teasingly questioned, "I'm not sure so about that."

We stopped for a drink downstairs at the hotel bar. I told her the story about Anna, starting with the dream then the Hotel, the trip to see the Twins and all that. How were the Twins? she had asked. Well, I had said, I am not sure they were really Twins, but I had a coin that they really liked. I showed her the coin.

"Wow," she said, examining the coin. "Well, there's your God. Inscribed on the money. How strange is that?"

"There's more to this story,"

"Indulge me," she said, nudging close like she was settling in for a bedtime story.

I felt the lush fabric of her dress against my shoulder, then continued the Anna thread and told her virtually everything except the parts about her being naked. She was curious about the woman and the tea, the questions she posed. I didn't tell her what she said about her. You can't share everything all at once. Some things are better in doses.

"What about the labyrinth tattoo on Anna's back? How did you know about that?"

"It was all kind of strange. It was sort of like this little glimpse. Maybe something I was supposed to see."

"Hmm," she scowled. "Seems very odd. Do you know if she really has a tattoo like that? Or the double axe?"

"I don't know. If you meet her, then maybe you go for a swim or do something women do."

"Do something women do?" Marta playfully called me out. "Like shop or sunbathe?"

"I didn't mean it like that."

"I know. I'm just teasing. It's fun and easy to do," she said. "Is that all?"

"Almost," I said. I wanted to bring up the part about the jewel just right. I already felt like I had made a hash of the story in the first place, omitting the part about the gift and playing off the whole thing like it was something from a dream, a quest and Anna was helping me get Marta back, which it was in a way, but in another way, I didn't know what it all meant.

"It's a crazy story," Marta remarked as she took a sip of her daiquiri. "You somehow believed Anna could help you win me back, all because she was in your dream."

"She's very insistent. And besides, there was one more thing. This. This is for you."

I brought the wondrous green stone from my pocket, and in that moment its embodiment of cool energy, that lustrous radiance became apparent, transfixing the gaze of Marta by its charm. Anna had been right, more than she knew, for in Marta's presence the stone was all the more intense, sparkling, emitting a commanding allure.

"Wow," Marta said softly as she examined the stone, turning it over, rubbing its smooth surface. "It's stunning. Whatever it is. Like nothing I've ever seen. Thank you. I don't know what to say. It's beautiful, David."

"Moldavite," I said. "It's a special gift for you."

She leaned over and kissed me so quickly I barely had time to react, but the kiss lingered long enough so I could, but not so long it seemed outrageous. After all, we were in public, and Marta wasn't the public kind of person and neither was I.

"How did she know?" Marta asked. "Anna, I mean. She must have had some idea."

"I thought about that too. I can't explain it. Maybe Anna was merely just the medium, the vessel within which one travels to the needed place."

"And here I thought when I first saw her with you," she began. "Well it's maybe not important what I thought, I was just happy to see you were still alive."

"I am," I affirmed. "It's been quite a day though. I've

missed you unbelievably."

I had the feeling that I had already expressed that numerous times, but that was okay. The moment was magical, though, there in the bar, right across from the boardwalk and the beach and the sounds of the surf crashing ashore. There was a light breeze, too, coming off the glimmering water.

"We could just live here, couldn't we?" she said, pretending in that moment that things were different, that our lives were different. "Get out of the city permanently, forever. You could do the same thing, just remotely, via the SIM or whatever. It wouldn't matter where you were. You could connect to the people."

"The people? What people?" I joked.

"Oh, those people you work with. You're part of it, you know, so you'll never be able to drift too far. That would be too much."

"You really think so? I'm not sure I'm as useful anymore or if ever I was."

"You're just saying that," Marta said, then reconsidered. "But maybe it is true. Maybe you are no longer essential. Especially if the network remains the same."

"How else would it be, if not the same?"

"All things can be changed, can they not? Not drastically maybe, just tweaked, even a little bit. Maybe so that people are less reliant on the SIM," she mused, sipping on the last of her drink.

"Humankind was always meant to be a little messy," I said. "Not so perfect. Not so machine-like. We're not engineered that way. Just look at me."

"Yes," Marta said, turning to me. "Let's look at you.

You're a bit of a mess, aren't you?"

We sat on stools at the hotel bar, side by side. I dropped my hand down and squeezed hers, gently, then returned my hand to the counter. In the mirror above the bar, we looked at each other and our expressions. I felt again as if I was in a dream, but I had been feeling that for a long time, so this was a different kind of dream, a much better one. And whatever it was, I didn't want it to end.

"Like that," she said. "It feels so real and genuine, you touching my hand, not forced nor programmed. I like that."

"Because it was. Because I wanted to touch you and I still do."

"I know, but it is always about more than saying something is. It's the action. And not just the action, but something in the action and the moment, the feeling behind it."

"Come on, let's go," Marta said suddenly before I could say anything. "Let's take a little walk. It's such a beautiful night and I want to feel it, the breeze, the air. . . no more drink."

"Even though it's not real."

"Isn't it pretty to think so," she said.

Then she just smiled so radiantly, Marta in her sparkling dress, when it caught the light just right. She rose first and I followed. We stepped out into the night, the blissful night, and we held hands as we walked along the boardwalk towards the vicinity of the lighthouse.

I didn't think too much about it, but a woman smiled at me as we walked. She wore a necklace outside her dark blouse with a symbol, unmistakably the flower of life with its concentric, equal, overlapping circles. They seemed to dance in the light, but maybe I was looking too closely. There was something captivating about her, though, and later I would think back to her, but during the moment, I merely just saw her then returned to the magical night, Marta and I, seaside, on our way to the lighthouse.

"How were the songs?"

"I really liked them, which surprised me. Some more than others of course. And especially that last song. Very sweet. I listened to them on the way here to get in the mood."

"What do you mean?" I asked.

"I was conflicted, a little unsure about things, but the music made me feel better, a little more sure."

"Nice. That last song was the Nick Cave one. Nick Cave & the Bad Seeds, a particularly moving song. The best songs have this power that takes you to another place. That's why music has always been a salve."

"I never listened to that much music, so I wouldn't know," she stated. "But I liked what you made."

"Did I listen to a lot of music?" I asked. "I must have listened to a lot of music over the years."

"Of course," she said. "On headphones mostly. I never really thought too much about listening to what you were listening to. I just watched you. That seemed to be the important part. I'm sorry if that sounds creepy."

"What do you mean? The fact that you know more about me than I do, at least, the observable me. That does make me feel a bit weird. But I suppose that's exactly what the network does too."

"True," she said, "But with the network, I suppose people feel it's anonymous, just like we've always said in all of our advertising. Sure, you're watched and tracked, but it's an anonymous you too."

"We believed that?"

"We still do," she said.

"But not our thoughts. We still own those," I said, more to myself than her.

"Not directly, but to the extent your thoughts might manifest some change in the body, then maybe to a degree. We can learn a lot through observation."

"It is true," I concurred. "I'd rather have you watching me than anyone else."

"Thanks," she said. "I learned a lot. Even about me."

"So how did you listen to the music?" I asked Marta with curiosity as we stopped along the boardwalk at a section with a retaining wall, the ocean lapping up against the barrier, between lamp lit posts.

"Oh, in the SIM," she said. "I took a walk in a park I built especially for my SIM. It's a place I like to go by myself. Very peaceful. Trees and greenery, sort of like an english garden at a manor house."

"Sounds peaceful. I can imagine you in that yellow dress you were in, walking where we walked."

"Not exactly," she corrected me.

"Oh, what were you wearing then?"

"Nothing," she said casually, but with a little bit of provocation. "I mean, just a pair of black panties."

"Really?"

"Sure. It's so quiet there; no one around. I do that from time to time. You ought to try it. Good therapy."

"Hmm," I said. "That's different. Not at all the attire I imagined."

"Do you want me to send you the SIM file? I suppose you would like that."

"You can do that?"

"Yes," she said then paused for effect. "You know I am just kidding. I wasn't walking around in lace undies listening to the tape you made. I was just trying to get a reaction, which I did."

"Oh," I said, so easily gotten.

"I was dressed in a horse-riding outfit," she added.

"That's interesting."

She nodded. "What's interesting? It fits the environment. Boots, pants, the longer jacket."

"Sounds nice. I wish I could have been there to listen to the songs with you."

"Someday, perhaps," she said, "It was nice to walk and listen to those songs. I pretended I was looking for my horse. I wished you were here, wasn't that one of the songs? And for the record, I did have on something black underneath."

"I'm never going to live that down, am I?" I said, sheepishly, liking that she pretended too. I was always pretending things, things that would likely never be. Pretend was its own kind of fantasy, a survival technique. I pretended one day we would listen to those songs together and walk in the park, just her and I.

"No. Because a woman's fantasy would never place such emphasis on an article of clothing worn or not worn," she looked to me, back against the retainer wall, the blackish sea beyond her glowing with *Noctiluca scintillans* and other bioluminescence, the moonlight too.

"I know, it's ridiculous, even juvenile. I admit it. It's silly and objectifying," I said, feeling ashamed. I had, of course, never thought about it from a woman's point of view.

"It's okay," she teased. "It's simple. But know this. You have to do a little more, no, a lot more than that to turn me on."

"How am I doing?" I asked as I touched her elbow.

"I'll let you know."

"Can I get a hint?"

"I am warming up to you," she said, planting a soft kiss on my cheek.

"What else?" I enquired.

"Well," she said as she looked to the lighthouse then back to me. "Maybe a woman wants to feel special. Like she's the only one."

The lighthouse long since lost its casting light, and though it was now abandoned, still retained a certain kind of charm, jutting up at the point, this dirty white stone structure, lit by street lamps and nothing else. We looked off into the distance for a long time, each in our thoughts, but she smiled so sweetly at me and took hold of my hand.

She was right, of course. I thought again about what she said, how even if I had said she was the only one, something about that would have rung untrue because it was just an idea not supported very well. And right now, what was needed, was not ideas but in things, like William Carlos Williams had said. Things, but what things?

As we neared the hotel, I looked to my left, away from the sea to the ancient town square and there was a statue of the Gorgons as part of a building, those mythical sisters with the venomous snakes for hair who turned those who looked at them to stone, and thus, acted as protectors of that structure. Medusa was the most famous and the only mortal one. Maybe my lodestar was Perseus, the hero who slain her. In some way, perhaps Star was Medusa and she needed to be slain. I discarded that thought almost as quickly as it came, but all the same, it did occur to me. They were just statues, though. In the network world, they meant nothing. In my mind, they were clues from Emrik because I knew tomorrow when Marta and I walked through the square there would be no such statues, no such pretend things.

"More clues," I said to Marta because I wasn't good at the other stuff, the stuff I needed to be good at.

"You really think so, where?" she asked. And I pointed to the Gorgons. Stuff only I would know. They seemed rather innocuous, but all the same a bit creepy in that semi-darkness, streets lit in the night by the sidewalk lamps and otherworldly lunar illumination, casting shadows, obscuring the images into depictions of the grotesque, rendering the imagery into a kind of hazy glimpse.

"More Emrik. I'm convinced of that. All these images that he knew would mean something to me, that are outside the realm of the network, just a little code here and there that's been written over, absolved of its purpose."

"Or someone else? You want it to be Emrik, but it may not be."

"Anna, perhaps?"

"Ah," she said, poking me in the ribs as she did. "Here is that less serious side. Let's see more of that. Yeah, I suspect it is Anna. Trying to lure you into her vast building."

"Her vast building?"

"Yeah, that's a metaphor," Marta said jokingly. "For you who like to speak so vaguely."

"I know, that's why I liked it."

I smiled as we returned to that electric night, the sudden sense of my lodestar pulsing in my head as I pushed on, headlong in that darkness. In my mind, I saw a tunnel, a long dark tunnel, dank and damp, smelling like hell, but it was the promise of what was at the end that kept me going. It wasn't the grotesque world that I saw in my mind, but something else, something real and alive. Something extraordinary.

Extraordinary like when we were back in the room and she slid out of her dress, then slowly removed her dainty panties and stood naked before me, shining in that half-light coming through the window, moonlight as our protectorate as we touched then entangled ourselves and all the while, though my eyes were closed, I imagined looking deep into her hazel eyes, swimming in them as the sweet melody of the ocean outside our window rocked us like a soft song.

Afterwards, I lay beside Marta, listening to her breaths, the beating of her heart. She was flat on her back, and I on my side, tracing the outlines of her body, doing figure eights on her chest, circling her gentle curves, eyes closed, imagining as I touched her skin that we would remain forever with these bodies of ours, basking in paradise, and yet, my mind too flashed to the absence of that. Perception is reality, I told myself. Just to be sure, I moved lower and touched Marta's inner thigh, breaking the flow. She opened her eyes with a befuddled yet amused expression as I moved up again towards infinity, drawing a line from her vulva to belly button to the great recurring, station to station. In another life, I thought, it was not that I wouldn't notice Marta, rather it was that she would not notice me, but I would know her eyes anywhere, wouldn't

I?

"I thought you said such things were childish?" I said, knowing that she knew what I was talking about because she always knew everything about me, even the things I didn't know.

"They are in some contexts. I was wearing them because they made me feel sexy."

"What's the difference?"

"I am wearing them first for me, and second for you."

"I don't mind you not wearing them at all."

"I know, David. I know," she reassured me as she touched my arm and moved it back towards her.

"What do we know?" I said. What did I know about anything?

"We don't look as good as this," Marta said to me as if reading my thoughts, or maybe it was because I was so closely studying her body with my fingertips. "Not you or I."

"In real life," I said as I resumed where I had been exploring, on her stomach again moving slowly up. She had loosely attached the jewel I gave her, looped it with some string. It had been tossed to the side, but I returned it to her chest, between her breasts, commanding and magnificent.

"Something about it," she said softly, faintly, reaching for the jewel. "I like to feel it close to me, like it's a part of me."

"It is something special, isn't it?" I said. Maybe it was an amulet, meant to protect her. What had that woman said. It might be for her, meaning Marta.

She nodded as I looked at her, closing her eyes again. So I closed mine and resumed what I was doing, exploring the station, her station, the one I had finally seemed to reach.

"But what is real life anyway?"

"Well, there is that," I said, touching her body, moving my fingers to where her heart was. "I don't care so much about what's out here, it's what's in here."

I thought about how we really looked, how a lot of the time, I didn't even know what I looked like. I did not actively seek out my image. Now and then, to my dismay, when I happened to catch a glimpse of myself, some of the time I was surprised. I had to remind myself who I was, what I looked like. It's not that I didn't know what I looked like, but the mental image of me was just different than the physical actuality. And I don't know why. But Marta was right. What was real life?

She drifted off to sleep. I listened to the sounds of her breathing as it blended with the melody outside and lifted my hands off her. Moonlight shone through the window of our room. I covered her up with the sheet and tried to get some sleep too.

I must have drifted off. I thought I would lie awake forever thinking about innumerable things, some unmentionable, the unknown, for example. At some point, I got up and flipped through my notebook. I found some interesting passages:

Why is it that we can't distinguish between a dream and reality? And when we do, we wake up. We might experience lucid dreaming or we might not. And when we wake up, all of that intensity, what we dreamt, quickly fades and we are back in real life. How quickly the mind adapts and that dream of moments ago goes lost.

Existence precedes essence. "We are the novelists of

ourselves..."

I awoke early, Marta nestled against me, breathing so peacefully, so beautifully content. At least, that was how it seemed to me. Would it be any different outside of the network when we were our true selves, assuming she was planning to go that far? I moved cautiously, so as not to disturb her, slipping out of bed and to the window to look out at the sea. Why wouldn't she go that far?

She was still asleep, though she had turned her body in a different direction. I tried to remember how I dreamt. One of those dreams that seem so vivid, but then when you awake, after a few moments, the lucidity drifts away and then nothing can be recalled. Just like I wrote in my notebook. Not that it mattered much, but something in my dream seemed to be important, so essential in its secret knowledge that I could not possibly forget.

At first all I recalled were fragments, something about a statue made of various materials that was smashed into bits and pieces by a large stone. And the wind then seemed to pick up, discard those remnants into oblivion. And I all did was watch and wait, in futility, in forever a freeze. Last night, I saw the Gorgons, but that statue in my dream was not quite that. It was something else.

And then there was another part of the dream, more of that same driving in the desert with my companion, searching for something. I remembered trying to look into her eyes, but she kept turning away, not allowing me a glimpse.

I glanced again to where Marta slept. I looked around my belongings and was surprised to find I had swimwear. That seemed like a convenient way to avoid the issue of whether I should go for a swim or not, but there they were, a pair of swim trunks. Long ago, I established I didn't even know myself, yet I distinctly remember in my notebook the phrase: Know Thyself. Well, I didn't know myself at all. I hadn't expected to find swim trunks. I didn't think I swam.

I left the room, crossed the boardwalk to the coolness of the early morning sand. With barely a pause, I ventured out into the water, wading cautiously at first, but once I cleared the rockier parts, the sand at my feet enticed me deeper into the surf. I imagined Marta joining me, though more carefully, sidestepping little bits of rock, staying firm against the pull of the tide before finally submerging herself after a long internal debate.

What, I wondered, could this feel like if you didn't know what it was supposed to feel like? They said the SIM fed off our imagination. But how did it work when we didn't know? The sense of weightlessness, being supported, however fleetingly by the water, was something I remembered that I treasured. How could such a thing translate to the SIM? I would have to see. There would be time. Was this how I remembered as a kid, diving into the lake off of a boat?

Marta came close to me and we floated together, in each other's arms, something that added another layer to the feeling of being weightless. Floating in space, I couldn't believe that I could feel so much for someone that I had known for such a short span of time, as if time meant too much and didn't matter.

Holding her close, wrapped in my arms, floating in the ocean with the fat old sun looking down upon us, if I could capture time, just like in the song then that would be the moment I would take. Except, I was imagining even this moment. Marta was asleep in the room, and here I was, in the water, floating, feeling weightless, feeling like I was with Marta and yet I was not. But I must have been with someone at some point, like this. But when, and where?

When I returned to the room, Marta was awake. She had put on one of my T-shirts, though a little big for her, and sat pensive by the window, like I had been earlier, transfixed by the sea. What was it about the sea? Calming, yet full of mystery and promise. That was how I saw it. Everything and still nothing too. Mystical and magical.

"I saw you," she said. "Swimming. You looked very happy."

"The sea," I said, "such a thing to behold. Each morning when I awake, I instinctively go to the window as if making sure it is still there and it's not an illusion."

"I know. I'm drawn to it too. There's a power there we don't understand."

Like so much else, I thought. All of this stuff we think we know, deceive ourselves into thinking we do as if our deceptions will prove the point. Some things held an almost instinctive, natural pull, and the sea was one.

"Where do we go from here?" she asked me, turning to face me. "This is all kind of new to me."

"We'll figure it out. There are clues all around us. I have a couple of ideas."

"I wasn't talking about that," she said.

"Oh," I said. "What were you talking about?"

"You and me," she whispered. "Maybe I am endangering everything. I don't know if this is what I am supposed to do. And then last night?"

"I wouldn't trade it, not for anything. You're the only one," I said, knowing they were just words and in time, would mean more to her than they did now if I just allowed myself to be loved.

I kissed her on the cheek, leaning over to her, briefly touching the small of her back, tenderly caressing. I've got reservations about so many things, I thought, but not about you, for you, you are my lodestar.

Yet still, I wondered what the network would do, if anything, other than seek to protect itself when the time came, when we found a way out. The whole balance, of births and deaths, all of life was managed on some level, but I wasn't really sure if anyone understood how. Not even Marta. And anyway, we couldn't worry about what the network would do. We. I liked using that term. We needed to worry about ourselves. We. Marta and I.

After coffee, we departed for our walk to the church, passing through the quiet, still sleepy streets, both of us with a bounce in our steps as if some great adventure awaited us. Marta wore a cute, summery dress. I was also dressed for the seaside, in shorts and shirt with sandals, which felt odd to me. Not my normal attire by any means, which made me slightly uncomfortable, but also new, like a different person.

For a while, we walked hand in hand, arms swinging slightly. It seemed to me we were close to where I was with Anna, that chill, the narrowing of streets, but it still wasn't the same, though the streets were different. Maybe not noticeably, as in some clear division, but suddenly the paths were cobblestone and uneven, ancient. There were no signs, but if we looked up to the hill, we knew we were headed in the right direction. Churches up on hills needed no maps. We chose a few wrong streets, but that was part of the fun, coming to a dead-end at one point before retracing our steps and trying again. Marta was so playful, loving the game, darting about like Anna had been, energetic and dare I say, the happiest I had ever seen her because we both knew something.

No God. No religion. And yet, churches still remained, stood as embodiments to another world, marvels of architecture that were models too for the future, and yet, never repeated, never built again. Maybe they were just reminders, markers in some elaborate game. See, behold what once was.

The sunlight, now obscured, shone through in glimpses, interstices between structures because there was a crack in everything. As we walked along the darkened streets, we peered into dark windows, shade covered, but generally saw no one else except for an innocuous old man walking a small dog, who at first glance seemed more threatening, maybe because of the growling of his dog, that small dog ferociousness that is anything but that.

He nodded as we passed him, turning his gaze to the very direction we took, which led us through a row of buildings to a winding pathway, that seemed to go upward forever, like some grand staircase, till we finally hit a clearing followed by the church, white steeple, so clear and pure, bathed in some special kind of light. Surely sunlight, but it seemed like something more. A quietude, hushed and serene greeted us, came forward to meet us, offering air that was both cold and warm, depending where you stood.

"The elevation?" suggested Marta, instinctively clutching the jewel around her neck. "That must be why the air feels so different."

"Either that, or religion was real, is real, and this is how that presence appears. Maybe we'll see an apparition of the Holy Spirit."

"An apparition?"

"Yeah, why not? The presence of something, an angel maybe. Something spiritual. You know."

Incarnate. Nothing incarnate, I thought.

"Actually, I don't," Marta said. "Unlike you, when I was young, religion was already on the fringes."

"True. I just read a lot about such things. I'm not that much older than you, you know?"

She gave me a look. I liked the look. An angel incarnate. But I wasn't religious and such things we imbued as it was, made in our mind that something out of nothing. We loved someone in the mind and that was how it endured. Time was otherwise cruel.

"It's oddly beautiful up here, isn't it?"

We walked up to the stone building that was the church. The front door was naturally locked. Such places were always locked. If anyone had keys, then that would be Evey and Evers. They had so many keys, I imagined, to go with their clocks and telephones and other contraptions. Actual keys. I only had one key. And I knew as I pulled it out, that it wouldn't fit.

"Where did you get that?" Marta asked

"I found it amongst my things. A key, a coin, and a pair of flashlights."

"Imagine that," she said, and reached for my hand.

Now Marta held my hand, moving me around to follow her about the exterior of the church with her energetic steps, the light curls of her hair bouncing in unison. There was no one else here. We had the entire place to ourselves.

And so our voices, when we spoke, seemed much louder than they were, amplified by the surroundings, so we took to whispering, sometimes akin to intoxicating sweet nothings in each other's ear and other times pure nonsense.

Our mood was rapturous amid the picturesque square beside the church until a noise startled us. We looked at each other. I thought I saw a face in one of the lancet windows, ashen, then a shadow that passed behind stained glass and disappeared. For a while we didn't speak, nestled close to each other so that I could hear the rhythm of Marta's heart as it pounded, a tempo so wild and unruly, I thought of that missing horse from her SIM, imagined that it was a wild horse. I thought of after we made love, that pulsing of passion, and then gradually all became more sedate, more stoic as the silence returned.

"Well, there's your apparition," she said.

"Indeed," I agreed, not believing, like I had willed the thing into existence, but it was all supposed to be in fun, like pretending to awake spirits with an Ouija board. Had I done that sort of conjuring before? I must have. I must have done so many things. Probably even Lando had been a part of that, acting as the spiritualist.

"Was it real?"

"Well, that's the thing, the whole thing, it's supposed to be half-real, religious in nature. Like seeing a ghost, but ghosts aren't real."

"Don't say it," Marta said.

"Say what, that it looked kind of like Emrik, in a weird way?"

"Yes, you said it."

"You saw it too then?" I asked.

"It's true, I did see it this time. But I don't think it's supernatural or anything like that. Whoever and whatever it really was, somebody programmed it. We were meant to see that."

"By whom?"

"Who else would want you to see that other than me? Who else might be trying to help you."

"Helping us," I corrected her. "We're in this together."

We. I squeezed her hand with mine. We did not linger much longer at the church. In practical silence, we quickly retraced our steps back to the hotel, each in our own thoughts, bypassing street signs with nary an inclination about anything except getting back to the hotel.

So we saw a face, possibly Emrik. What did that signify? That we were on the right track? That he's still alive and hacking into the network? That would be amazing if that was true. Maybe this was a hack from long ago, so long, that it was not a hack, but part of the network itself.

"What are the chances. . . " Marta trailed off.

"I thought about that too. It was the noise that triggered us. Otherwise, the whole thing would have been pure chance."

"But it wasn't pure chance. It was calculated. It was a reasonable assumption to think you would visit the church."

"Of course," I said, though, I hadn't suggested it. The oracle had. That was what I was now calling that strange woman who Anna took me to. Perhaps our choices were not as clear cut as they appeared.

"Yeah," Marta said. "You're very predictable that way. The things that interest you will always interest you.

You're like no one else, David. And I'm not just saying that. That's why you were part of the original eight."

"And why weren't you part?"

"A bit too young at the time, perhaps. Though certainly Emrik lobbied hard not to have me on the team."

"Really, why would he do that?"

"You can figure that one out."

"He liked you or didn't like you?"

"Of course, he liked me," she said, as if it could not be any other way. "But not in that way that others did. He liked me better outside of the group."

"Strategic. Always thinking farther ahead than anyone else," I said, not really thinking too clearly what she had said. *Not in the way others did.*

"Exactly."

We reached the end of the grid of streets and were now in the main square. Water was once again within sight. Great statues stood. Such a lovely spot, so grand and spectacular. I was happy to be out in the sunlight again. Something about the semi-darkness, the cold of the side streets terrified me, and I didn't know why.

"The best groups are often not full of the most talented people."

"Emrik was my mentor," I said, thinking I had said that before, that we already had this conversation. And maybe we had. Everything that happened always happened again.

"I know. Mine too. He spoke very highly of you," she said, then muffled her laugh.

"What? Why the laugh?"

"He even said I could trust you, that you were one of the good ones."

"But I am," I said. "Aren't I?"

"Of course you are," she said. "In fact, I am going to buy you a new shirt. As a gift. How about that? Reciprocate. Like that word? Wait here."

I watched as she sauntered off in her summery dress, glancing back once as she veered off to a jewelry store, casting what I detected was a rather mischievous smile in that glance. Maybe it was true, I missed a lot, but I did not miss that nor the three weavers, a little inset to a storefront she casually passed. I looked again, just to make sure, and there they were in their white gowns at a loom weaving fabric, three women, engrossed solely in their craft, turning that thread into something more, and then ultimately something less with the simplest of a cut.

They were the Fates, incarnations of destiny: three sisters weaving the lives of the world, the beginning, the middle and the end, in their thread of the loom, individually known as the spinner, the allotter and the inevitable, or death. And there they were. Another sign from Emrik? The irony, perhaps, because our world, the old world, was now the new world and there was no place for such things. The network was the ultimate spinner of all fates. Maybe even mine. No matter what I tried to do.

I turned away from there to look around, get my bearings. They called it Tartini Square after a musician of that name, a violinist, actually. I found that fact interesting. I supposed I could go into a SIM and see him play. But that wouldn't be real, even if everyone said it was because the network would piece something together and say it was all real and none would be the wiser. I would never know the truth, if there was such a thing because there were no facts, only interpretations.

Across from me was the Archives Building. A well-apportioned building with a low bank of steps to the entrance. In the daylight, no menacing gargoyles, rather some innocent cherubs stretching from the eaves of the second story building. In my head, I imagined Medusa, the most notorious of the Gorgons. But maybe everything in my head was also only for show, for in the daylight, the grotesque looked perfectly inviting. There I was standing in the square no more than a hundred yards from the entrance, when who else should I meet, however fortuitously, but Star. With her blond hair and linen white dress, she looked almost angelic as she thrust herself into my path so that I was nearly touching her.

"David," she said, as if I wouldn't see her, couldn't see her, that I would somehow miss the one that everyone always saw wherever she was, screaming out like the red fire engine number nine blasting down the street for the onlookers and the gawkers and the café culture glitterati.

"David," she said again. "Just what are the chances I would run into you here, the Seaside, of all places?"

"I don't know Star," I said, trying to look past her for Marta, but not trying to appear like I was. "Must be fate."

"Of course, it is fate," she replied, touching my shoulder. "Everything is fate."

I didn't know what to say, but I must have said something or gave off the look, the impression that I had things to do. And I did, but not necessarily now, as I waited for Marta, not sure if I hoped or not, that she would intervene.

"Well, I know you're busy and things ended kind of awkward last time. Boys will be boys. But we must all have dinner. I'll find Lando and let him know. He's around here somewhere. In the Archives Building I think."

I gazed into her eyes as she inched closer to me, was lost then for some segment of time before recovering. I didn't know why for that moment I was mesmerized, caught up in her, like a spider and fly. There was that metaphor again, emblematic of those who use flattery and charm to disguise their true intentions.

"That's where I was thinking of heading," I casually said, breaking away from her.

"Well, that's where he is. Looking for some maps. It seems this used to be a fortified city and he's developed quite an interest in history. I'm here for the architecture. Lovely, isn't it? Not as good as Las Vegas. We had such a lovely time, didn't we?"

"You don't say?" I said, not even mildly amused, ignoring most of what she said. I took it all in stride, for a moment accepting that perhaps I was resigned to my fate, or my fates, as it were. The three of us, the unchangeable, the ever evolving moment and the impossible, that future looming large but so precariously dangling off the edge, casting off its brightness as mere embers, though all the while too hot, too wonderful to touch.

Lando emerged from the archives building. Star spotted him first and I followed her gaze. In his hands, he carried something, which in a moment I would learn, were maps, actual paper maps. Of course, we all had the ability to have them on our comms, these maps, but like all information, they could also be useless attention grabbers.

"I thought it such a novelty," Lando said, offering the maps to me, "Surely something you would appreciate, which is why I collected what little they had for your perusal when I saw you outside talking to Star."

"Thanks," I said, accepting his offer.

"Can you imagine," he continued, "how they used to always print these maps up? What a waste of such a precious resource. Paper. It amazes me the way people used to live. So thoughtless and unintelligibly."

"Oh Lando," Star said, "Leave David alone. He may be a bit of a relic, but he's our relic. Aren't you, darling?"

"Surely I am."

"Darling," she now said, addressing Lando, "He'll join us for dinner. He even has a new friend, don't you David?"

"Uh," I paused, caught off guard, but I shouldn't have been. I should have known. After all, the network was as Marta said it was, an all-seeing, all-knowing, supposedly impartial entity. I had said then, the network is a panopticon. What's that, she had said? What's that, Lando was saying, as he socked me in the arm. Sorry about the other night. Yeah, don't worry about it. Is it true?

"Of course, it's true," Star stated as if all-knowing, too. "I can tell such things. I know things. He has that look about him, not so depressed, like she stripped those colors right out of his blues."

"Well, she who strips such things," Lando said, amused at Star's phrasing. "I can't wait to meet her. Tonight, even!"

I nodded to them, held onto my new maps and waited, then watched as they made their leave, Lando and Star, perhaps the perfect couple and everything I would never be, not Marta and I at all, though we were perfect for each other too. Weren't we? I asked that as she emerged from a shop.

"What's up?" Marta said happily as she came to me, a few bags in hand. "Look. I've got a proper chain now. No more strings attached."

"Nice, that's cool."

"All these things, so cool," she joked to me. "When it's so warm out."

That was the one word I used she thought so strange because it seemed to insert itself all of the time. It was just a filler word, one that outlasted hip and dig it and some of those more far-out expressions.

I reached out and touched the silvery chain she proudly wore. Then I told her about Lando and Star, the maps I had and how I inadvertently made dinner plans I didn't want or mean to make. She nodded and said okay, and before she could say anything else, I told her I needed to go into the Archives Building.

"Be careful," she added.

"I'm always careful," I responded.

"Hmm," she said, shaking her head and smiling as if to deny my claim. "Come here."

I had stepped away, but then stepped back. She leaned in and kissed me, quick, but efficient, that faint trace of loveliness lingering on my lips as she moved back to where she was. I danced in her eyes for a moment or two, maybe longer, I don't know.

"I bought you a shirt," she said, reaching into her bag. She pulled a blue linen shirt. "A little gift for you."

"Thanks," I said. "It's lovely. I like the color. It's kind of blue."

"Kind of blue, it's really blue," she said. "And be careful, I really mean it."

"I'll only be about ten minutes or so. I just want to check something out."

She nodded, indicating she would still be there,

waiting for me. And I knew she would. We couldn't blend in, nobody could. When that eighteenth century English philosopher coined the term panopticon, he was talking about a prison in which a single guard could see what every prisoner was doing at any given time, so that no one ever knew they were being watched. Marta had immediately picked up on it, the basis, she said, for the modern surveilled society. And here we were, still in a prison, never knowing who the prisoners were and who were the guards, but maybe it didn't matter.

Once inside the Archives Building, it was deathly quiet and cold too, as if a refuge from the brightness of the sunshine and the afternoon heat. I figured that was why most people were inside, a quick distraction, a place that was literally cool and not for history.

I saw them gathered around an old topographic model of the city. Some wore special glasses that allowed them to see some sort of layering. Looked like a gimmick to me. Those without the glasses seemed to admire the constructed model, which I understood, because it was an impressive rendering of the medieval architecture of the city. I was sure that it seemed more real than what you could see with the glasses on. And yes, maybe I was a relic, holding positions that were contrary to reality, but I needed to hold on to my books and notebooks, even my old coin and skeleton key.

With its high ceilings and huge columns at the entryway, this place would have been a governmental building at various times, back in the age of monumental construction. Now it was just a museum, although limited in use. I noted that sections of the building were closed, which was curious to me, something off limits.

I tried the door, but it was locked, imagining lower levels that were dark and musty, and whatever was there, if there was anything, would be covered in dust. Without missing a beat, I inserted the key. A skeleton key in theory is a kind of master key, one that has been cut in such a way that opens multiple locks, reduced as it were, to the essentials, down to the bone.

The lock slowly turned and the door opened, leading to a surprisingly well-lit landing. I descended the first set of stairs, old stone steps that wound around and around, and finally down. That made me think I was missing something, for the whole city was full of secrets, layers upon layers. I just needed to go deeper, stumble upon what I was supposed to find.

And I saw it, maybe only because I was supposed to see it, but there was a passageway, semi-hidden, like an illusion, a narrow slip through a pair of large, angular stones, that from most angles, looked non-existent. And maybe the passage didn't always exist. But at this moment it did, and that was all that mattered.

This stairwell was dark, everything I thought the other would be, murky and dank, with no real light, and I had left my flashlight back at the room. I felt along the cold walls and worked myself down the stairs, running my fingers along the rough stone, its coarse, uneven features, and if I didn't know otherwise, I would have thought I was touching something else. What? I didn't know for sure. Limestone, I presumed, yet, parts of it were suddenly smooth as if polished. Of course, limestone could also be polished like marble.

When I reached the new level in complete darkness, something glowed in the corner of the room. I slowly walked, one foot hesitantly in front of the other to that corner of the room where I found a huge collection of stones, in a light blue hue, shimmering. Upon contact with my hand, they became bright and more illuminative. I grabbed a few of them. That blue light lit just enough of the room for me to note its sparseness. Like everything in this world, whatever used to be here had been cleared out, made to look clean, maintained and perfectly tidy.

I had to admit, the stones were quite handy as I walked about the room. I came across a much cruder version of the map upstairs carved into the rock itself, with huge trenches linking parts of the city, the tunnels I suspected (or hoped), leading from the church in various directions, all across the city, some seeming larger than others, but the largest seemed to lead to the various gates. In some cases, the tunnels seemed to go in circles too. That would be the maze that was talked of by the oracle, these intricate turns and pathways to nothingness.

I thought about the labyrinth, the idea that Daedalus constructed it so elaborately that he barely escaped the Minotaur contained within it. In general, labyrinths and mazes were used interchangeably, but there were differences. It was thought that a maze was multicursal while a labyrinth was unicursal. The representation before me seemed to have plenty of dead ends, but if there was a center, then it was the church. Though the church was hardly centered as it was constructed high upon a hill with one side a cliff and the sea below.

Assuming the way could be found, a few tunnels stretched out far beyond the original walls of the city. And one tunnel in particular went farther than the map allowed to show. As well, there was a tunnel that seemed to lead to where Evey and Evers lived. Their house connected to a tunnel that led directly to the lighthouse, no winding paths or misdirection.

I went and gathered a few more stones and strategically placed them about the map so that I could study the big picture, and though the stones did not emit as much light when not touching my hand, the glow was sufficient. What an amazing piece of work, whoever carved such a thing, I marveled.

The maps from Lando were meant to distract. They were not complete. They did not show me the things I needed to see. In the early nineteenth century, an Englishman told the story of diverting hounds chasing a rabbit by some particularly strong-smelling kipper, or red herring. Star mentioned the gates, as if to let me know something, and Lando had maps. But they were just red herrings. The bigger thing was these tunnels and where they led, and perhaps the more telling, how one would navigate them.

A noise startled me. I listened for scurrying, thinking that it might be a rat. I hated rats. A long ago memory came to me, how I used to always imagine getting bit by a rat when I was in a dark place, and how I would have to get a tetanus shot, one every day in the stomach, for fourteen days. That was the part that terrified me.

I thought I heard steps or a scuttling but couldn't be sure. I could imagine a whole lot more than rats, yet that didn't make any of it more real. I had what I needed though, confirmation. I just needed a way to access the tunnels. Not I, but we: Marta and I. We.

I quietly retraced my steps, up the circular flights of stairs that seemed to wind even more than before. How much of life just was like that, going in circles, I wondered. We did the same things over and over yet hoped for something different. Even now, I felt like I had been here before.

As I stepped back outside, from the dull drab interior of the building to the brightness of the square, to Marta leaning so casually against a post, brilliant in her blue, summery dress and sandals, I considered.

I considered that even the map I saw was likely not accurate, at least not to scale, for it captured how things were according to an artist's point of view, a mere rendering, for who could have such complete, perfect knowledge? No one. Though that was the way of things. All these things we thought we knew, we were told as much, but so often there was more to the story, more going on than we knew, like the secret tunnels and passageways. Just how deep did it all go? I thought about Alice.

That was the question Alice asked, was it not? Wonderland was something I knew. Marta? Not likely. Definitely not Lando or Star, but Emrik would have known. Not that it mattered much, all this literary stuff. Still, that was my contribution to the group, all of this useless knowledge, useless except as a context for human history. That had been my role: the resident relic. They were all so very right. I was a relic, but I wasn't alone.

Rousseau, the French philosopher, didn't have much faith in the progress of the world, believing that institutions corrupted humankind. And the natural order was therefore doomed by the inextricable failure of society. Perhaps the world was ultimately doomed, but not in the way he imagined. We can never seem to imagine where we will be, not ourselves as individuals nor as individuals within the society.

Despite everything, what may or may not come to be, I was lured by its undeniable beauty, charmed by the square with the statues, picturesque buildings, little cafés, and its life. Just look at it all, I thought. And yet, contained within these walls, burning so bright, beckoning with all of its wonder, I knew was just a jilted lover, tempting me to come a little closer, to get so near I couldn't escape its grasp. That was the lure of the network, it's game. And there, against it all, fighting for me, with me, was Marta.

"Hey," I said to Marta as I neared, noting her slight change in appearance. "Nice sunglasses."

"When in Seaside, they say," she smiled. "Did you find what you were looking for?"

"Yeah," I said, nodding.

As I looked to Marta, I longed for something else, for some other path. I just wanted to get in a car and drive, though I hated driving. That was an improvement to the modern, network era. No one had to drive. But I still just wanted to drive, get on the road and drive out of all of this, just her and I, maybe the radio song and no place to be except where we were, wind in our hair and the open road.

"Hey, remember when you said there was no way out?" I asked.

"Yes," she said "One, no one is looking for an exit and two, even if they were, no one knows exactly where the boundaries are."

"Makes perfect sense," I agreed. "But what if I told you I had found a way, that it is possible to circumvent the system?"

"Do tell," as she leaned closer as if to kiss me, but

instead put her ear close to my mouth.

"Underneath the city is a system of tunnels that was built centuries ago. At one time, useful for times of war, for transporting troops and who knows what else," I whispered.

"Go on," she said eagerly.

"The tunnel system was later changed into a bit of a labyrinth, as a test of some kind, I assume. And if we get down to the tunnel level, then we can navigate our way through the labyrinth."

"What then?"

"There's an exit of some kind, I know there is. An underground railroad line, long since abandoned, something. There has to be."

"How do you know all of this?"

"The oracle told me and I saw it in a room in the Archives Building, but I also remembered it too like I had found it before, this underground train moving from station to station."

"Are there really stations?"

No, I thought to myself. Not really. There are probably not stations, but that was my metaphor when I was searching for a way to reach you, and now that we are searching for a way out, there are stations too because that's how I think.

"I don't think so. That's just an image that sticks in my head. It's probably a set of tracks and an old rail car if we are lucky."

"Where do we find a tunnel?" Marta asked, moving back away from my ear to face me.

"The Twins know, I think. Or they are involved somehow. Perhaps the Archives Building, the lighthouse, and the church too."

"What's the catch? By labyrinth, do you mean a maze?"

"I am not exactly sure if it's multicursal or unicursal," I said, "If that's what you mean."

"One path or many," Marta said. "Let's hope there's more than one way."

"In theory, the unicursal labyrinth has only one way in and out, and it's more ornamental."

"In theory," she laughed at me. "Ornamental. That's a good one. Every network likes a good puzzle. I don't think it will be easy to decipher. What we'll find will be more like a maze, and it won't be easily navigable."

"Well, we have to find a way," I said.

"What?" she asked, assessing the look I was giving her. "And how?"

"Anna," I said.

"What about Anna?" she asked.

"Well, she had that labyrinth tattoo on her back."

"She might," conceded Marta. "It could have been part of the simulation, though, that place, wherever you were. I still don't understand how it all connects and why she showed you her back."

"I don't know either," I added as we left the square and made our way back to the hotel, not wanting to delve any more than skin deep.

I liked the colors on the various buildings, little etchings and blotches of pastels on the shutters. Not all of the buildings were off-white with red roofs. That was something I noticed as I walked. From a distance, things looked so similar. Close up, among the details, I appreciated the nuance.

We saw so little, did we not? All of this world, this colorful cornucopia before us, and yet we retained so little, focused on one thing at a time, and then our minds just filled in the gaps because those finer details were not necessary, and really, that was not so different than the network either. The network captured everything, mostly, too much of everything, but now and then, it had to fill in the gaps when something wasn't transmitting properly from its world of sensors and images, its readings and renderings. Like us, it simply made do.

"I am a little nervous," Marta admitted.

We were back in the hotel, side by side, looking out at the sea and its tranquil blue waters. Below us a clattery of noise, indistinguishable, and yet if I concentrated, I could make out certain sounds. And beyond, beyond us was everything.

"It's kind of a game of cat and mouse," I said as I slid my arm from her shoulder to her waist.

"And curiosity killed the cat," Marta said, uneasily, but I blunted that thought out and reassured her as best as I could, without words, just swift action. "Isn't that the expression you used?"

It had been. So as much as I craved all that surrounded me, I was still curious about what was left of the other world. Curiosity might kill the cat. That was a riff on an old saying. And this world, of course, wasn't as real as everyone thought, the picture was deceiving. Maybe it was only a matter of time before things fell apart. That was the ultimate eventuality, the network be damned. The network sought stability, not advancement. But all things were in flux.

The network had changed us all, and whether it made

us into who we were really supposed to be or not was open to debate. Were we in fact, still human, if all of our flaws were smoothed over, so all that we really were, was the gloss and the gleam, the glistening of the sheen?

"Hey," she said, "I need to get dressed for tonight."

I watched her for a moment as she looked at what she was going to wear, spread out on the bed. She gave me a look, kind of like, I don't want to be weird and go to the bathroom, but can you look somewhere else? I marveled at her modesty, happy that I continually found things to be amazed with.

I laid down to rest for a moment, closing my eyes, trying to picture what dinner with Lando and Star would be like, but all too easily drifted. I was hung up on details, minor details, conversations that might happen, exact phrases until I just skipped them over entirely.

And I was back on the desert highway in the truck, seemingly in the middle of nowhere, that desert highway, the heat of the day. I kept trying to get a glimpse of my companion, but it was always somehow incomplete, like the file had been blurred. All I could see was that she had a pale orange jersey-like dress. In earlier versions, she had been in denim and T-shirt.

We pulled off the road, some kind of stop. Dust everywhere, the ground like it was on fire. At a bench, a woman sat. I knew who she was. I was trying to tell my companion, but I couldn't speak. I wasn't in water, but it was still like I was floating, treading water, trying to get to the top to breathe, to get a better view. The woman was the oracle. I could tell by the way she looked at me.

Then Lando appeared out of nowhere. I swear he just emerged out of the distance like there was a door or some kind of secret entrance. He pulled out a long gun, and while looking directly at me, shot the oracle. I turned back to my companion, and I could almost see her face.

That was when I awoke, Marta leaning over me, letting the jewel around her neck dangle on my chest. Except it wasn't Marta. No, it was. She had on makeup. That was something women still did, even in a world like this. Her elegant dress had half-moon patterns, black gauzy material with straps and gray moons. She looked irresistible.

She held a pair of fancy trousers in her hands and the blue shirt she bought for me. It wasn't anything like a tux, but I thought back to a time long ago, on a cold wintery night, all dressed up with pointy shoes, joking with friends as we walked on a frozen street to a wedding of all things, something that there never would be again. That must have been when Eddie and Beatrice were married. I hadn't thought of them in so long.

She watched me as I dressed, helping to straighten my collar when I struggled. We could have this world of dinner party delights, dressing up and going out, all gussied up, among friends and good cheer, among whomever we wanted, living or dead. Christ. We could go hang out with Gandhi and the gurus, meet the music masters of the golden era, the Beatles, Lennon and McCartney, Jagger and Richards, Dylan, Bowie, Tom Waits, Nick Cave. Whomever we wanted. We could do it all, Marta and I. We.

We had it all. Once, didn't we? What had I hoped to find? Maybe it was okay to just be how I was, be here like I was now, go through the days as I am, knowing I could see the world differently than almost anyone else, that none of it was really real, but that was okay. Why was it more authentic to leave this world, to that other place? And what made it more real there? Because the conditions were harsh and life was hard and full of suffering? Did that make it more authentic? Was life only meant to suffer? Was it only the good art that came from suffering? I recalled how that was such a twentieth century idea. And yet, it stuck with me. Perhaps I had studied that period too much. *To live is to suffer,* maybe was something someone like Nietzsche wrote, but to *survive is to find meaning in that suffering.*

"David," Marta said, knowing how I felt while I struggled to understand. "You need to believe. I believe in you."

"I know," I said, but not in a manner that convinced anyone. "But why me?"

"I don't know. I sometimes ask myself the same thing, but about me. All of these people are living the perfect life, the dream, yet here I am. How did I get here? And despite all my doubts, all of the times I second guess myself, I reach the same conclusion. That I am here because I want to be here. I'm here because I believe in you."

"I am not remarkable. I don't know anything."

"That's not true. What did the oracle tell you? You told me all about her. What did she say?"

"She said I knew all the answers, but I acted like I didn't," I said uneasily. Why hadn't she said something else?

"Hey," she said and kissed me, that chain dangling near me, the jewel on its end touched me in such a way as Marta touched me too. "What do you know? Tell me one thing you know to be true?"

"Tell me about love first," I said, as I closed my eyes and felt that jewel, her jewel, the real Marta, close to me.

"Love," she said. "Love is complicated, remember?"

I loved her. I wasn't sure at the beginning. I didn't believe in love at first sight. And it wasn't love at first sight, anyway. Along the way, there was a moment though, more than a moment, of uncertainty, of confusion, but then too, there was also a solitary instance of clarity, and that was the moment I knew, when she was, when she became my lodestar, but I didn't know that was the moment until now.

"I know you are my lodestar. And that's a force that is more powerful than the network."

"I hope so," she said.

She smiled. I could tell, even though she looked away, a radiant smile that powered the night now descending upon us with its massive talons, its darkness like a reclusive animal turned restive. I could feel it. We both could. It doused any rush of inspiration, like a cool breeze escaping from the dark sea, a chill spun over us, clouded, shrouding my hopeful thoughts so that they too fell off, disappearing like an exhale. The walls felt like they were closing in. The time, the forever time, was there like the man in black with the scythe, the grim reaper.

We held hands as we walked, and though the heat of the day had since faded, I still thought it should have been warmer. Marta wore a shawl over her dress and carried a little purse, small but still big enough for two flashlights. Beside us the dark waters, flashed with illumination from the scattering of lights. When Marta squeezed my hand, a sense of calm returned, for no matter what, I had Marta, the lovely one, my lodestar.

As we walked, I knew that nothing anymore would ever be simple, that even this moment was special. So, I squeezed her hand, relishing in the simplicity of the gesture, the causality, the reverberate feeling. That such simple pleasures would never be so simple, both terrified me and excited me, for it meant that we had to create the world anew. The true definition of ambivalence meant being torn between two powerful ideas, and in this instance, all that was lost and all that could be regained. In modern parlance, the word had come to mean something different, a sense of not really caring one way or another, but we cared. We cared all too much.

Before I could consider anything more, there before us, were Lando and Star, stunning as ever. And what did it matter what she wore. She was always stunning as ever. Even Lando was sharply dressed. I admitted that much as well. Perhaps they were the prototypic couple.

Star bowed gracefully as her white gloved hands reached out to greet Marta. I shook Lando's hand, then we alternated, and I kissed Star on each cheek as Lando did the same customary greeting to Marta. Before things were in the least bit awkward, Star took charge and we followed her to the restaurant, which was situated directly across from the water, almost like our hotel restaurant, with the boardwalk separating, only this place was much farther up the coastline, closer to the lighthouse. Lando followed behind, in back.

And here I thought we looked so glamorous, but that was before we saw Star and Lando, for they elevated the game to another level that before that moment, had surely not existed. Her sequined, semi-transparent dress shimmered in antique white, the same shade as Lando's suit. Even the minor details remained striking, be it the cuff links matched to her earrings, Star's bracelet, her necklace sparkling between her flattering décolletage, on down to their shoes: Star in heels that seemed to make no noise as she moved yet had an edge sharp enough to cut. Lando's shoes were pointy just like they had been long ago on that cold night on the slippery steps.

No surprise, they had reserved the best table, perched a little bit higher than all of the rest, up a small expanse of stairs, overlooking the boardwalk and with clear lines to the sea. Champagne on ice was waiting. I stared at the bubbles in the bottle through the clear tub full of ice that kept everything cold. I couldn't see the bubbles, but I could hear them. That made them seeable. And soon we were toasting with the chilled beverage, and after the clink of glasses, tasting that bit of sweet paradise.

We made small talk about the seaside, about the little town and all of its old structures and oddities. And yes, it seemed a little surreal to me, but as long as Marta was okay with everything, then I was fine too. It was only Star and Lando. And not the Fates nor the Gorgons or strange figures in windows.

"How long are you two staying?" Marta asked at one point.

"As long as it is interesting," joked Star. "Of course, really, you can be anywhere and then go anywhere, so it doesn't matter to me. Lando wanted to come here; he said it made him nostalgic."

Lando was more direct, though *nostalgic* would never have been his word. Maybe it would have been mine. Wasn't I the one so good with words, so much in another place and time? For a moment, I thought about writing, not anything specific, just words, one after another, sentence upon sentence, station to station in some remote place.

"We knew David was here. We just thought we would drop in and have dinner with you both, given that we had not met the lovely Marta before and were curious who this *mysterious* woman was."

"Well, here I am," Marta spoke brightly, evincing not a shroud of hesitation. I, on the other hand, was conscious of every word I spoke, every thought I thought.

"How did you guys meet?" Star asked, her eyes flickering with interest. "It's so quaint, being a couple, isn't it?"

I didn't audibly or visibly sigh, but internally, I did, but I liked that she recognized us as a couple. Better to let Marta explain this one. I hadn't even thought of the best way to answer this question. The simplest explanation obviously was best. Occam's razor. Nothing without necessity. We both knew that it was easier to maintain a simple lie than a more complex one.

"A coffee shop, the one near your office," Marta said, looking affectionately at me. "We kept running into each other there. We were on a similar schedule, I guess. And after a while, I decided he wasn't merely a stalker but possibly an admirer."

"Well, certainly he didn't approach you," Star said, laughing ever so slightly.

"No. He was a bit too distracted to do that."

"And just what do you intend to do while you are here?" Lando asked me. He was always direct, so that troubled me none, but more so than usual, his expression betrayed such sincerity.

"Swim," Marta answered, resting her hand on my hand on the table.

"SIM?" Star asked.

"No," Marta calmly clarified. "David and I mean to swim in the ocean every morning. Other than that, we have no plans."

"But you'll get all wet," Star exclaimed. "You should try it in the SIM. Solves all kinds of issues."

Marta just looked at me and smiled.

"Yes, that's true," I conceded, "but there's something about it all happening in the same space that I like. Just like now."

"Well, it seems the same to me," Star said, throwing a smile my way, "Whether I kiss you here or in the SIM, it feels the same to me. In fact, sometimes I forget what's acceptable in one world is not so much in the other. In fact, I challenge you. Touch these."

"Oh, such a distraction," Lando said. "I'll do it later for you."

"Darling, you know I am. Thanks," Star enthused

I suppose Star wanted to make Marta feel jealous, and Lando wanted me to feel inferior to him, all because of Star wanting to be the star. She was not my lodestar, though. As I looked at all of us at the table, then took a sip of champagne, my gaze moved beyond, out to the sparkle of the sea, half-lit by the stars and the remainder, a shimmering of lights from civilization, such that it was, debating now how real one experience was to the other, when they both had been altered. Nothing was real. Nothing was authentic. That was the thing. Except my lodestar.

"Speaking of distractions, David and I are going to go

to the bar for a whiskey." Lando remarked, eyeing Star with a sense of devotion I had never bothered to notice.

"Of course, darling," Star said, batting her eyelashes. "We prefer a little girl talk, anyway. Don't we Marta?"

Marta smiled warmly, touched my hand briefly as I got up to go with Lando to the bar. With a subtle glance, she soothed my sense of alarm. She was a big girl. It was true. In her eyes, she told me something else. Be careful, perhaps. I knew when she worried about me, I should be worried too.

"Such a lovely woman," Lando said when we were out of earshot.

I didn't know whether he meant Star or Marta. And I didn't ask. I just agreed. It didn't matter anyway, what I said or didn't say. What mattered most was how I felt. Yet, as we stood at the bar waiting for our drink, when I looked back at Marta, there she was. I always expected her to know I loved her. She knew that, didn't she?

"Don't get too attached," Lando said. "Nothing lasts forever. Sorry to be blunt. I don't think Marta is the right girl for you. Maybe she just feels right."

The remark caught me off guard. We touched glasses and I sipped the smallest bit of whiskey, I could, surprised how good it was, how much I seemed to crave the sudden taste of whiskey, like all the nights of drinking whiskey had come back to me, all at once, and in more ways than one. And they stung.

"The way I see it," Lando continued, "she's just a distraction. You might think she's leading you in, but she's leading you astray. She's not what you think. Resist."

I didn't look at Lando. I stared at my drink. When I looked up at the bartender, she looked like the oracle. That wasn't possible though. I turned to survey the bar, the sea of faces, but it was starting to blur. I thought I saw a man in black, though I thought I saw a lot of things, so it could have been anyone, like the man on the moon. But I had seen that man in black before.

"We can help you," Lando continued on. At least, that was what I think he said. I wasn't listening. He said something about being friends, such good friends and he was always there for me. And it didn't have to be like this.

I looked up to him, into his eyes, so far and deep into them, I was no longer looking there, but somewhere else, in something else, a series of moments that spun like circles into a single black dot drawn by a thick pen.

Everything fell upon me, crashing into me. I felt the pressure, the tightness of being surrounded and unable to move. I collected myself, calmed my thinking by focusing on breath, breathing each breath as measured as the next. I sipped the whiskey glass, forgetting it had been in my hand, or had it? I thought I was sipping tea, though surely this was not tea. I was sipping whiskey. Lando and me. Where had the oracle gone? Was she still here?

I drifted, I dreamt. I felt I was on a train speeding across a track suspended high above the world, passing station after station, never stopping. The whole world was a blur, an image that coalesced then came apart in a pulsing rhythm, repeating and repeating, focused one moment then obscured the next.

Lando tapped me on the shoulder, gave me a look like he knew of the burden I carried, if that was what it was, and for a moment he seemed sympathetic. I could see that in his eyes as if he understood my predicament, even shared it to some degree. Was the human race worth saving, and if so, in what form? Maybe to him, this was what saving the human race looked like.

I needed Marta. I just *knew* I needed Marta. I blunted out the train, Lando, the whiskey, all of it, and walked, however unsteady as I moved, a thousand images flashing through my mind, some meaningless, some bizarre, some I could not explain. The man in black, the dream of the desert and a truck with a mysterious companion, the station, Marta's legs like an endless spiral staircase, winding around and around, in a maze, section by section, layer by layer each with rooms full of books and other useless things. Was it just another elaborate ruse and I was a lab rat, running on a treadmill. They said lots of things were discovered because of lab rats. I didn't know what any of those things were. Maybe the original network was tested on rats. They didn't terrify me per se, but I could see their fangs and the coming of the plague was imminent.

And so I reached, I breathed in and out. I was adrift at sea, unmoored, and the waves kept pushing me around. Yet I remained, and though surely I could move, I certainly could, I did not stir. I looked out and I looked in, but I saw nothing. Maybe I was the thing that was not real and my sense of consciousness was an illusion. How could I be sure? *I think therefore I am.* That was what Descartes said. That assured me of nothing. What am I? Oh, great Cartesians, this body and this mind?

Or maybe I was real and nothing else was? In that regard, disconnecting myself from the network meant I had to create my own world, fill it with people and things as I saw fit. And so all of this glamour and glitz was all in my mind. And that meant Marta, even the lovely Marta was a conception of the ideal, that I truly did make her up.

But I couldn't ever create something as good as her. Not in a thousand tries.

I breathed, conscious of the action as if voluntary and vulnerable to lapses, closed my eyes and reopened them, wondering but not knowing all would be the same, just hoping something would be different, some little thing, something aglow.

Marta's hand touched me, bringing me back to life as she so often did. Still the walls were closing in and everything shrank, smaller and smaller. And there was no way out. The time was running out. All of the things I tried so hard to do, to get done, to keep it all together, were coming apart and helplessly I watched the unraveling, the loss of sands from the hourglass, unable to alter the course of events.

We were in the desert again. Who was with me? I wanted to be better, to be good. Couldn't I just have another chance? I would play it differently next time around. I wouldn't think so much. I wouldn't challenge the center. I wouldn't have all these questions. I would accept it. I would be just like you wanted me to be. I promise. Just let me do it again, I pleaded. To God. What God?

I squeezed Marta's hand and I guess that was like when people say they had to pinch themselves to make sure it was real, turn on that light to know it's not a dream. In her eyes I saw a world dangling on a string, by a mere thread, and that lonely light flickered, faltered then fell. I was falling. I thought about Marta, the first time we met, that little dream of mine that was real, that sparkly dress, the fallen world fluttering about like paper mâché.

And she was very real. Something about the way she touched me, both her hands cradling mine, gently massaging the back of my hand. Inside, I felt a surge from the pit of my stomach. I squeezed Marta's hand again and she squeezed back, and as if her lips were on mine, I breathed a breath like no other breath, so bitter and so sweet.

When I opened my eyes, I felt a sense of déjà vu, the world before me was of two kinds, completely perfect, gleaming brilliantly on one hand, but in parts, broken up, disintegrated, a crumbled spectacular ruin.

Star looked at me with a horrified expression, hands to her face. Lando calmly sipped his whiskey with a wry smile. He made no effort at first as we got up, Marta guiding me. When we reached the landing, I thought I heard him move. The first set of stairs had been fine, but the final set looked like they would crumble with the slightest touch and yet we descended them quickly, without problem and were out on the boardwalk before I looked back and saw Lando atop the balcony where we had been, grinning broadly, like a man with a cigar who just won big at the tables in his white suit.

I staggered, so did Marta trying to support me. I fell against her as we moved, no one on the streets as if they had been cleared, as if the people were mere debris and the constant gardeners meticulously cleaned them up. An eerie silence enveloped us. Like we were going into a SIM, those few moments of absolute nothingness. But this was no SIM. Or was it the greatest SIM of all, the master SIM?

"To the lighthouse," I croaked. That was a sound I didn't know I could make.

In the distance, sounds returned, that fluttering of drones moving in like a mob. Up ahead, Evey and Evers stood by the lighthouse. He had a walking stick. They looked like they were expecting us, as if they knew all of their lives we would be here at that exact moment in time. There was no shock, no alarm, not even as the drones landed and the alternates sprang out.

A gunshot rang out, its echo lingered long as I turned first to Marta. Please not her. God. I was praying to God again. Evey collapsed near the entrance of the lighthouse, bullet through the head. Evers was expressionless. He knew, as we all did, that she was dead.

Lando looked at me as if in warning then raised his gun again. The alternates too, stood there waiting, half a dozen of them dressed in matching military regalia. Another shot. Evers stepped in front of me, took a bullet in his shoulder, then lurched inside as I shut the door. It all happened so fast, first Evey and then Evers. But Evers wasn't dead. He was just losing lots of blood, a deep dark ruby red, and like a river, it flowed as I crossed over it.

I pictured Evey on the sidewalk, bleeding out, outside the lighthouse, the moonlight gazing down on her, but I was in too much shock to feel any of the real pain, even as I looked at Evers, stoic as ever as he held a rag from his pants against his shoulder. I swear he grinned, undefeated in his moment of defeat.

"Go on," he beckoned us on. "This is no longer my time."

He waved us away again. I lingered, guilt ridden as I set this whole thing in motion so long ago, by my actions and mine alone, oblivious and nescient of the ramifications. How else did I think things would end? Did I expect to get away scot free, that there would be no casualties? I was callous and selfish, so determined to see out an end that I didn't even understand.

"Evers," I said. "I'm so sorry. About Evey. And you too. Thanks for all your help. I wish I could have done something more."

"Thank you," Evers said. "We only do what we must, what we must do."

He reached out for my hand. I put the old coin in his clasped hand, while with his other hand, he gave me his walking stick, his staff. He smiled as the blood spilled out of him, flowed as all things flow and nothing abides, such blood.

And I held his hand till Marta dragged me away, her voice doing its best to soothe and yet convey urgency. At the door, there was banging. I knew it was only a matter of time before Lando got through. Those old locks were trickier than anyone thought, even the network. Analog, I reminded myself. Analog versus digital. Again, the world took on its shape, two shapes at once, two versions of the same thing, a splitting of the real, one astride the other.

"We gotta go," she urged again, her hand replacing Evers. "There's no time."

I took a quick look around, the interior of the lighthouse merged back into one scene, no longer separate. Communications equipment of some kind. It looked ancient, stuff I remembered from my childhood, those old radio shack computers with the flashing triangle, simple and primitive. A desk with old style monitors. A blinking light, like some sort of radar or sonar, pulsed and flashed as it swept across the screen. I heard the drilling as Marta frantically opened doors. More shots rang out.

In what looked like a closet, there was a broom and dustpan, a bucket and a manhole covering. Marta adeptly lifted the plate aside, handed me a flashlight, and climbed down the ladder. As I followed her, I couldn't help but let it slip into my thoughts. Lando had pulled a gun. They didn't even exist here. They weren't supposed to because there had been no need and yet he had one.

We came to a landing. I had never seen Marta with such a look of focus, a driven intensity. While I seemed hesitant and unsure, she moved ahead, undeterred by the matter at hand. She seemed to know her way around. From the landing where we stood, there was another opening and a ladder, so another layer below we went, emerging in a dank, dark chamber that smelled like death and felt like the room in which I met the oracle, that air that wasn't air.

The necklace around Marta's neck glowed more incandescently. She must have sensed it, because she took it out from beneath her dress. The light glinted off the limestone walls of the tunnel. For a moment I was transfixed by its power.

"I know the way," Marta said to me. "I don't know why or how, but I know the way."

I didn't ask why or say anything. I just watched as she touched the walls of the tunnel, then strode confidently ahead. I flashed my light against the walls, saw motifs and symbols. Even my walking stick at its top had a serpent eating its own tail. I saw the same thing on the walls.

At the first split, we took a new direction, not the route that led along the outer portion, where above us was surely the boardwalk and the oblivious people, but the part that led within, to the heart. At that trailhead, we found a cart loaded with electronics, dry goods and even some clothes. Marta stepped out of her block heels and put on a pair of sneakers.

I started to roll the cart, but Marta stopped me. She heard what I heard. Voices behind us, somewhere echoing against the limestone walls of the tunnel, seemingly from every direction. It was impossible to know how near or how far.

"Too loud," she insisted. "Let's just fill these packs."

Two knapsacks. I stuffed clothes and the dry goods in them, while Marta examined the electronics. She decided on a few processors and a strange tool, then grabbed one of the bags.

I clutched the other and we forged ahead.

We came to another junction. I flashed my light to the walls and saw Anubis, the Egyptian god of death and the underworld. Unmistakably, with its jackal head and body of a man. Among other things, he ushered souls into the afterlife and was also present during the weighing scale, where the determination was made of how worthy a soul was.

On the opposite wall was Osiris. There was no green skin depicted. Maybe at once there had been, but all the same, I knew the hieroglyphics. At some point, Anubis ceded the underworld to Osiris. Osiris took over the tasks at hand, but was also considered symbolic of rebirth, of the cycles in nature.

Marta didn't see these things nor did she think twice about which way to go as we came to yet another place to choose and then another. I trudged along in the rear, listening for sounds. In the distance I thought I heard something, but I was paranoid, on edge, so that may have been my imagination. I didn't say anything. Marta could hear it all just as well as I, two sounds, one like a scuttling and the other, a kind of whir, mixing together, rattling off of the walls.

The sounds grew louder and nearer. Marta stopped, moved over to the wall and crouched, motioning to where she was. She put her hand to her lips and pointed to a red light emitted from a mini drone flying slowly towards us in the darkness, then past us. We would hear a few more after that but none as close, so we moved on. There were too many options, not an infinite amount, but still too many places for them to go.

Marta kept choosing pathways. Sometimes it felt like we traced our steps back and we were just moving in circles because I saw some of the same symbols, or variations, like Thoth with his ibis head. At a hairpin turn, we saw a crashed drone. Marta smashed it till its red glow dimmed. That's where I shone my light in Thoth.

Occasionally we came to parts of the tunnel that were wider sections, landings of a kind, stations I thought, some of which had ladders that led up to another layer. Marta ignored all of these until we heard the scuttling.

She climbed up on the ladder and I followed. We watched and waited as a spider-like thing scampering near us, stopping momentarily by the ladder. I wasted no time, thrusting the staff with the pointed end square in the back. Marta leapt from the ladder and pulled that strange tool from her knapsack and plunged it into the side of the thing. Convinced it was dead, she put its remnants in her bag.

Neither of us spoke. We just kept moving. My mind thought of everything that it could, but at such a speed that maybe I thought of nothing at all, but what lay ahead. That wasn't true. Whole thoughts emerged then disappeared. I thought of Dylan, and how I would never hear another one of his songs, but at least Marta got to hear one. Certainly not his best, though that was how it was going to be for now. We would have to make do with what we had. And all I knew for sure that we really had was each other.

When I first met Marta that night in the bar, I thought about that. And now here we were, in the thick of it, wandering around, like rats in a cage, trying to get to the cheese or whatever was supposed to be at the end of this, not knowing what it was going to be, only knowing that we must know. That night seemed long ago, so innocent, that first drink, the first time she touched my hand and that feeling, even then, that told me she was someone to be reckoned with.

When she looked back and saw me smiling, I couldn't help but wonder what she thought. That I was thinking of something, that I was lost in my thoughts. But really I was doing whatever it is the brain does that keeps us alive.

It turns out that mapping the brain doesn't tell us as much about a person as we thought it would. There had been an assumption that all brains were the same, but they were not. Knowing the patterns of the mind tells us very little about how a person will perform a task. Once we abandoned our initial picture of the brain, that was when real progress was made.

We feared what we didn't know. I thought about Anubis and the afterlife as we walked, as I moved along following Marta through the maze. The great unknown. Was it more comforting to believe something that was not true? I supposed it was if you didn't know it. And in a way, that was the beauty of the network. At the end of the day, we were our brains and the cravings we desired, both emotional and physical, began and ended there.

At some point, I felt tired and devastated. The initial adrenalin faded, the numbness of what happened, its shock or whatever you wanted to call, became unabsorbed, and like a fresh wound, opened up and flooded me. I remembered being in that room with Anna, with the oracle, trying to recall everything she said, though there hadn't been much and she seemed to suggest I knew all of the answers anyway when I didn't.

I thought about every conversation Marta and I had, as we wandered the endless corridors in the tunnel for what seemed like hours, our talk of the network, of humanity, of love. I had no doubt that she knew which way to go. My only doubts were where we were going. Was this realm truly beyond the manipulation of the network or not? Now and then, I shone my light against the walls as if the depictions meant something.

I saw a man with a stick, serpents and dragons, fire, some sort of burial in the sky. I saw topiary patterns, figures with wings, ouroboros as infinity, recurrence. I don't believe Marta saw anything of this. Now and then she stopped, knowing one of those things was nearby, and she was good in a way I never expected, disabling those creatures with that strange tool. Occasionally, I had to use the staff as one surprised us and came scuttling along the walls or ceiling. They were crafty buggers.

All the while Marta remained in a trance, had that look in her eyes that I knew not to disturb. She seemed to move without moving, knowing instinctively which turn to take and what to do. Somehow the stone around her neck guided her. That was something I didn't understand. But there were a lot of things I didn't understand. And though I wanted to talk, to say something just to remind myself I had a voice, I didn't want to break the spell, the fluidity in Marta, her momentum. The way she moved, ethereal, barely touching the ground while each step for me was more akin to the weary kind, a trudging along.

In my mind, I had great conversations with her. We talked about childhood and love, humanity, the digital world, what she found amazing, and music too. I told her music was a kind of history, yet also a language that moved beyond the limitations of words. She told me her perfect day, her fantasies and realities. I told her everything about me, but she already knew half of it. We talked of everything and anything, she both teased me and taunted me.

I quickened my pace so that I was nearly beside her, but it wasn't so much that, rather that she had stopped. We had reached the end and were in a circular room with a high ceiling that rose toward a point we could no longer see. In the middle of the room a small flame rose from a fire pit surrounded by stones, its wisps of smoke rising and disappearing upward.

Our eyes had been accustomed to a kind of darkness, that being in this room offered a respite. There was a lightness here, not just from the flame, but the room itself. Two separate pathways veered off. The way we came was not one of them. There was no going back, not now and not ever.

I hadn't noticed until now, that Marta no longer wore that beautiful evening dress with the half moons. She had on a pale orange jersey-like dress, outside of which hung the stone, more radiant than ever. Like her. Her hair seemed the same, though her body was slightly different. I wondered about her eyes. Were they still that hazel color that so intrigued me? And what about me? How was I different? I wore denim and a T-shirt. I didn't know what else because I still felt like me, the same thoughts and ideas as ever floated through me, coming from I don't know where, but I knew they were mine.

I felt that raw emptiness scraping against me and I wanted desperately to be numb, to not feel a thing, but that was never possible. We always felt something. There was never nothingness. And some things, there were things that you could not possibly imagine, though we tried, didn't we, to picture what might, what could be. And sometimes we made it worse, sometimes better, but never really as it was. And this was as it was. Bleak and devastated, a semi-dark ruinous landscape stretched out before Marta and I. *Dum spiro spero*, I said softly to myself and reached for Marta's hand, but I couldn't find her hand. Instead, it was a cold steel rail.

Everyone knows, you have to derive your own meaning out of your existence, that the essence comes later. Such meaning remains born out of experience, what we lived and breathed and saw and did. In short, how we lived. I surmised that meant I would spend the remainder of my life rebuilding the world with Marta, our world, whatever that entailed. I was okay with that. I knew who she was, and I had learned who I was.

I had grabbed hold of a handcar, that was the cold steel rail, then let go and moved towards her, towards a reflection. She seemed to understand what I could not as she stood over the flame. Off to the side was a pooling of water, so very clear I tripped on something, fell back, but she grabbed me and held me upright as I watched a world of images on a screen flash on by, but that was all in my head, everything I saw, my whole life in a rapid blur that slowed down the moment I saw Marta's eyes staring into mine. They were always the same, even in a dream.

Two paths diverged, and we chose one of them, but we would never know what was the other way. That was real life. We didn't waver or hesitate. I thought nothing of deliberation. I just looked into her eyes, she back to me. *I love you Marta.* I said to her.

I've always loved you David, she replied.

I helped her up on the handcar, then pushed down on the lever as we slowly gained speed, then a little more and we shot forth into darkness, our flashlights lit and pointed ahead, but to what we didn't know.

My mind raced, moving on a tightrope across a precipice of hope and disillusion, feeling clarity and calmness one moment followed by despair and derangement the next as we rushed into madness until I saw an opening from the darkness, and in the distance a figure stood half in and out of the light, dancing like a flame.

Marta moved closer to me, into my arms, as the handcar slowed. The figure dissolved, if it was ever there. Uneasily, we stepped off the platform and walked forward, hand in hand, out of what seemed like a cavern, into the light, into a vast emptiness that stretched forever.

All was not lost. All was never as lost as I thought it was, as I thought it might be. There was something up ahead, something in the distance. We both saw it. And that thing we saw made it known to us, that we had a purpose, that the dream was not lost. I reached for her, my lodestar.

ABOUT ATMOSPHERE PRESS

Atmosphere Press is an independent, full-service publisher for excellent books in all genres and for all audiences. Learn more about what we do at atmospherepress.com.

We encourage you to check out some of Atmosphere's latest releases, which are available at Amazon.com and via order from your local bookstore:

This Side of Babylon, a novel by James Stoia
Within the Gray, a novel by Jenna Ashlyn
Where No Man Pursueth, a novel by Micheal E. Jimerson
Here's Waldo, a novel by Nick Olson
Tales of Little Egypt, a historical novel by James Gilbert
For a Better Life, a novel by Julia Reid Galosy
The Hidden Life, a novel by Robert Castle
Big Beasts, a novel by Patrick Scott
Alvarado, a novel by John W. Horton III
Nothing to Get Nostalgic About, a novel by Eddie Brophy
GROW: A Jack and Lake Creek Book, a novel by Chris S McGee
Home is Not This Body, a novel by Karahn Washington
Whose Mary Kate, a novel by Jane Leclere Doyle
Stuck and Drunk in Shadyside, a novel by M. Byerly
These Things Happen, a novel by Chris Caldwell

ABOUT THE AUTHOR

Daniel Hagedorn lives in Seattle, Washington, where he was born and raised, with his wife and elderly dog. An alum of Pacific Lutheran University with a couple of humanities degrees, he now splits his time between writing and helping various businesses and entities do what they do. He has written a number of novels, poems and countless other musings. This is his first published novel.